Christmas with You

Christmas with You

A Four Irish Brothers Winery Romance

Nan Reinhardt

TULE
PUBLISHING

Dedication

For my darling daughter-in-law, Les, my daughter-in-spirit, who coached me on all things theater and acting and who never fails to come to my aid when I need a word from someone a generation (sometimes two) younger than me. Thank you, lovey!

Chapter One

HOLLY SANTOS SET her chin in her palm, gazed around the Tea Leaf Café, and breathed a satisfied sigh. It was small and, okay, maybe the wide-plank wood floor needed a refinish and the tin ceiling could use a new coat of paint, but it was all hers... or it would be in—she glanced at the screen of the laptop sitting on the table in front of her—another two hundred and thirty-one months. Her teeth worried her lower lip. The ceiling would probably be okay for another year; so would the floor, but the bigger concerns were the two old industrial refrigerators back in the kitchen. It was a coin toss which one would go first.

However, this morning, she could breathe, and stretching, she gave the little computer a thumbs-up. Finally, the ledger was starting to hold its own—no profit yet, but the fall tourist rush had pushed her a little ahead, just as Aunt Susan had predicted when she'd sold Holly the Tea Leaf Café on contract back in December. River's Edge, Indiana's economy depended on tourism and the autumn weather had been particularly beautiful this first year of being a merchant.

The opportunity to buy the tearoom in her hometown

had come at moment in her life when she'd been at a crossroads, trying to decide whether to stay in River's Edge or move back to Cincinnati. Her dad's sister had tossed the idea out one night over a family supper and Holly's widowed mom had literally squealed with delight.

"Do it, sweets!" Melinda Peterson's face had lit up for the first time in nearly two years—since Holly's dad had died.

Holly had thought long and hard for a solid week, alternating between terror and possibility. Two years earlier, Clive Peterson's cancer diagnosis had brought her back home with her tween son, Mateo, but the chasm between her and her father had barely begun to narrow before the cancer stole him away. One big reason she'd accepted Aunt Susan's proposition had been Matty, who'd fallen in love with his grandparents, the mighty Ohio River, and all things River's Edge. She'd never seen him so happy and that alone had been enough for her to take the plunge.

The Tea Leaf was already a thriving endeavor when Holly took over. For years, Aunt Susan's business acumen had kept the little shop a charming place for tourists and townspeople alike to relax and unwind, but she was ready to retire. Holly's associate's degree in restaurant management provided lots of ideas for updating, such as putting the whole business online with a point-of-sale cash register and a new app that made inventory a snap. She'd added a new line of herbal teas, increased the lunch menu to include more vegetarian selections, and haunted auctions and estate sales all along the river to find a variety of china teacups, saucers, and plates to add a little color to the plain white bone china Aunt Susan had always used.

She glanced up, frowned at a cobweb that had formed overnight in the wide bay window, and made a mental note to get it with the duster before she opened at ten. The sun hadn't begun to lighten the sky yet, but it was October and mornings stayed dark longer. The only other place with lights on was Mac Mackenzie's Riverside Diner. Like Mac, Holly arrived at four thirty to start her day. The rich scents of cinnamon and butter wafted from the kitchen in the rear of the café, just as Alexa reminded her that her rolls were ready to come out of the oven.

"Alexa, stop." The chiming shut off as she closed out the ledger and thrust her fingers through her hair. Pulling the weight of it up into a messy bun, she secured it with the elastic she invariably had around her wrist before adding *call Callie for a trim* to the to-do list on her phone and hurrying back to the kitchen.

AIDAN FLAHERTY PEERED at the clock on the dashboard of his jaunty little MG—six fifteen. Too early for Mac's. Besides, he wasn't looking for breakfast anyway, or even a cup of coffee. He wanted tea—strong hot tea. *Lapsang*

souchong, to be exact, and even as gourmet as Mac Mackenzie was, Aidan was pretty certain he wouldn't find that particular variety of tea at the Riverside Diner. He drove a little farther up Main Street, past dark and shuttered shops, stopping in front of the Tea Leaf Café. When he'd been in River's Edge a couple of months ago for Sean and Meg's wedding, Conor's wife, Sam, mentioned that she'd found his favorite tea at this frilly little place.

There was probably no point in checking, but he pulled into an angled parking space in front of the Tea Leaf anyway. Peering out the windshield at the café tucked cozily between Noah Barker's Hardware store and The Bookmark bookstore, he couldn't help smiling. The café had been there forever, with gingham curtains at the front bay window and an attractive display of tea tins, squat teapots, and thin china cups and saucers.

Wait. Is that a light on in the back?

Looking around, he didn't see any other cars parked nearby, but there was a lot behind the row of buildings that served several businesses as well as public parking. He got out of the car, closing the door quietly behind him. Yes, there was a light on in the back. Face pressed against the glass door, he tried to see if anyone was moving around in the space behind the high-ceilinged public area of the café. Yup, someone was there. He could see a slim shadow on the louvered doors that separated the public and private spaces. The posted hours said the place opened at ten, but if someone was inside, maybe he could convince them to make him a cup of tea or at least sell him a tin of *lapsang souchong* that he could take with him to Conor and Sam's.

He raised his hand to knock, but then hesitated. Was it rude and arrogant to assume he might get the proprietor of the shop to open up at six fifteen in the morning just because *he* wanted tea? Probably. Aidan had become too aware of the whole celebrity entitlement thing ever since he'd read an article online several years ago about famous people making unreasonable demands. But he wasn't asking anyone to sort all the yellow M&M's out of his candy dish or drive fifty miles to find exactly the right brand of Tahitian bottled water; he just wanted, no, *needed*, tea.

He was still debating when a face suddenly appeared in the glass. A damn pretty face with peachy cheeks and huge eyes under a fringe of dark bangs.

"We're closed," the woman mouthed and pointed to the hours list painted on the door between them. "Come back at ten."

Aidan debated for a few more seconds, then pulled out his phone and typed *I'm desperate for tea. Can you open the door?* into his Notes app and held it up for her to read. Okay, so he *was* arrogant, but she was here and he had to have some fortification before he faced his family.

She gazed back at him, eyes narrowing. Hating himself, he turned on the Aidan Flaherty celebrity grin and waited. In LA, that smile usually got him more than he ever asked for, but it didn't seem to be cutting much ice with Miss Tea Leaf.

"Please?" he mouthed and held up one finger. "I just need one tin of tea." Shoving his signature narrow-brim black fedora back off his face, he offered another boyish grin. In for a penny, in for a pound as Da used to say. And now it wasn't just about the tea. He was curious about the petite proprietor whose expression was softening just a touch. She looked ever-so-vaguely familiar.

After another moment, she reached up and slipped the lock, then bent down and released the foot latch at the bottom of the door. "You can turn off the charm, Flaherty," she said as she yanked the door open. "The only reason I'm doing this is because your sister-in-law buys tea here and she's a nice woman and our mayor."

Ha! She recognized him. Aidan couldn't help the little victory smile that crossed his lips, although he gave it his best try. *Thank you, Meg!* He came in and stood aside as she relocked the door. The scent of cinnamon and something else heavenly wafted toward him from the kitchen, and his stomach growled, reminding him that the last food he'd eaten had been fries from a fast-food drive-through somewhere in Missouri. "Harney *lapsang souchong*, if you have it, please."

"I've got it." The woman, who was small but shapely as any Hollywood actress he'd ever seen, bustled over to the counter. When he started to follow her, she held one hand out behind her. "Stay put. I'll get it for you."

"Thanks so much." Aidan wiped the smile off his face. She wasn't giving him an ounce of quarter, which was fair, given the imposition he was presenting. "I really appreciate you doing this. Normally, I don't ask someone to make special accommodations for me, but—"

She gave him a deprecating glance. "Sure you don't, rock star." Her tone chilled him to the bone, which he was sure was her intention.

Chastened, he took one step into the shop, scanning the dim room. "This is nice. Are you the new owner? What happened to Suz?"

"She retired." She hit a switch under the wood counter next to the baked goods case and a series of can lights turned on overhead. Then she tapped on the screen of an electronic point-of-sale register that sat on the counter. "Loose or sachet?"

Aidan hated tea bags. "Loose and a tea ball if you have one, please."

She gave him another raised brow. "It's a tea shop, so that's a safe bet, now, isn't it? Stainless or mesh?"

"Mesh is fine, thanks." In spite of her chilly demeanor, he gave the cordialities another try. "I haven't been in here in ages, but when I'm home I don't get out much. When did Suz retire?"

She snapped open a brown paper bag, preparing to drop a tea infuser on a card and the tin of tea into it as she waited for the register to boot up. "About ten months ago. I took over on New Year's Eve." She drummed her fingers on the wooden surface of the counter, keeping her eyes focused on the register screen.

"How did I miss that?" Aidan tried the celebrity smile again to no avail.

The woman smirked. "You're a busy guy. I'm sure the goings-on of a tiny tearoom are pretty far off *your* radar, even if it is in your hometown." When she finally met his gaze, he realized her eyes were violet—like Elizabeth Taylor violet. They were amazing and sensual and...

"You have beautiful eyes." *Oh, good God.* The words were out before he could stop them. Immediately, he backpedaled. "I'm not coming on to you, I swear, it's just this is the first time I've actually seen someone with violet eyes. I-I mean... in person." Heat rose in his cheeks. *Blushing!* Holy crap. He didn't blush anymore—hadn't in years.

She scanned in his purchases. "Come on, rock star. All those Hollywood starlets and groupies and not a single one had eyes the same color as mine?" Her voice dripped sarcasm as she held out her hand for his credit card. "It's thirteen sixty with tax."

He fumbled in his wallet for his Amex Black Card. "Why do you keep calling me that? I'm an actor, not a rock star."

"I'm using it generically." She passed the card back to him with another eye roll. "We don't take Amex. What else have you got?"

Biting his lip to keep from expelling a frustrated breath, he handed over his VISA, the one where two percent of the money he spent went to save the redwoods. If it impressed her at all, she hid it well as she tapped the card on the screen, thrust it back at him, and turned the screen around so he could sign it with his finger. He hated doing that. His signature always ended up looking like his six-year-old niece, Ali, had written it. "Thanks so much for opening up for me."

"Don't expect me to do it again." She walked swiftly around the counter to the door, twisted the key in the lock, opened it, then stood glaring at him, one hand on her slim hip.

In that moment, Aidan could have sworn they'd met before. "You look really familiar. Do I know you?"

HOLLY SANTOS DRUMMED her fingers on her hip bone, waiting for the great Aidan Flaherty to get the hell out of her tea shop. She wasn't sure why she'd even opened the door to him except that he was Meg and Sam Flaherty's brother-in-law and she really liked both ladies. Plus, Sam was helping her with her father's estate, which had turned out to be the nightmare from hell because of that huge white elephant of a showboat down on the riverfront.

At that moment, though, she seriously could not believe

Aidan was asking *do I know you?* What an ass. He'd only spent every summer of his teenage years in her presence, the jerk. Her conscience nudged her. Well, okay, so she was behind the scenes on her dad's showboat, painting scenery and building sets, plus she was five years younger than him, but she *was* Clive Peterson's daughter. Nobody had been more enamored of Clive's talent and direction than Aidan Flaherty and Clive had adored Aidan. His *golden boy*—the son he'd never had, who'd followed in his footsteps and beyond.

He peered at her; those amazing blue eyes wide with curiosity sending a frisson of sensation through her. Oh no! She *wasn't* going there. That old crush was so far in the past, it dripped gray cobwebs.

"Do I?" he repeated and she realized she was staring.

"Nope. Don't think so." She jerked her head toward the open door. "Enjoy your tea."

Brow creased in a frown, he strode through the door, pausing when he got outside to turn that heart-stopping smile on her. "Thank you for this. You saved my life." He tipped his hat in a gesture so classically Aidan Flaherty that she almost smiled back.

Instead, she bit back the smile that rose to her lips and merely nodded as she closed the door and locked it behind him.

He stood outside for a moment longer, gazing at the shop, a bewildered expression on his too-handsome face before giving a small shrug and getting into the dark green sports car parked in front of the Tea Leaf.

She backed away from the door, then moved forward again. What? Was he driving the same MG that his character on *LA Detectives* drove? Surely they didn't let the actors take props home with them. Although if you were making over a million dollars an episode to dazzle the female fans of a stupid TV cop show, you probably got to do whatever you wanted.

She straightened her shoulders and marched back to the kitchen to put a third pan of cinnamon rolls in the oven and start mixing up the hummingbird cake. Glancing up at the clock some minutes later, she saw that it was nearly seven—time to call home and wake Mom and Mateo so he could get ready for school.

Mom's sleepy "Dammit, Hols" made Holly smile for real.

It was the same thing every morning. Holly called home right before seven and Mom resented the hell out of being awakened five minutes earlier than her alarm. But Melinda's good humor usually kicked in within the first thirty seconds and today was no exception. "Okay, no worry, Headmistress McGonagall, we're up."

Holly could picture her mom sitting up and stretching, her gray-streaked blond ponytail falling down around her face. "Harry Potter this morning? Nice. Every morning, I'm somebody new, but always wicked."

"I read. My list of fearsome disciplinarians is endless, darling daughter." Melinda Peterson's voice faded as Holly heard covers rustling and her mom moving around. "Matty! Haul it out, kid."

Holly smiled, picturing her twelve-going-on twenty-four-year-old son curled up under his covers peacefully snoozing through the insistent beep of her mother's alarm. Why the woman still used that annoying clock radio was beyond her when a cell phone served the purpose just as well and she could pick a quieter or at least a gentler chime. "Mom, turn off the alarm clock."

"Gotta pee; hold on."

Holly hit the speaker button on her phone, and set it on the countertop next to several trays of filled croissants that were rising. The ham-and-cheese were almost ready for the oven, but the chocolate ones needed a bit more time. Scones were next, then pumpkin bread, but that could wait until Layla and Fran arrived in—Holly glanced up at the clock above the door—about an hour. The restaurant would be filled with the scent of baking pumpkin bread when they opened at ten and the place bustled with autumn tourists.

The Tea Leaf Café was open daily, except Mondays, from ten to three, although *she* invariably arrived by six a.m. The menu claimed baked-fresh-daily desserts and breads, so generally the three large ovens were turned on and preheating long before dawn. She loved the tearoom hours, though, and a great staff that allowed her to be home for supper and homework and family time each evening and to have all day Sunday with Mateo, which suited Holly just fine.

"Okay, kid's getting dressed." Melinda's gravelly voice came through loud and clear even over the sound of the one-hundred-cup-capacity electric kettles that were beginning to heat up on the counter on the other side of the café's large kitchen.

Holly smiled. "Thanks, Mom. His iPad is charging on the dining room table and there's a permission slip there for the shipyard tour that the sixth grade is going on next week. Make sure he puts it in the folder in his backpack."

"Will do." Melinda had wandered downstairs to the kitchen—Holly could hear the water running and the coffee grinder.

"Also please see that he eats more than a bowl of cold cereal. At least—"

"A banana or some yogurt or an egg," Melinda interrupted. "Hols, I've been getting the kid off to school for damn near a year. I know the drill."

Holly closed her eyes, immediately remorseful. "I know, I know. I'm sorry. It's just... he's in a weird place right now."

"He misses your dad."

"He's not the only one." A pang went straight through Holly's chest at the mention of her father, whom she missed and perversely, for whom she still harbored resentment even though Clive had died nearly two years ago. She and her dad had been estranged for years after she'd gotten pregnant at the tender age of sixteen. Quitting school, marrying Leo Santos, and moving to Cincinnati with him had been a bad choice, but who made good choices at sixteen?

However, when Clive developed liver cancer, Holly had made the drive every weekend to visit him and the relationship had healed somewhat, thanks mostly to her son, who'd immediately fallen in love with his grandfather. Clive was still Clive, though, opinionated and full of himself, and Holly had never stopped resenting his obsession with theater and most especially the *River Queen*.

"I know." Mom's voice was contrite. "But if we could only get rid of that damn boat, maybe Matty's attention would turn to something else and he could let Clive go."

Holly sighed as she poured the batter for the cake into three round pans. "Mom, we're trying. Sam's got Becky Cavendish listing it all up and down the river. He hasn't been going back there again, has he?"

Melinda didn't respond right away and Holly's heart sank. She wasn't sure why Mateo found comfort in her dad's old showboat dry-docked out on the shore of the Ohio River; it wasn't like the child had ever spent any time on it. A couple of times since Clive got sick, he had been on the boat with her, but that was after the old tub had been permanently dry-docked and Clive was running it as a bar. Shuttered and locked up tight when her dad became too ill to manage it, the *River Queen* had suddenly become Matty's obsession and Holly's greatest worry. More than once, Holly or Melinda had gone down to the river to find him wandering on the deck of the old behemoth.

"He hasn't disobeyed you, but I walked down with him yesterday," Melinda confessed finally.

"Mom!" Holly hated the sharpness in her tone, but what was the point in encouraging Mateo's fascination with the boat? It was dangerous for him to be climbing around on it and no matter how she had the thing rigged, he still managed to find a way to get up onto the deck. "You're not helping when you take him down there."

"I figured it was better if we went down together and just sat on the dock for a while. That way, at least—" Melinda broke off midsentence. "Hey, kiddo. Where'd you find that shirt?"

Apparently, Mateo had come downstairs. Holly removed a pan of hot cinnamon rolls from the oven and replaced them with the tray of ham-and-cheese croissants. "Good morning, sweetie!" she called.

"Hi, Mom." Matty's voice, still sounding a little sleepy, came through the speaker on her cell phone.

Holly's curiosity was aroused by her mom's comment about his shirt. "What are you wearing, Matty?"

She could hear the hesitancy in his voice. "A T-shirt from Grampy's boat. I found a big box of them in the closet in your room." His voice suddenly changed from timid to challenging. "I got one that fits... mostly."

Holly hovered her hand over the hot cinnamon rolls, debating what to say. "Which one did you choose?" She pictured her son's smile. *Pick your battles*—she'd been living by that credo each passing day lately. Going through the box in her closet wasn't a hill she was willing to die on. Not this morning.

"The orange one with the black picture of Grampy's boat on it. It's awesome." The delight in his voice came through loud and clear.

"Does it come down to your knees?" Holly rolled her eyes heavenward.

"He picked an adult small and it actually fits him pretty well." Melinda's voice was slightly muffled. "Man, kid, you are growing like a weed, but you're still not too big for hugs from Grammy. Are ya? Huh? Are ya?"

Envy spasmed through Holly as she heard Mateo laughing while Melinda was clearly hugging the stuffing out of him. Her little boy was growing up. "Gotta go mix up scones, baby. Have a good day at school and please come right here as soon as you get off the bus. You can earn some money today, okay?"

"Doing what?" Mateo's tone was suspicious.

"Just show up. We're going to have fun." Holly intended to put him to work clearing out the container gardens in front of and behind the café, then refilling them with the mums she was going to buy at the orchard after she closed up. "Love you, Matty."

"Love you, too, Mom."

Holly touched her screen to disconnect, then gathered the ingredients for cranberry scones, wondering idly as she mixed the batter what Aidan Flaherty was doing wandering around River's Edge at six in the morning on a Tuesday in the middle of October. Shouldn't he have been back in LA shooting episodes of that TV cop show?

Chapter Two

SUNRISE PAINTED THE eastern sky all shades of pink and orange as Aidan sat in his car in the parking lot of the McDonald's on the highway above River's Edge, munching an Egg McMuffin and sipping his tea. He could've been sitting at the counter at Mac's Riverside Diner, enjoying an omelet and Mac's famous truffle butter toast, because it was Tuesday, after all. He could even be lounging in Conor and Sam's roomy breakfast nook, eating waffles and sausage while he teased Ali and made silly faces at baby Griff. Either place, he would've had his tea in a real mug or cup instead of a cardboard container.

He was a rank coward, no question about that.

He was also rank in body and spirit. Although he'd showered at a couple of the motels he'd stopped at along Highway 40, he'd kept such odd hours driving that he hadn't bothered at the last one. Instead, yesterday, at two in the afternoon, too exhausted to drive another mile, he'd checked into a dingy mom-and-pop motel in a town some-where near St. Louis, fallen fully clothed onto the bed, and slept for twelve straight hours. Then he'd checked out and began the last leg of his journey home, figuring he could shower in his brother's sparkling-clean guest bath if he simply got on the road and drove. It hadn't even occurred to him that he'd be arriving in River's Edge at the butt-crack of dawn.

He peeked at his phone propped up behind the gearshift—almost eight a.m. He could probably head down to Four Irish Brothers Winery, let himself in, and wait for Conor and Sean to show up. Conor had given him and Brendan new keys to the place at their last "board meeting," which took place on New Year's Eve as they sat on barrels in the cellar toasting Da with port.

By now, Ali was already at school, Sam would be getting little Griffin ready for the day. She was probably on the phone with Meg. They usually rode together in the mornings—Sam and Griff to her law office on Adams Street, Meg to her mayor duties at the town hall.

He slumped down, closed his eyes, and laid his head back against the smooth leather of the seat. Everybody was doing normal today. Everybody but him. He had no idea what normal was anymore or would be ever again. The muffin and egg turned to ashes in his mouth as memories of the previous weeks washed over him. He'd sucked it up, been professional through the whole fricking mess, but now that it was well and truly done, despondence overtook him.

His cell chimed with a text. "*Call me*," and a smiley face. Mason Riverton, his agent. Moaning, he picked up the phone, then set it back down again. He was not in the mood to deal with Mason's fast-talking morning exuberance. It was five in the morning in LA. Nobody should be sending smiley face texts at five in the morning.

He'd left messages with everyone in LA—he was taking a break; he'd be in touch, so there was no need to return the three dozen or so texts, voice mails, and emails Mason had sent over the last five days. His PA, Philomena Murphy, had probably gotten his belongings out of the cottage in Malibu and into storage by now and turned the keys and garage door openers into the management company. He would miss that little piece of heaven on the Pacific, the early morning walks on the beach, the sunsets over the ocean, but he simply couldn't spend another moment in California.

Five days ago, after shooting the last scene of *LA Detectives*, all he'd wanted was to get in his car and drive east to Indiana and home. But now that he was nearly there, he couldn't seem to make himself trek those last few miles to Four Irish Brothers Winery. He had no doubt his brothers and new sisters-in-law would shower him with love and sympathy. Sean would bluster about how Hollywood was a racket and how glad he was that Aidan was well out of it. Conor would immediately suggest he join them at the winery, while Sam and Megan offered tea and sympathy and Ali and baby Griffin covered him in hugs and kisses.

But the humiliation of being written out of *LA Detectives* was still raw. It wasn't only that he'd lost the part; it was how they'd done it—without even a heads-up. He sipped his tea, remembering that dismal day two weeks ago when he'd read the script for episode ten of the current season…

"You killed me!"

Aidan Flaherty stormed into the writers' office at 3Guns Studios and tossed his script on the table where three men and two women sat, laptops open in front of them. Empty cardboard cups were strewn among crumpled papers, fast-food bags, and overflowing ashtrays. The last bastion for chain-smoking writers reeked of cigarettes, french fries, and stale coffee. Aidan nearly gagged. If he weren't so pissed, he'd open the window and turn up the ceiling fan that twirled lazily over the table.

"Okay, Aidan, hold on. Just chill." Gary Weiss, the head writer, raised one finger, but didn't look up from whatever he was typing.

Aidan fumed for all of ten seconds before he released a frustrated breath and shoved the lid down on Gary's computer. "Dammit, Gary. Talk to me."

Gary yanked his fingers out of the way. "Look, our ratings have dropped and we need to bring in some fresh faces." He didn't meet Aidan's eyes.

"So you kill off the only guy on the show to win a Golden Globe and *an Emmy this year?" Aidan threw up his arms, pacing the small stifling room. He was furious, barely able to take a breath. Why would they kill* him *off? His character got more fan mail, more hits on Twitter and Instagram. His Facebook page was always buzzing. For the past couple of years,*

he'd been avoiding popular Malibu eateries because it was impossible to finish a meal in peace. He loved his fans, but sometimes it would've been nice to go out for a steak dinner without being hounded for selfies and autographs. When he didn't want to be recognized, he covered his signature blond mop with a baseball cap instead of wearing his fedora and put on old-fashioned aviator sunglasses, but even that didn't keep people—okay, women—from figuring out LA Detective's *Pete Atwood was in the house.*

Pam Stokes reached out to stop him. "Think of it as going out on top, Aidan. You can write your own ticket in this town now." She pulled him toward her, winked, then patted his jeans-clad butt.

Aidan hopped away as if he'd been burned and glared at her. "Keep your hands off!" Pam had made passes at Aidan since she'd started writing for the show two years ago and he had deftly avoided her innuendos and groping. Today, he didn't have another ounce of polite patience in him. But she only chuckled.

"Who told you to do this?" he demanded.

"We're the writers, kid." Gary lit up a slim brown cigarette. "Nobody tells us what to do. But we had approval from the carpeted offices, so take it up with them."

"Dick okayed this?" Aidan couldn't believe director Dick Leonard had let them write his character out of the show. He'd hired Aidan for the part of Detective Pete Atwood five years ago. The two of them had become fast friends on the set. Hell, he'd come over to Aidan's cottage in Malibu just last week for poker

and never mentioned it. He'd drunk plenty of Four Irish Brothers Winery zin that Aidan had brought back from Indiana though. Bastard...

Without another word then, Aidan had grabbed his script and stomped out of the writers' room, letting the door shut behind him with a rather unsatisfying thud. He'd heard one of the other writers moan, "Actors, sheesh," as the door closed. The others' chuckles had sent another shaft of ire through him, but he'd made it through the table read that day and rehearsals and the days of shooting.

The indignation and anger were gone now, leaving a huge empty hole in place of all the good piss-off that had gotten him through his own death scene. And he had died with panache, no denying that. Being shot in the chest offered the chance for a heart-wrenching scene between Pete and his long-time partner Angel Rodriguez, played by the lovely and still-employed Janine Garcia. Janine's tears had been real as Aidan had gasped out that he'd always loved her and how sorry he was they'd never have a chance to be together—lines he'd improvised. Dick loved it so much, he'd kept it, to the loud disapproval of the writers, who'd written him in typical Pete Atwood smart-ass mode even in his death scene.

The episode would air right after Thanksgiving hiatus and give fans something to chew on for weeks. As far as he knew, the news that Pete Atwood was dead hadn't broken yet, although the TV industry was terrible at keeping secrets.

Didn't everyone know someone significant was going to die long before Matthew Crawley crashed his car on *Downton Abbey*? No doubt word had gotten out that *LA Detectives* was losing an important character. In a moment of true childishness, he hoped fans would assume the victim was Detective Frank Hughes, played by veteran TV actor and asshole deluxe Adam Paxton. But, no, Adam had strutted around the set smirking while—

A knock on his car window jerked him back to the Mickey D's parking lot and he turned to see a young woman peering in. "Hey?" She tapped on the glass again. "Hey? Aren't you that cop? The one on TV? Pete At-Atwater?"

Aidan came within a second of simply shaking his head since she didn't even have the name of his character right, but another girl came up behind the blonde, a huge smile on her face. "It's him!" She gripped the blonde's arm. "It's Pete *Atwood* from *LA Detectives*!" Elbowing her way to the window of the little MG, she stooped down. "We love you, Pete!"

Pinning on his celebrity smile, the one that showed off his dimples and made hearts race all over America and Canada, Aidan rolled down the window. "Good morning, ladies."

They clutched each other and giggled, jiggling with excitement. "Can we get a picture with you?" the blond one asked while the other one bit her lip and sighed.

"Sure." Aidan opened the car door and got out, surreptitiously scanning the parking lot as he did so. Most of the cars were in the drive-thru and the people in line weren't paying attention to the activity in the corner of the parking lot, where he'd deliberately parked to avoid being recognized. How had these two figured out who he was?

Oh, crap, the California license plates on Pete's distinctive MG! A dead giveaway and it's no secret that the actor who plays Pete Atwood is from a small river town in Southern Indiana.

At least ten pictures and a couple of autographs later, he was back in the car while the two girls scurried off. Aidan watched out of the corner of his eye as they high-fived each other before getting into an older compact car. No doubt they were both on their phones letting friends know that Pete Atwood was haunting the parking lot of the McDonald's on the highway, so heaving a huge breath, he buckled up and turned the key in the ignition.

Sam and Meg and the kids would surely be gone by now, and Conor and Sean would be up at the winery inspecting fermentation tanks or maybe out in the vineyard checking to see if hardening over had started. Conor would open up for visitors and Sean would head into town to open the tasting room down on the river. Brendan might still be at home instead of in his office at the CIA or FBI or wherever the hell it was he worked in Washington, so they could FaceTime him into the conversation, and he'd only have to tell the story once. He sped out of the parking lot. He wanted to talk to all of his brothers together.

HOLLY UTTERED AN oath, wiped down the chalkboard sandwich-style sign she'd leaned against a table, and started lettering the specials for the third time.

"Little trouble there, boss?" Server Fran Peale nudged her shoulder as she passed by with a tray of salt and pepper shakers that she'd filled.

"Did those get good and dry overnight?" Holly stood back, eyeing the blackboard as she spoke. "And you put rice in the salt, right?"

"Yes, boss." Fran began distributing pairs of shakers, taking time to refill packets of sugar and sweetener on each table from a basket she had hooked over her arm as she went along. Stopping for a second, she gave a Holly a grin. "You know, it's only the specials board. It's not going to be hanging in the Louvre. Doesn't have to be great art."

Holly bent over the board, carefully sketching before filling in a border of ivy with green chalk. "I know, but it's fun to make it look pretty and unique."

Fran nodded. "People do love your specials boards." She set the last set of shakers on table twelve by the big bay window. "I smelled quiche when I got here. Which is it?"

"Mushroom, bacon, and shallots and brie and spinach." Holly wrote the words in elegant lavender script on the chalkboard as she said them out loud. "Cranberry scones today, ham-and-cheese croissants, along with all the usuals."

Suddenly, the back door flew open and Layla Burton raced in, rosy cheeked and breathless, her blond curly hair wisping around her face. "You'll never guess who I met up on the highway!" She pulled out her phone, tapping the screen with trembling fingers. "Look!"

Holly shook her head as she and Fran exchanged a tolerant smile. At eighteen, Layla was about as starstruck as any college freshman could be. Ever on a vigilant celebrity watch, the girl lived and died for the newest editions of *People* and *Us* magazines, and swore she saw famous people wherever she went. Hard to believe because, seriously, how many celebrities hung out in River's Edge, Indiana?

Fran glanced at Layla's phone, then did a literal double take, grabbing the phone and scrolling through several pictures. "Holy Toledo! Is that—"

Layla nodded. "It's him! He was sitting in his car at Mickey D's. We knew it had to be *somebody* because of the little sports car and the California plates, so we got bold and peeked in the window."

Without even looking at the pictures, Holly knew immediately whom she was referring to—had to be Aidan Flaherty. She kept quiet as Layla waxed eloquent about how sweet and gorgeous Aidan was and Fran nodded and swooned, appropriately appreciative.

"Do you want to see the pictures?" Layla stepped over to where Holly was finishing up the specials board, holding out her phone.

Holly gave the phone a quick look to verify her hunch. "I've seen Aidan Flaherty, thanks." She picked up the board, lugged it to the front, and shoving the door open with her butt, set the A-frame sign outside on the sidewalk.

Layla followed her and leaned against the doorjamb. "But it happened this morning! You know what that means, right?"

"He eats fast food, just like the rest of us peons?" Holly ventured a guess as she moved the sign closer to the building and turned it this way and that.

Layla released an exasperated breath. "It means," she explained with exaggerated patience, "that he's in town. Probably visiting his brothers and laying low as usual, but he's here!" She bounced on the balls of her feet. "Depending on how long he's here, there's a good chance we'll get to see him again!"

"Yay." Holly backed a few steps away from the blackboard in an effort to see how easy it was to read from a distance and bumped right into Mae Boyle, owner of The Bookmark, who was wheeling a cart full of sale books out onto the sidewalk in front of her store next door.

"Yay, indeed." Mae grinned, clearly misunderstanding the genesis of Holly's acerbic cheer. "It looks great, Holly!"

Layla had followed Holly down the sidewalk and was shaking a finger at her. "Your enthusiasm for the only person in the entire town of River's Edge to ever make it big is a bit underwhelming."

Holly turned to return Mae's smile. "Good morning, Mae! It's a good day for tourists!"

"Sure is!" Mae went back into her shop as Holly gave Layla a withering look.

"Seriously, Layla? The *only* person from River's Edge to make it big?" She crossed her arms and tapped one sneaker-clad foot. "So we're dismissing a governor, two US senators, various congresspersons, a best-selling author, a Pulitzer-Prize-winning journalist, an artist whose work hangs in the MOMA in New York, a woman who's currently writing number-one hit songs for several famous rock bands?" Holly ticked each item off on her fingers. "Not to mention at least fifty small business owners all over town who might find that comment slightly offensive. *Me*, for instance?"

Layla sighed, looking at Holly pityingly before she headed back into the Tea Leaf. "Point taken about the business owners, but I'm talking about *real* stars, not politicians from the eighteen hundreds and boring writers and painters for pity's sake."

Holly followed her in. "Oh, so sorry. For a minute I thought we were discussing *all* the accomplished citizens of River's Edge."

Layla glanced over her shoulder. "Why do you hate Aidan Flaherty? I mean, seriously, Holly, what's not to like? He is yummy." She smacked her lips.

"Did I say I hated Aidan Flaherty?" Holly came around the back of the counter to rescue a tray of scones that Fran was wrestling into the glass case. "Here, Frannie, I've got it."

Layla went into the kitchen to put on her gingham apron and tuck her order pad and a pen into the wide front pocket.

"Pull your hair back, Layla," Holly reminded her as they brushed shoulders in the doorway. "And make sure you wash your hands after you do it."

"What's your problem with that delicious hunk o' man?" Layla pursued the question while she stood in front of the mirror in the small bathroom outside the kitchen, putting her blond curls into a high ponytail.

Fran brought two trays of cookies to the display case. "Didn't he used to be in the plays your dad put on when the showboat was running?"

Holly came in with another tray of goodies—chocolate croissants this time, always a big seller. "He was, but I never really knew him. He was onstage and I was backstage. Besides, he was a lot older than me. I'm not a big fan of TV. I hate all the violence. I'd rather read or spend time with Matty." She was avoiding the question, but she really wasn't up for a conversation about Aidan Flaherty. His presence in her shop that morning had discombobulated her more than she wanted to admit. And talking about him would only make her wonder and the wondering would bring up the crush she'd successfully quashed for most of her adult life.

Living in Cincinnati had made not thinking about him easy, but since she'd been back and in contact with most of his family again, the old feelings had crept in. She'd even dreamed about him a few nights ago. Not a sexy dream, but definitely a romantic one, except that in the dream, he was still that swaggering high school kid who could act with the talent and panache of Olivier and she was herself now—a twenty-eight-year-old divorced single mom who hadn't had a date in over five years.

She blinked and shook her head to clear it. It was time to open up. What did it matter if the great Aidan Flaherty was in town? He never stayed long. At least that was what she was counting on.

Chapter Three

"CAN THEY GET away with this? How does your contract read?" Sean was pacing the concrete floor of the wine cellar, having fallen into attorney mode as soon as Aidan spilled his guts. "Do you have it with you? Let me take a look at it. They're all a bunch of rats out there. Who knows what kinds of shenanigans they pulled to be able to write you out?"

Conor tossed his hands in the air with a decided *pshaw*. "It doesn't matter, Ace. You're home and now you can stay here and be a part of the business and"—he paused to gaze into Aidan's eyes—"well, I mean, if that's what you want to do."

Aidan couldn't help grinning. Sean's reaction was exactly what he'd expected—bluster and indignation. So was Conor's immediate invitation to become an active participant in Four Irish Brothers Winery. Unfortunately, Bren had an early meeting and couldn't join them via FaceTime, so Aidan would have to tell the story again. He addressed Sean first. "Dude, they were perfectly within their rights, I promise you. My contract was up for renewal... or not.

Mason and my attorney have it all under control." Then he turned to Conor. "Right now, helping out here sounds fabulous to me. I need to put my hands in the dirt and be as far away from LA as I can."

Sean plopped down on a barrel, outrage rolling off him in waves. "Those bastards. I can't believe they killed off Pete Atwood—the only motivation I have to ever turn on a TV. *You* are the whole reason that show's ratings are so high. Aren't you the only one who's won an Oscar or whatever the TV equivalent is?"

Aidan chuckled. Sean didn't watch television. He never had, even when they were kids. He was always reading with his Walkman earbuds keeping him in his own world while the rest of them watched their favorite shows. Later when he was in high school, he was at basketball practice or on a date or studying with Meg. The fact that he realized there *was* an award for television acting and that Aidan had won one spoke volumes about how proud he was of his little brother. "It's an Emmy and, yes, I was the only one. It pissed Adam off no end that he wasn't even nominated this year and that his *supporting* actor won one instead."

Conor smirked. "I'll bet the table read for your last show was the highlight of *his* career on *LA Detectives*." He had absorbed more knowledge about Aidan's job, or at least the jargon, than either Sean or their other brother Brendan simply by virtue of the fact that he was at home and heard more about it from Aidan when he came to River's Edge on hiatus. Sean had only recently returned to the fold after leaving his Chicago law firm, while Brendan still lived in Washington, DC.

"He was pretty cocky, that's for damn sure." Aidan rolled his eyes. "I'm sure he's convinced the writers are going to concoct a romance between him and Janine, Lord help her."

"He's the one they should've written out." Conor plucked the fedora from Aidan's head and ruffled his hair. "You'll stay with us, Ace. The guest room in the basement can be yours as long as you need."

"He can stay with Meg and me, Conny." Sean paused his pacing. "You can have your old room, Ace. Meg hasn't gotten to it yet, so it's still the way Char left it."

Conor guffawed. "Um, trust me, you're don't want to live with the newlyweds. You never know what you're going to interrupt when you go over there. They're enough to gag you."

"*This* from the guy who salivates visibly whenever his wife crosses his field of vision?" Sean gave him an over-the-top-of-the glasses mock glower and went to the office to pour three mugs of coffee from the pot he'd started brewing right after Aidan's arrival. He handed Aidan a steaming mug. "Here, drink this. You look like hammered crap, kid. You can follow me back to the house and we'll get you settled. I gotta figure out which sheets are for the bed in there, and I need to toss the towels in the dryer, but I can set you up."

Aidan inhaled the dark brew. Although it smelled great

and he appreciated his brother's concern, he really hated coffee. He set the mug on the barrel next to him and offered his brothers a weak smile. "I don't care where I sleep, honestly, but what I really need is a shower. I've been driving at night and sleeping during the day since I left LA, so my circadian rhythms are a little off-kilter."

Conor's deep slug of coffee made Aidan cringe inwardly, but he tried not to show it, especially since Conny said, "*Our* guest room it is, Ace. You'll have the basement to yourself. Private bath, *clean* towels, and Sam always keeps that bed made up. But, truthfully, I don't think you should go to bed right now. You'll do better if you get back on Indiana time right away."

Sean nodded in agreement. "He's right, Ace. It's like when you travel to Europe and you land in Paris or Munich at nine in the morning local time. They always tell you to stay up, even if all you want to do is sleep. Let's get your *circadian rhythms*"—he air-quoted the term with a wry grin—"back on Eastern time."

"Have we fallen back yet?" Aidan never could keep track of that because California was always three hours earlier than Indiana no matter whether DST was in effect or not.

Sean shook his head, gulping the last of his coffee and sauntering into the office to refill his mug. "Not until the first Sunday in November."

Conor followed Sean into the office to warm up his own coffee, calling over his shoulder, "Go on down to the house and get settled. Go in through the screened porch. Key to the back door is under the basket next to the boot tray. Come back up here and I'll fill you in on where we are, postharvest. After that, you can drive into town and follow Sean around the tasting room for a while. When Steve and Liz get here, I'll come down and we can have lunch at Mac's or the tavern." He ambled back out into the cellar, sipping. "It's all going to be okay."

Sean came out and slung an arm around Aidan's shoulder, surprising Aidan with how much stronger his older brother had gotten in the past months, or wait, had it been over a year? It had! Almost a year and half now since Sean's near-tragic shooting in Chicago. He looked great. He wasn't even limping anymore. Work in the vineyard built him up like no personal trainer ever could. Aidan gazed into his oldest brother's blue eyes, noting, not for the first time, how much life in River's Edge and marriage to Mayor Megan Mackenzie agreed with him.

As a matter of fact, both Conor and Sean exuded peace and happiness, and he longed to warm himself at their lives for just a little while. They both demonstrated how life could turn from tragedy into something wonderful. Although he'd never compare his loss of a TV series to Conor losing his first wife to cancer or Sean being shot by a client's crazy ex, he couldn't deny this moment was the lowest point in his own life so far.

That realization suddenly struck him with the force of a

Mack truck. How hard he'd worked at his acting career—going to New York from college, years of struggling to get to auditions while holding down two jobs. He'd lived with his friend Dean from college and four other aspiring actors in a cramped apartment on the Upper West Side; working days at a bookstore and nights as a server at a wine bar near the Theater District, running to casting calls and trying to find an agent.

He played small roles in dozens of off-off-Broadway productions and summer stock around New England before being cast as Stanley Kowalski in a revival of *A Streetcar Named Desire* on Broadway. It had been a fluke—he'd gone to the open audition because the part was one he'd played several times before, never believing for a moment they'd cast a relatively unknown actor in the lead of a Broadway production. But he knew Stanley inside out. It was a meaty role and as he watched the auditions from backstage, he was shocked at how limp the performances were. Where was the passion Williams had written? When had Stanley Kowalski become such a wuss? Clive Peterson would have been waving his signature cigar and shouting, "Tennessee Williams is rolling over in his grave! Do the play as written!"

He'd given an audition Clive would've been proud of, putting all the passion he had inside him into his interpretation of the crude and volatile Kowalski, losing himself in the role to the point that he went past his allotted time. No one stopped him, and the actress reading the role of Stella just rode along, clearly caught up in the final scene of the play. He was panting and dripping sweat when he finally ended the scene with his arms around her and one hand groping her breast exactly as Williams had written in his stage directions.

The director's assistant called him that evening while he was working. They offered him the role and a salary that meant he could quit the bookstore and the wine bar and sign with an agent. He loved the play and everything about working on Broadway. *Streetcar* opened to rave reviews from the New York critics, especially for the unknown newcomer playing Stanley Kowalski.

When 3Guns Studio director, Dick Leonard, saw the play several months later, he'd come backstage to introduce himself and invited Aidan to brunch the next day. His offer of the role of Pete Atwood on the hit cop show *LA Detectives* was too good to pass up. In less than a month, Aidan was in Los Angeles, and with the help of his new personal assistant, Philomena Murphy—Phil—settling into a small cottage on the ocean in Malibu, and being groomed to play the smart-mouth foil to Adam Paxton's gruff character on the show. Now here he was, unemployed and for the first time in his life, unsure of what he wanted.

"Ace? Hey? What is it?" Sean's voice dragged him back to Four Irish Brothers and the wholehearted acceptance and love of his family. Right now, *that* was what he needed. Not another role on another cop show like his agent was pushing.

Or a gig on one of the bachelor reality shows that were so popular—another bright idea from Mason. Not even going to New York to audition for the revival of Neil Simon's *Chapter Two* that Marc Chambers was producing—something he'd thought about seriously as he drove across the country. He wanted to be *offstage* for just a little while… or maybe forever. He didn't know anymore.

"I'm so glad to be here." The words came out slightly choked and Aidan swallowed hard, determined not to show how emotionally frail he was to his brothers. Not that they wouldn't be sympathetic, they would. But he was here to garner strength, to figure out where he was headed, something he couldn't grasp onto in LA.

Sean grinned and winked. "We're happy you're home, Ace. Head on down to Conny's and get settled. I'll be in town whenever you're ready. We'll hit Mac's for lunch, maybe meet the girls. They'll be thrilled you're home."

HOLLY BLEW A breath into her bangs as she flipped the sign on the Tea Leaf's door to *Closed* as the last customer departed. She loved how easy it was for people to linger over tea and scones, but was equally thrilled when they paid the check and moved on to wander the shops in River's Edge. She paused for a moment, relishing the bright blue October sky and the red, yellow, and orange leaves on the trees at the park in the center of the square. They hadn't started falling yet and her town glowed fiery with autumn.

As it happened, fall was becoming the best season she'd had at the Tea Leaf Café so far, but that wasn't a surprise. Tourists filled the town from Chautauqua at the end of September right through the holiday season. According to the other town business owners, things were pretty quiet from late December through March, but spring brought folks back for the Redbud Festival in April and tourist season started again. Even so, in the dreary winter months, Holly had served plenty of tea to the townsfolk, who divided their time between Paula's Bread and Butter Bakery and the Tea Leaf if they were looking for delicious baked goods.

She gazed down the street observing, with a small smile, the hubbub of out-of-towners along the sidewalk, exploring shops or heading down to the River Walk for a jaunt along the wide ribbon of the Ohio River.

Oh, damn, the chalkboard.

Stepping out into the warm fall sunshine, she meandered to the sign, all the while keeping an eye out for Mateo, who was due to arrive at any moment. As she folded the board, a familiar whistle brought her attention to the park in the center of the square.

"Hang on, Mom, I'll get that." Mateo looked both ways and then crossed just a few feet from the crosswalk, hurrying toward her.

She leaned the sign against her hip and enfolded her son

in her arms. Lord, he was as tall as she was, although that wouldn't be hard. At exactly five feet tall, Holly was shorter than most people. But Matty had grown like a weed since they'd moved to River's Edge. He wasn't her little boy anymore. At twelve years old, he was becoming a young man.

Her heart ached for her son, growing up without a father, although because Clive's focus had always been the showboat and his own acting career, so had she. When she got pregnant and her parents turned their backs, she'd hoped for more from Leo Santos, who'd scooped her up and taken her to Cincinnati to live with the grandmother. Turned out, he was no different from Clive, abandoning his son to pursue auditions and cattle calls. Clearly, Matty was happier here in River's Edge, but Holly still worried about him constantly and about Melinda, who sometimes seemed so lost without Clive.

"Hey, kiddo." She handed over the sign. "You stopped by home and changed your clothes. Thanks for that."

Matty looked down at his torn jeans and Warner College hoodie. "Well, you said you had a job for me and I figured it would be a dirty job because they always are."

Holly laughed and ruffled his dark hair. "You're so mistreated."

Matty rolled his eyes, then grinned that Santos grin—the one that had charmed her right into Leo Santos's arms when she was sixteen. "Don't I know it." He backed into the door, shoving it open with his butt, and leaned the sandwich board against the wall behind the counter. "Right here okay?"

"Perfect."

He scanned the glass case. "Did you make brownies today?"

"Nope, but I saved you a chocolate croissant. It's on the prep table in the kitchen."

"Do I have to save it for after?" His expression was so wistful that Holly shook her head.

"No, go eat it now while I close out the sales report for today. We can work for a bit and we'll hit the bank night drop on our way home." She tapped the screen on the point-of-sale register to generate the report. "Help yourself to milk or lemonade."

"Milk with chocolate always, Mom." Mateo headed through the propped-open kitchen door to where Layla and Fran were packaging up leftover pastries and Ethan was filling the dishwasher.

"Amen to that, dude!" Ethan offered Matty a wet high five, while Layla and Fran caught him up in hugs that made the poor kid squirm as Holly looked on from the dining room. The two women adored Mateo and never missed an opportunity to tease him, which he always tolerated good-naturedly. The four of them chattered while she closed out the register and collected the cash from the drawer under the counter. Credit card sales were in the program in the register and would go automatically to the bank.

It had been a good day. Plenty of traffic. Even a line for tables at lunch, which wasn't unusual. Because it was too chilly to use the outdoor seating, customers received a pager and were encouraged to wander the shops right around the tearoom. Mae Boyle at The Bookmark, Janet at the Yarn Basket, and Clyde at Antiques and Uniques, across the street, had all invested in the long-range paging system with the agreement that the Tea Leaf hostesses would send customers to their shops to peruse as they waited for a table. So far, it had worked out perfectly if the bags that diners brought in with them when they were paged were any indication.

Holly had been impressed with the business owners' sense of camaraderie and cooperation in River's Edge. It certainly had been much more cutthroat when she'd managed the restaurant in Cincinnati. But here, Mac at the Riverside sent customers to the Tea Leaf and Holly reciprocated in kind. They both offered coupons for Paula Meadows's bakery or for a free drink at Hutchin's House tavern, a discount on goods at the Yarn Basket and other shops, or a tasting at Four Irish Brothers Winery. *Four Irish Brothers Winery.*

Releasing a huge sigh, Holly shook her head to get rid of the image of Aidan Flaherty that had been haunting her since early that morning. Damn him anyway for that smile, which had set her heart racing ages ago when he'd tweaked her braids backstage on the *River Queen*, and then dared to have exactly the same effect on her fifteen years later. She'd been

Matty's age the first time he'd sauntered onto the deck of the *River Queen*, oozing charisma.

Aidan had had a job on the *River Queen* every summer when he was in high school and college. And always, he'd been the star of the show, whether he was singing, dancing, or acting in one of the old-timey melodramas that Clive produced on the showboat's stage each season. He'd broken more hearts than any other kid in the cast or crew, although Holly had to admit that he'd never been any more conceited than any other actor who played the showboat. In fact, Aidan had worked his gorgeous butt off, not only onstage, but helping out belowdeck, maintaining or repairing the giant diesel engines or taking his turn cleaning the theater, which unlike his time onstage, were paying gigs. He was an incorrigible flirt though, and it seemed, even to her twelve-year-old observance, that he never met a female he couldn't charm.

And charm them he did, both onstage and off. The incredibly talented Aidan Flaherty was a huge draw for showboat audiences up and down the Ohio River—audiences were sure he was headed to Broadway or Holly-wood. Inevitably, he had a pretty girl on his arm everywhere he went.

Her dad's Showboat Summer course was one of Warner College's most popular classes. Clive always had a waiting list. Even people who weren't majoring in drama or theater signed up, and when they got a spot, it was eye-rolling time for the kids who were actually there for the experience and not the hot guys and girls. Holly recalled the theater majors whispering in frustration when girls who *weren't* enrolled in the drama school got a spot, but gave little effort to their stage crew or costume shop or set-building duties. Instead, they trailed after Aidan Flaherty as he rehearsed for shows or elbowed each other as he passed them on deck and gave them a wink or a dimpled grin. Girls in the audiences often followed him from town to town, and more than once she'd glimpsed him up on the top deck, making out with the flavor of the week.

Over the winters, she'd focus on school, keeping her distance from him, which wasn't hard since she was way too young to drink wine and the years between them meant their paths rarely crossed, even in River's Edge. Each summer, she'd vow that season would be different. She wouldn't give two hoots about Aidan Flaherty. But then he'd return, more handsome than before, and her tender young heart ached when he looked through her to whatever sorority cutie had caught his eye.

And here he was—back in River's Edge, and still making her heart pound.

Damn him.

Chapter Four

A T FIRST, IT was the hushed whispers that woke him…

Didn't you tell him not *to go to bed?*

I did tell him. Looks like he dropped his bags and fell across the bed.

Poor baby, he must be exhausted. Should we wake him?

We have to or he'll have his days and nights mixed up for ages.

Ali! Wait!

Aidan emerged sluggishly from a dream where he was being chased through the streets of LA by Adam Paxton, who turned into Mason, who changed into Clive Peterson, who somehow transformed into a huge curly brown dog that caught him and covered his face in slobbery kisses.

What the hell?

When he opened his eyes, the creature, that wasn't really huge at all, had its front paws perched on his chest and was blowing dog breath into his face. With a groan, Aidan put both hands up to push the dog's face to the side. "Ugh! Where did *you* come from?"

"It's me and Lily, Uncle Aidan!" Ali's voice came from the chair across the room. "We've been waiting hours and hours for you to wake up." She shrugged as she sauntered over to the edge of the bed, her dark braid slung over one shoulder. "I guess she couldn't wait anymore." She shook her finger at the dog, who Aidan realized was barely out of puppyhood. "Lily! Get off! Heel. Sit."

The dog, her stumpy tail wagging vigorously, jumped down from the bed and sat on the floor, compliant to a fault, even though she was barely able to contain her excitement over someone new in the house.

Aidan peered out the window, but the screened porch off the walkout basement hid the sun or it was getting dark… or it was already dark. He couldn't tell. He rubbed his eyes, then stretched, glancing up to see Conor hovering in the doorway, holding a grinning baby Griff.

"You fell asleep, Ace," Conor observed, coming into the room with his wife, Samantha, at his heels.

"I feel like I could sleep for a week. C'mere kid, give us a hug." Aidan extended his arms to Ali, who leaped into them, giggling when Aidan kissed her on the cheek as he sat up on the edge of the bed.

"I'm so glad to see you, Uncle Aidan!" Ali squealed. "You've been gone forever! Look how big Lily got."

Obediently, Aidan eyed the dog—a miniature Australian Labradoodle with curly chocolate-brown fur and a face that made even the most macho of men go *awww*. Lily had still been a scampering puppy last time he'd been in River's Edge, which was back in June for a brothers' weekend. Griffin was only two months old then but wow, the baby had grown, too!

"I'm glad to see you too, Princess Alannah." With a groan, Aidan rose from the bed, then knelt on one knee in front of the little girl, his eyes downcast. "Knight Aidan at your service, your majesty."

Ali broke into peals of laughter, her dark eyes glistening. "You don't have to bow. I'm not a princess really, Uncle Aidan. That's make-believe."

"But you're wearing a crown." Tiredly, he sat back down on the bed with an *oomph*.

"It's not a crown, it's my ballet tiara." She twirled around showing remarkable grace for a six-year-old. "See?" She pirouetted across the big bedroom, landing next to her stepmother, who caught her before she fell.

"Ali, chill out, honey. Let's give Uncle Aidan a moment or two to wake up, okay?" Sam patted the dancing child. "Welcome home, Aidan, it *is* good to see you." Setting Ali next to Conor with a warning look, she came over to hug Aidan.

Sam looked amazing—tall and slender—her auburn hair up in a messy bun. Motherhood agreed with her. She fairly glowed with happiness.

He stood and stepped into the embrace. "Thanks, Sam. It's good to be home."

"Did you find everything you needed?" She gazed around the room. "Towels? Soap? There are extra toothbrushes in the vanity drawer and more clean towels in the bathroom closet."

Aidan chuckled. "Conor was right. I literally dropped my bags and fell on the bed, so I haven't needed anything yet."

"I heard Da tell Sam that you weren't supposed to go to bed." Ali frowned and scooted closer to Aidan and Sam. "You should always mind Da 'cause he doesn't tell us stuff just to be mean; he wants to be sure we're safe. You know, 'cause he loves us so much."

Conor grinned. "There you go, Ace, out of the mouths of babes."

"You've really brainwashed this poor kid, haven't you? Hey, hand over that baby." Aidan scooped Griffin out of Conor's arms and swung him around. "Dude, look at you! You sure have grown! You must have the Flaherty appetite. And where'd you get all that hair?" He brought the little boy to his shoulder, pressed a kiss to the top of his dark head, and inhaled the scent of his nephew—shampoo and that sweet essence that was unique to babies everywhere. "He's got your eyes, Sam."

Sam's joy in her son shone on her face. "He does, doesn't he? Those are Mom's eyes."

"How *is* Carly? She and Mac still an item?" Aidan patted Griff's diapered butt, enjoying the solid feel of the child against his chest.

Sam gave him a wry smile. "Yep. Those two are hilarious together. Mac actually lets her in his kitchen. He's trying to teach her to cook, but so far she's only mastered truffle butter and bacon."

Aidan rubbed his stubbled cheek against Griff's hair. "It's a start."

"Sam keeps telling us what a diva Carly was in Chicago, but she sure doesn't show it now." Conor leaned comfortably in the doorway. "I caught a glimpse of her out behind Mac's yesterday picking up trash in the parking lot."

Sam gasped. "*My* mother was picking up trash? With her bare hands?"

Conor nodded. "Yup. Well, she had those latex gloves on… but who wouldn't, right?"

Sam shook her head. "She continues to amaze me. Here, Aidan, let me take that guy. Supper's almost ready, if you want to join us. It's Ali's favorite—"

"Sketty and meatballs!" Ali screeched.

"Ali, you interrupted," Conor scowled.

"Oops, sorry, Sam." Ali grabbed Aidan's arm as he handed over baby Griff. "Come on, Uncle Aidan. Aunt Meg and Uncle Sean are coming, too, but you can sit by me!"

Conor rolled his eyes as Ali dragged Aidan past him toward the stairs.

Aidan tugged his arm loose. "Honey, hang on. I need a shower and some clean clothes. Sam, do I have time to grab a shower?"

Sam nodded with a smile. "I haven't started the pasta yet and Meg and Sean aren't here, so go ahead and get a shower.

We'll eat in about thirty." She herded Ali up the stairs.

"Welcome home, Ace." Conner cuffed him gently on the shoulder and followed his family.

Aidan gave the rumpled bed a longing glance before tossing his duffel on it and yanking out clean jeans and boxers and a waffle-knit shirt, scowling at how wrinkled everything was. He'd lived out of the duffel all the way across the country, stuffing dirty clothes into one end and trying to keep clean items separate at the other. He tossed a pile of underwear, socks, and shirts on the bathroom floor; at some point, he was going to have to do laundry. The rest of his clothes should arrive in the next few days. Phil had taken care of packing his entire wardrobe, along with some of his personal stuff, and shipping it to Indiana when she'd cleared out the cottage in Malibu.

As steamy water sluiced over his body, Aidan thought about how grateful he was for Philomena Murphy, who'd been hired by 3Guns Studios to be his personal assistant. At first, he'd been uncomfortable having someone at his beck and call, until Phil patiently explained that he was paying her a tidy sum to look after his needs and she was starting to feel extraneous. So he'd let her find him the beach rental, then rent some furniture, and hire a housekeeper.

Eventually, he turned a good bit of the posting to his social media over to her because he simply couldn't keep ahead of Facebook, Instagram, and Twitter. As his salary increased, so did Phil's, along with her responsibilities.

Before he knew it, she was doing his grocery shopping, updating his wardrobe, keeping his calendar organized, and even bringing him his favorite tea and granola on the set.

When he was overwhelmed with personal appearances, Phil worked with his publicist, Heather Gable, to manage scheduling. She picked out clothes for him to wear on late-night talk shows, morning show gigs, and other celebrity appearances. She arranged fittings for tuxes when he confessed that he'd only ever owned two suits in his entire life and had always rented tuxes when he'd needed them before. There wasn't much call for formalwear in River's Edge, Indiana. Adding stylist to her repertoire of skills, Phil used his Hoosier style to create a casual, country-boy sexy look for Aidan that had Hollywood buzzing, women swooning, and young men scouring their local Targets and Kohl's for plaid flannel shirts, long-sleeved henleys, and suede desert boots. The *LA Detectives* costume designers picked up the look for Pete, allowing Aidan to wear a lot of his own clothes on the show.

Aidan sighed deeply as he toweled off. Phil had been invaluable and he missed her. They'd shared a fond farewell when he took her and her partner, Chloe, out to dinner before he left LA. Phil was in great demand as a PA and had already been interviewing other celebrities for a new position even while she was getting Aidan packed up and ready to leave. She'd been desperately disappointed that he was bugging out, convinced he'd regret leaving LA. But she also knew him well enough after all their years together to see how much he needed time on the river with his family.

Laughter wafting down the basement stairs reminded him that he needed to get his butt in gear. It sounded as if Sean and Meg had arrived.

"MATTY, THIS LOOKS amazing!" Holly stood back to admire the pots of yellow and gold mums Mateo had planted in the heavy concrete urns that flanked the doorway to the Tea Leaf Café. "Nice job, kiddo."

Mateo brushed his dark hair off his forehead with the back of one gloved hand. "I scooted two of them down by the window. All four of these giant pots by the door seemed too crowded as big as these flowers are."

"It's perfect, kid. We're all ready for fall now." Holly slung an arm around her son's shoulders and pressed a kiss to the side of his head, noting once again that he was only an inch or two from being her height. His father was tall and brawny, so Matty came by his size honestly. Leo Santos. Tall, gorgeous, charming, and completely irresponsible.

She shook her head to clear her ex-husband's handsome image from her mind. Instead, she grabbed Mateo's hand and hauled him through the tea shop, through the kitchen, and out the back door to admire the work he'd done there.

"These look perfect, too, honey!" Once again, yellow and

gold mums stood sentry around the door, this time in giant gaily painted terra-cotta pots that she'd brought from home. Her mom had finished painting them a couple of nights ago and the pots and mums added a real pop of color to the parking lot that she shared with Mae, Noah Barker, who owned the hardware store, and Janet.

Mateo stood back to admire all four doors as Holly smiled in satisfaction, noticing that Noah had managed to get the dumpster moved over to the far corner of the lot, closer to the alley just like they'd all discussed. The dumpster was a necessary evil, but it didn't need to be up by the buildings trashing the ambiance of the shops. Sure, it was a parking lot, but that didn't mean it couldn't be attractive, since customers entered and exited from both the front and the back.

The back of the block was a riot of fall colors with Janet's red geraniums and Noah's pots of lavender and purple mums. This year, Mae had gone with dahlias in a mad variety of colors, so the yellow and gold mums that Matty had potted and placed strategically completed the colorful décor in the parking lot.

Matty nudged her shoulder. "Mom, can we walk down by the boat on the way home?"

When she turned her head, the expression on his face was so wistful, she bit back her immediate objections. "Sure. Let's take the River Walk, then follow the path down to the boat." She handed him her cell phone. "Text Grammy and tell her we're about an hour from home and that we'll scare up supper when we get there." She led the way back into the shop, turning off lights and locking the front door before returning to the back to do one more quick check of the kitchen, set the alarm, and leave the premises.

She really wasn't in the mood to see that damn showboat, but better to take Matty herself rather than have him wandering around down there all alone. His fascination with the old tub really worried her. She'd call Becky Cavendish in the morning. Maybe they could drop the price or advertise it in other big cities—anything to get the stupid thing *off* their plate.

The River Walk was busy with tourists, the air filled with the scent of the river and fall and popcorn. The autumn street vendors had set up at either end of the long paved path. She bought a small bag of caramel corn for Matty, rationalizing that he'd earned it by working so hard planting mums. His appetite was huge right now anyway, so she wasn't worried about ruining his supper. The kid was going to grow again, which meant a trip to Target for new jeans and shirts soon.

Companionably, they strolled along the wide walk, chatting about Matty's work at school and what she was going to bake at the tea shop the next day. Her heart warmed at the sight of all the folks either walking or sitting on benches enjoying the mighty Ohio River on a perfect October evening. Since tourism drove the town's economy, a crowded

River Walk meant customers in the shops, restaurants, hotels, and B and Bs.

They stopped to admire the Cotton Mill Inn that had opened over the summer. It looked fabulous, exactly as Gerry Ross, the hotelier who'd bought and restored the old place, had promised. It had been full up from the moment Gerry opened the doors. She and Matty and Melinda had eaten at the restaurant several times already and found the food delicious. Mayor Megan Mackenzie... er... Flaherty had been right all along. When Holly moved back, her aunt Susan had filled her in on the debate among the townsfolk about whether allowing the old factory to be turned into a hotel was a good idea. Frankly, Holly believed it to be a boon to tourism and a great reuse of an eyesore on shore of the river.

"Hey, Mom, is that Gram?" Matty pointed to a person standing in front of an easel, chatting with a group of tourists in the distance.

Holly squinted in the fading light. Sure enough, her mother, wearing a paint-spattered old shirt of Dad's over jeans and a worn T-shirt gestured excitedly with her brush, nearly hitting one woman with the paint-filled tip. The lady stepped back, smiling, as Matty and Holly approached.

Melinda grinned. "Matty! Hols! Thought I'd catch the sunset tonight. The colors are marvelous already." She tilted her head toward the heavy paper taped to a board that balanced on the easel.

Melinda's specialty was watercolors. She created amazing flower, street scenes, and landscape paintings that sold well in several shops in town as well as in the little gallery over on Cleveland Street. She'd done one-woman shows in Louisville, Jeffersonville, and Cincinnati and sold a lot of pieces off her website. Holly was incredibly proud of her mother's talent, although sometimes it was frustrating when Melinda forgot meals or to keep an eye on Matty. Thankfully, Megan Mackenzie Flaherty, who was not only the mayor of River's Edge, but also a first-rate CPA, kept track of the sales invoices and receipts that Melinda tossed haphazardly in a shoebox each year, so Holly didn't have to worry about that.

She smiled inwardly, too aware that her mother would say, *Hols, not your circus, not your monkeys*, if she knew that Holly worried about *her* finances. But Holly worried about everything from Mateo to Melinda to the Tea Leaf to the weird noise the sump pump was making at their old house up on the hill. *Worry* sometimes felt like Holly Peterson Santos's middle name.

Most especially, she worried about the *River Queen* and what the holy hell they were going to do if they couldn't sell it.

Chapter Five

"MATTY, SLOW DOWN!" Holly called after her son, who was practically race-walking down to the River Walk with a load of Melinda's framed prints. "If you drop those, your grandmother will kill us both!" They were back on the River Walk helping Melinda set up for the Halloween Hoopla, the annual town celebration that happened the Saturday before Halloween.

"I've got them, Mom." Matty disappeared around the corner, headed for Melinda's booth.

She pulled the rest of the watercolors from the back of her SUV, glancing at her smart watch as she shut the hatch. Only five p.m. They still had plenty of time to set up. The festival didn't officially start until six, but no doubt Matty had made plans to meet up with his buds.

He had eschewed buying a costume this year, preferring instead to wear an oversized, shredded flannel shirt from Melinda's collection, torn jeans, and a black wig. His grandmother had obligingly painted his face green, so his Incredible Hulk look was complete. He'd been looking forward to the costume contest for several weeks, going through closets to find exactly the right shirt to destroy, stuffing the shoulders and arms with Melinda's old stockings filled with plastic grocery bags to create the impression of muscles, and sharing pictures with his grandmother so she could see how he wanted his face to appear.

The River Walk was abuzz with activity—vendors setting up booths, tourists and townies milling about, costumed children running up and down the path. Mayor Meg stood on a makeshift stage near the Warner mansion, laying out the ribbons and trophies she would award to the costume contest winners. When her handsome husband, Sean Flaherty, set another box on the table and dropped a kiss on her forehead, Megan leaned back against his chest. The gesture tugged at Holly's heart, and reminded her that Aidan Flaherty would probably be around tonight, although he'd been mysteriously absent from town in the two weeks since he'd arrived.

At least as far as she knew.

It wasn't like she'd been watching for him or hoping to see him. Well, not really. But neither Layla nor Fran had mentioned seeing him and as starstruck as they were, they'd certainly have been full of Aidan Flaherty news. Since Four Irish Brothers Winery always had a booth at the hoopla, chances were good he'd be manning it with Conor and Sean.

Maybe.

Hopefully.

She shook *that* nonsense out of her head as she approached her mom's booth with the last of the watercolors. Melinda and Mateo were hanging framed pictures on the pegboard that backed the stand Clive had asked a student set crew to build several years ago. He'd whitewashed the pine boards himself, though, and Melinda had used the same cranberry-red paint Clive had used on the *River Queen* to brighten the stand. *Artist Melinda Peterson* was painted across the front, and the kids had added shelves inside to hold extra pictures. The stand always made a good impression and this year, Melinda landed the prime spot in front of the stage where all the events would happen. As fate would have it, the Flahertys' booth was…

Well, damn. They're right next to us.

Holly avoided staring as she set the extra framed watercolors on the shelves in Melinda's stall and helped fill the pegboard with priced pictures. Matty showed up with the last box for his grandmother—a deep carton of matted watercolors. Those sold without frames at a lesser price and usually always went like hotcakes at town happenings.

"Thanks, honey." Melinda pulled the various sizes of prints out and stacked them neatly in baskets on the counter. "Did you bring my face-painting box? It was on the front seat."

"Right here." Mateo held out the toolbox that held Melinda's brushes and face paints. "Mom, can I go find Max and Cory now?"

Holly turned from the picture she was hanging. "Yes, but

60

check back in an hour."

"You know, if you'd let me have a phone, I could just text you a check-in." Matty gazed at her, anticipation gleaming in his eyes.

Holly gave him a quirked brow. "Anyone could kidnap you and use *your* phone to check in with a ransom message or a threat. I need to see your sweet little face, kiddo. Well, it's actually not all that sweet right now, but even so, bring your incredible green butt back here in an hour. Got it?"

Mateo gave her that look of frustration and disgust only a tween could muster, then immediately switched to a smile. "Got it." He raced off.

"He's really working the phone thing, isn't he?" Melinda grinned as she set out her face-painting supplies.

"Yup." Holly placed the last print, straightening the ones around it so they all hung perfectly symmetrical. "But I have all the power." She raised her arms in a body-builder pose. "I am mother!"

"Yeah, good luck with that." Melinda dismissed her antics with a hand flip. "Go next door and get us a bottle of Riesling and a couple of glasses."

"It's a little early, don't you think?" Holly glanced over at the Four Irish Brothers Winery booth where Conor and Sean were stacking coolers behind the curtain that backed their stand. No sign of anyone else though. Not Sam or Alannah or Meg or… anybody.

"It's after five, Hols. Go get us some wine before all the

cold bottles are sold." Melinda turned away to greet a little girl and her mom who were looking for face painting. "What do you want on your face, sweetie?"

With a sigh, Holly crossed the few steps to Four Irish Brothers Winery as she dug in her cross-body bag for her credit card.

"Hey, Holly!" Sean's dimples sent a shiver up her spine—not because it was Sean, but because he was a Flaherty and in spite of being taller and broader and darker than Aidan, the smile was the same. So were the blue, blue eyes. "What can we do for you? Want to try our zin?"

"Tempting, but Mom sent me for Riesling." Holly offered up her VISA. "A cold bottle and two cups if you don't mind."

"Oh, here, have a taste of the zin and tell us what you think." Conor appeared at his brother's shoulder and held out a disposable tasting glass of rich red wine that resembled the communion cups she remembered from church camp. Except at camp it was grape juice, not the delicious zinfandel that Four Irish Brothers Winery was becoming famous for along the Southern Indiana Wine Trail.

She savored the smooth flavors of plums and dark cherries and spice on her tongue before swallowing. "Wow. I can't believe I haven't tried this before now. It's amazing."

Conor and Sean high-fived each other, then Sean grinned. "Thanks. We're pretty proud of it."

Certain Mac Mackenzie had a grill full of brats with

peppers and onions set up somewhere along the River Walk—she could smell them cooking—she added a bottle of zin to her order. Melinda wasn't a red wine drinker, but Holly was, and she imagined this wine would taste great with a mustardy brat on a thick bun. "I'm going to go see if Mac's brats are done yet," she said as she signed the Sean's phone with her finger. "Want me to bring you guys some?"

Conor shook his head. "Thanks, but Aidan's supposed to be getting us some on his way here, so we're covered."

"Oh, Aidan will be here tonight?" Holly hoped her tone didn't give away the sudden breathlessness she felt.

Conor rolled his eyes. "So he claims."

Holly caught the odd expression the two brothers exchanged. "Is he okay? He came in for tea a couple of weeks ago, but I haven't seen him around town since." She tried to keep her voice neutral. "I sorta thought he'd gone back to California."

"He's still here," Sean said as he uncorked both bottles for her, sticking the corks back in upside down and placing a clear plastic cup over the top of each. "He's probably going to be here for a while."

"Hiatus?" Holly didn't really want to pry, but she was popping with curiosity.

"Something like that."

Just then a group of laughing and chattering couples came up to buy wine, taking Sean and Conor's attention away from her probing. She smiled and took her wine back to Melinda's booth.

Something had happened. She didn't know what, but something was going on in the Flaherty family, and she had the distinct impression that it had do with a certain famous TV star.

"I'M HERE." AIDAN plopped two foil-wrapped sandwiches on the back counter of the Four Irish Brothers Winery booth along with two large iced teas and two bags of chips. "Extra spicy mustard"—he pointed to one sandwich, then the other—"regular yellow mustard."

"Geez, Ace, did you come by way of St. Louis?" Conor scowled over his shoulder as he poured three cups of mulled wine for waiting customers. "We're starving here."

Aidan looked up at the vintage four-dial lamppost clock set on a pole at the start of the River Walk. "It's only seven." He sat down on a cooler and sipped the beer he'd nabbed from the River Rat Microbrewery's booth on his way to his brothers.

The hoopla was well underway. He'd had a hell of a time finding a parking space and ended up leaving his little MG up river in the big lot where the *River Queen* showboat was dry-docked. He wasn't about to confess how long he'd stood staring up at the huge boat, his mind drifting back to his days with Clive's acting troupe.

What fun he'd had playing mustachioed villains and strong noble heroes in the old-fashioned melodramas Clive had either written himself or found at the library. And the sketches and singing and dancing had been everything Aidan had ever dreamed of from the time he'd first seen Fred Astaire and Bing Crosby in *Holiday Inn*. Aidan had been younger than all the other cast members, but they'd respected his acting chops and other skills—especially the girls who were signed up for the Showboat Summer course. What a crew they'd been those sultry days on the river, playing to audiences in towns along the lazy Ohio.

The Ohio River hadn't always been lazy, but locks and dams that had been added since the early 1800s had slowed the swift-flowing water, making the river more navigable for barges, flatboats, and steamboats that traversed it over the years. Aidan had been one of the actors responsible for giving tours and lectures to folks who were interested in the history of the river and the giant paddle wheeler, which actually ran by huge diesel engines. He'd helped take care of those diesels, too, serving as pretty much a jack-of-all-trades during his summer vacations on the *River Queen*.

Thankfully, although disappointed, Da understood that Aidan's true passion was theater, not winemaking, but he did insist Aidan help with harvest every fall. In the last couple of weeks, Conor and Sean had just brought in the last of the grapes, and had been dropping broad, not-so-subtle hints that Aidan could be down in the cellar lending a hand with the grape press or up in the winery pouring tastings instead of sleeping until well past noon every day. Winter pruning would probably start soon and he should pitch in there as well.

It wasn't that he didn't want to help. He did. Sorta. But pulling himself out of bed in the mornings was next to impossible. In the afternoons, it was easier to lounge on the sofa in Conor's basement, eating taco chips, watching old movies on Netflix, and wondering what had happened to great filmmakers like John Ford and William Wyler and suave actors like Cary Grant and beautiful bold actresses like Barbara Stanwyck than to haul his tired butt up to the winery.

It *was* time for him to stop lying around, but he just couldn't seem to motivate. He'd never been so directionless. There had always been work he loved. Maybe he should have gone to New York instead of coming home. A twinge of guilt skittered through him as he sat on the cooler watching his brothers serve hoopla visitors while their sandwiches got cold, but he didn't stand up to help. That was not until Sean turned around and gave him the stink eye. So Aidan sucked down the last dregs of his beer, dropped the bottle in the recycle bin, set his fedora back on his head, and stepped up to the front counter.

Immediately, a group of giggling girls descended upon the booth.

Look! It's Pete Atwood!

You're Pete Atwood, right?

Squeals and more giggling ensued before…

Can you sign my T-shirt?

Come around here, Pete, let's do a selfie together.

Oh-oh, no, sign my… A bosomy redhead touched her fingers to her chest as she leaned over the counter giving Aidan, Sean, and Conor quite a display of cleavage.

Backing away slightly, Aidan smiled, then shrugged his shoulders. "I'm on duty right now, ladies, and my bet is none of you are old enough to be served. How about if you go enjoy the festival and I try to catch up with you later?" He gave them dimples and canted his head toward the River Walk, hoping the girls would simply move on.

Fat chance.

"Just one picture?" A little blonde in skintight jeans and a too-tight T-shirt begged, while the redhead continued to smile at him suggestively behind her.

Conor stepped in. "Sorry, girls. Tonight, he's just plain Aidan Flaherty and he's pouring wine, so unless you've all suddenly aged five years… Well, we've got customers waiting." He turned on the Flaherty dimples, too, and reluctantly, the girls took off.

But they didn't go far—just to the Warner mansion steps where they sat and stared at Aidan as he slid a menu down the bar to an older couple who'd been watching the exchange with wry expressions. "What can I get for you?"

The man chuckled. "A couple of glasses of pinot, please." He pulled out a credit card as Aidan poured. "Sucks to be you, eh? Women falling all over you?"

"It's not always convenient, my friend, but honestly, I wouldn't dare complain." Aidan handed him back the card. "Enjoy your wine."

By eight o'clock, so many young girls, grown-up women, and even men had crowded around the booth looking for autographs and selfies with Aidan that Sean finally groaned aloud. "Good God! Did someone tweet out a Pete Atwood sighting? You're going to have to go, Ace. You're bad for business. Nobody's buying wine. They're just here to see you."

"Okay, I'll head home." Aidan's conscience nudged him, even though he couldn't deny he was relieved to be released from booth duty. "Here, let me take these boxes of empties to your truck, Conor. Is there anything I can do at the winery to make tomorrow easier?" Sundays were big days at Four Irish Brothers, and Sean and Conor were already spread thin this weekend working the hoopla.

His brothers exchanged a look of exasperated tolerance they didn't even try to hide. "Yeah, I told Steve and Liz to just lock up at six and come down to the hoopla, so the racks in the tasting room need to be restocked." Then Conor grinned and tugged on the brim of Aidan's fedora. "Labels up, remember?"

"I know how to put wine bottles in a rack, dude." Irritation rose in Aidan, but he shoved it back down.

His brothers had put up with his utter laziness for the

last couple of weeks, and he felt an intervention coming on that he wasn't looking forward to. He *did* need to step up; he was too aware of that. The lying around feeling sorry for himself was going to have to end. Da would have tolerated it for about twenty minutes. Besides, he wasn't just disappointing his brothers; he was disappointing himself. The Flahertys had always been and continued to be hard workers. If he wasn't going to head to New York or back to LA, he should pull his weight in the family business.

However, tonight proved he wasn't going to be able to work with the public much until folks got used to the idea of his being there. He hauled three cases of empties up to Conor's pickup, making two more identical trips before dropping the key fob back with his brother. In between loads, he stopped to take selfies with fans and sign T-shirts, napkins, and even one woman's arm.

Conor and Sean's good humor was restored by the time he took off up the River Walk with a cadre of fans trailing him. He'd sign a few more autographs, do a few more selfies, then go back and get the racks filled in the winery and tomorrow he'd ask Conor for a job. Maybe plain old hard work was what he needed to get out of the funk he'd been in since he arrived in River's Edge. Something to keep his mind occupied while he debated New York versus LA.

He wanted to be back onstage. That much he'd realized. To feel the rush that applause brought, to delve into a character, and bring him to life before a live audience.

Television had been good to him, but Pete Atwood had become so one-dimensional toward the end, Aidan almost had barely needed to read the script. He wasn't sure he wanted to go to New York just yet though—the thought of auditions, arduous rehearsal schedules, and living in that huge bustling city sent a chill through him.

As he passed a booth just down from theirs, a smallish watercolor hanging on a pegboard in the back caught his eye. A stunning rendering of the old *River Queen* in her heyday, sailing proudly up the Ohio, flags flying and water sluicing off the giant paddlewheel on the back. The artist had captured the scene perfectly with folks running along the shore waving and people on the boat leaning on the rails of the top deck.

He walked closer, his little entourage right on his heels, giggling and chattering.

Ooh, pretty pictures!

I like that one!

Pete, are you going to buy one?

Which one do you like, Pete?

The slim young woman manning the booth arched one dark brow. "Can I help you?"

She looked familiar… really familiar sitting on a stool, legs crossed, her cheeks dappled with a pink hue from the sodium vapor lights that lined the River Walk.

"Um… I…" He pointed to the painting, flustered because of the group of nattering teenagers who'd dogged his every step since he'd walked away from the winery booth.

"That's amazing. Are you the artist?"

She cocked her head toward an older woman in a flowy flowered top and jeans who was chatting with a group of people about another picture. "No. She is." Even the voice was familiar.

He peered at the painting, which was signed in the corner, *MK Peterson* with a flourish. He blinked. *Oh, holy crap! Peterson! Melinda Peterson! Of course! Clive's wife.* She'd designed and painted amazing sets all those years ago. He leaned back to read the signage on the front of the booth. Yup. Clive's wife, who'd done all the sets for the showboat all those years ago. Her watercolors were striking. Seemed like he remembered seeing them in the winery gift shop area—paintings of the vineyards with the verdant hills in the background and scenes of life on the river. "Does she sell these up at Four Irish Brothers?"

The woman shrugged. "Probably. She has them in shops all over the area and in the gallery up on Main Street. She's amazing, isn't she?" When she met his eyes, it was obvious she knew who he was and equally obvious she gave not a single shit. She was one cool customer.

"She *is* great," he agreed, and stuck out his hand. "I'm Aidan Flaherty, by the way."

She offered the briefest handshake in the history of cordiality. "I know who you are." She gazed past him at the clutch of fans who'd followed him. "Apparently, everyone does."

Aidan scanned the crowd around them. The girls were crowded around the booth, sorting through a stack of matted, unframed prints on the counter while the young woman frowned, clearly prepared to rescue anything that might fall on the ground.

He shoved his fedora back, hoping the lock of blond hair that always fell across his forehead might work its magic, and offered the famous Aidan/Pete dimpled grin, but her expression didn't alter. "I have a lot of fond memories of that old tub." He pointed to the painting of the *River Queen*.

"I'm sure you do." Her tepid response was almost lost among the noisy prattling of his fans.

Are you going to buy that one, Pete?

Hey lady, do you have any others like it?

If I buy one, too, will you sign it, Pete?

Aidan couldn't think for all the chattering so he focused on the lovely dark-haired woman. "I'd like to buy it, please."

"Okay." She slipped off the stool and Aidan stepped back, surprised at how tiny she was—maybe five feet tall and *maybe* a hundred pounds. Her body was feminine and graceful, even in jeans, flannel, and beat-up Doc Martins. Her dark brown hair was styled in an adorable messy bun on top of her head and her eyes were... *violet*. Suddenly it struck him who she was.

The tea shop lady.

He gave it a shot. "I really enjoyed the tea. Thanks again for opening up for me the other day. You saved my life."

She took the picture off the pegboard and wrapped it in brown paper, taping the ends closed. "Oh, I imagine you'd have lived or found *someone* to make you tea." She extended her hand. "That'll be a hundred thirty-three seventy-five with tax."

He handed her his credit card and she swiped it on the little doohickey attached to her cell, then held out her phone.

"Sign with your finger, please."

He scrawled his signature while the girls behind him giggled and squealed. If only he dared to simply tell them to get lost. He could hang out, see if he could get the tea shop lady to warm up a little bit, even though it was clear she wasn't having it. But these girls were part of his base and nothing killed a career faster than being crappy to your fans.

Instead, he accepted the wrapped painting, nodded a thank you, and turned to walk away. Suddenly a vision appeared in his head—a petite preteen in a pair of crumpled denim shorts and a yellow *River Queen* T-shirt, her dark hair hanging down her back, her huge eyes shining. When a certain cocky seventeen-year-old actor sauntered offstage and patted her head with a breezy, "Hiya, munchkin," she'd blushed while her eyes turned dark with disappointment.

Those eyes were violet. *Oh. My. God.*

He turned, walked backward a few steps, and over the heads of his fans, called, "Thank you... Holly!"

Chapter Six

H E KNEW WHO she was! Holly barely had time to catch her breath from that startling, tantalizing fact when another voice drew her attention.

"Ms. Santos! Ms. Santos!" Mateo's friend Max was racing toward her with Cory right behind him. "Come quick! It's Matt!"

Her heart dropped to her socks. *Oh, dear God.* She grabbed Max by the shoulder. "What is it?"

Max gasped, his face red and streaming sweat even in the cool October air. "He-he fell and"—*gasp, gasp*—"and I think he's hurt bad."

Bile rose in her throat. "Where is he?" She glanced over at Cory who was panting, his hands on his knees as he tried to catch his breath. "Cory?" She slipped out from behind the booth. "Take me to him!"

Max pointed up the River Walk. "At the showboat. We were pretending we were monsters in a haunted boat and he—"

Holly didn't wait to hear the rest. She bolted up the River Walk full speed, dodging revelers, with a "coming through" as she raced to her son, Max and Cory in hot pursuit.

She barely noticed Aidan Flaherty and the group of girls following him, but the fear on her face must have been evident because he shouted after her. "Holly, what's wrong? What happened?"

Holly didn't bother to answer. Her entire focus was on getting to her boy. Darkness enveloped her as she slowed down, stepping more carefully on the dirt path that led down to the parking area where the *River Queen* was dry-docked. Panting, she reached the bottom of the hill and scanned the big boat, which was several yards away. "Matty? Where are you?"

"He's at the back, in the paddlewheel." Cory's words came out on a wheeze of air.

"How'd he get up there?" A deep voice behind her spun her around. Aidan Flaherty was there, sans entourage, eyeing the huge old boat. "Is there a way to board from the ground?"

"There's a set of rolling steps, the kind airliners use, up by the bow that the stage... uh... gangplank rests on so it can be boarded while it's in dry dock," Holly explained hurriedly as she rushed to the front of the boat and pointed to the platform, usually referred to as *the stage*, above their heads. The wide plank was meant to sit on a dock so passengers could board when the boat was in the water. "I have a locked gate at the bottom of it—"

"We climbed over it." Max's confession was accompanied with tears. "I'm sorry, Ms. Santos. I'm so sorry! We were just going to—"

Holly touched his hair gently. "That doesn't matter now, Max. I've got to get Matty."

Aidan was already at the bottom of the stairs, tugging on the padlocked gate. "Do you have a key?"

"Not with me." Holly put one foot on the bottom of the gate to heave herself over, but before she could get any leverage, Aidan swooped her up into his arms and set her on the step on the other side. Then, gracefully, he vaulted the gate, landing on the step right beside her.

"You boys stay down here." He pointed a finger at Max and Cory. "Come on, Holly."

Gratitude welled up in her as he grabbed her hand and tugged her up the steps to the stage, but all she could think about was getting to Matty. She pulled her hand away, and running down the main deck of the boat, past the windowed theater, she burst through the door at the back onto the stern, next to where the paddlewheel was attached. "Matty!" she screamed his name, trying desperately to see him in the dark. Dammit, there were no lights because the generator wasn't hooked up and her phone was back at Melinda's booth. "Matty!"

Suddenly a beam of light appeared behind her. Aidan held up his phone in flashlight mode. "Matt? Where are you, son?"

"Mom?" A tiny voice sounded below them and Holly's heart spasmed.

"Matty, where are you?" Her own voice cracked and she swallowed fear and the lump that was forming.

"Down here."

Aidan shone his light in the direction of Mateo's voice and she peered down into the beam, finally spotting a black frizzy wig several feet below them on a forked support between two of the huge paddles. He looked so tiny and helpless down there. Tears stung her eyes.

"Matty, are you stuck?" Holly couldn't see his whole body, just his head and shoulders.

"I think I broke my arm. It hurts so bad." Terror laced Mateo's tone and it tore at Holly's soul.

"I'm coming, honey. Hold on." She started to swing one leg over the stern rail next to the paddlewheel.

"Wait." Aidan put his hand on her shoulder. "Let me. I've climbed this wheel a dozen times getting off stuff we picked up on the river. Tree branches and such." He zipped up his black hoodie, took off his fedora, and handed it to her along with the phone. "Can you hold these? Keep the light shining on him, okay?"

Holly nodded, not at all certain what he intended to do, but at least he seemed to have a plan beyond leaping down onto the paddles, which was her instinct at the moment.

She stared, heart in her throat, as Aidan examined the huge old wheel, clearly mapping out a strategy for getting to

Mateo. He wasn't in celebrity mode now and he wasn't trying to impress her. He was simply a concerned adult trying to figure out how to rescue a kid.

Finally, he turned to her with a look of determination. "It looks like one of the steel braces broke and snagged him when he fell. It must've rusted through." He held out his hand. "Give me your scarf." But when she started to haul it over her head, he said, "No, no, untie it."

She untied the bit of silk fabric around her neck and handed it to him wordlessly. At this point, if he'd asked her to remove every stitch of clothing she had on, she'd have done it. Anything at all if it meant saving Matty.

"If his arm *is* broken, I'm going to need something to bind it with so I can carry him up," Aidan explained as he wrapped the scarf around his arm.

"Mom?" Matty's plaintive cry that seemed weaker than before sent a chill through her.

Holly released the last of her misgivings. "Honey, my friend Aidan is coming to get you." She shone the light on herself and Aidan, hoping to ease some of Mateo's fear. "See him? He's on his way down now. Just keep your eye on the light, honey, and do whatever he says."

She'd never once, in Mateo's entire life, asked him to trust a man other than her father—not even his own dad, who'd proved time and time again what an irresponsible butthead he was until she finally got a court order granting her full custody. That order was all Leo needed to abandon his son completely. But this was an emergency and, for reasons she'd figure out later, she had complete faith in Aidan Flaherty. He was going to rescue her son. For the moment, that was all she needed to know.

THE CLIMB DOWN the wheel was tricky. Aidan hadn't done it since right after junior year in college—his last season of summer stock with Clive and the *River Queen*. The good news was the boat wasn't in the water, so the buckets weren't wet and slick. But the bad news was that if he or Matt fell from the middle of the twelve huge paddles, which were actually called *buckets*, not paddles, they wouldn't have the river to cushion a fall. The ground below them was hard concrete, which meant at least a broken bone or two upon landing.

"Hey, Matt." Aidan was about four feet above the boy, balanced on a cross-member between two of the great buckets. "I'm Aidan."

Matt looked up, fear shining from his dark eyes in the light his mother shone down on them. Sure enough, one of the steel braces had snapped. Matt was just below it, balanced precariously in the V of a pair of crosspieces.

"We're going to get you out of there, but I need some information first, okay?" Aidan peered down, trying to assess exactly how the kid was positioned.

"Okay." Matt's voice trembled.

"How did you fall?" Aidan eased his way down to the next crosspiece.

"I slipped trying to get down to hide on this bucket. Then that rusty metal thing broke."

Aidan was close enough to see Matt wince as he pointed just past the bucket that was nearly parallel to the ground below. "Does anything else hurt besides your arm? Did you hit your head?" He could see blood seeping from below the black fright wig. Or maybe it was just the face paint. Hard to tell in the dark.

"I dunno. I just lost my balance and fell."

Crawling carefully over the wooden bucket above Matt, Aidan lay on his belly and slid to the crosspiece nearest the boy. "Hiya, kid." He offered an encouraging smile.

Matt's teary eyes widened. "You're Pete Atwood."

Aidan furrowed his brows. "Well, I used to be. You okay if I take that wig off your head?"

Matty nodded, sniffling as Aidan slowly removed the wig and dropped it to the ground. Yup. The kid had cut his head in the fall. And his left arm hung at an odd angle. Either it was broken or his shoulder was dislocated.

"Anything else hurting besides your arm and your head?"

"I-I don't think—" Biting his lower lip, Matt moved slightly before Aidan held up a hand to stop him. If the kid had injuries that weren't immediately visible, moving him could damage his spine or cause his arm to fracture worse.

Plus what if Aidan lost his balance carrying him? They'd both land on the concrete below. They were going to need some help.

"Don't try to move, Matt. Stay perfectly still." He looked up toward the light and kept his tone calm as he called, "Holly, Matt and I are going to need some help getting down from here. Please call 911. Tell them we need a ladder." He grinned at Matt. "I think that's going to be easier, don't you?"

"Oh, God!" Holly's stricken cry came down loud and clear. "What's happening? Is he conscious?"

"Matt, holler up and tell your mom you're okay." Aidan stroked the boy's hair off his forehead, trying to get a better look at the cut and goose egg that was developing there.

"I'm okay, Mom," Matt said obediently. The light disappeared and Aidan heard Holly's frantic call to 911, begging them to hurry.

It was getting cooler and the breeze had picked up. The musty, fishy scent of the river filled Aidan's senses with memories of being on the showboat. "You know, I used to spend every summer on this old tub." Aidan unzipped his hoodie, shrugged out of it, and gently set it around Matt's shivering shoulders with the hood over his head, all the while keeping his voice as casual as he could. "Your grandpa put on the best shows."

"It was a bar when we moved here." Matt's face was pale under the green makeup. "G-Grampy also had p-poker there on W-Wednesday nights."

"Ah-ha, the infamous floating card game. My friend Mac used to play." Aidan eyed Matt. The kid's eyelids drooped and his face seemed even paler. *Oh, crap.* The last thing they needed was the kid going into shock. *Keep him warm and keep him talking.* That was what he remembered from the first aid course he'd taken in college. He thought fast. "Nice Hulk costume. So, you're an Avengers fan?"

Matt managed a small smile and a nod. "I'll bet you hang out with all those actors, don't you?"

"Not really." Aidan squinted into the darkness. Where was the fire department? The fire station was only a few blocks away. "In LA, I'm a TV actor, although I did meet Mark Ruffalo at a party once. He was a super nice guy."

"Yeah?" Matt's eyes closed and his chin tipped down.

"Matt." Aidan lifted his chin. "Stay awake."

"So sleepy," Matt murmured.

"I know, kid, but you have to stay awake so you can tell the firemen what happened. Talk to me. Avengers. Which movie is your favorite?" He gazed into the boy's eyes, all the while pulling Avenger movies from the depths of his memory.

The light once again shone down on them, so Aidan called up, "Holly, name your favorite Avengers movie. Matt's thinking about it."

He looked up into her frightened face and smiled encouragement as he stroked Matt's hair back and began listing

Avenger film titles. Just as sirens sounded in the distance, she called down, "The first one—I loved Mark Ruffalo as the Hulk and… and"—her voice hitched—"he-he made a really cute Bruce Banner. What does Matty say?"

"I think he's all about the *Endgame*. Right, Matt? Hey, talk to me." Aidan held Matt's chin up, forcing him to maintain eye contact until two fire trucks and an ambulance pulled into the lot, lights flashing.

"Aidan Flaherty, is that you up there?" Fire Chief Frank Ashton's deep voice sounded from below the paddle wheel as a huge searchlight suddenly shone bright as day on the stern.

"They're right there!" Holly cried, using the phone flashlight to indicate Aidan and Matt's position.

"Hey, Frank, yeah, it's me." Aidan waved at the fire chief. "I think if you can get a ladder or cherry picker up to the bucket that's parallel to the ground, we're just below it. Or maybe the next one down, although it's tilted some."

Within minutes, Tierney Ashton and another EMT were perched on the closest bucket, peering down. "Aidan? What've we got?" Tierney shone a flashlight right on them.

Relief surged through Aidan as he explained what he believed happened, all the while holding onto Mateo as best he could.

"Will this paddle hold me?" Tierney gazed dubiously at the wooden plank, its red paint peeling.

Aidan nodded. "Sure, it's treated oak—pretty sturdy." He watched as Tierney and the other EMT crawled out onto the wooden board with what looked like a folded stretcher.

Matt's head fell back and his eyes slitted open. "It's not a paddle. It's called a bucket."

"Okay, good to know." Tierney grinned. "Hey, dude, how ya doin'?"

"My arm hurts." Matt's head tilted toward his shoulder, then fell backward again. "I'm tired."

"I know, buddy. We're going to get you out of here, get you all fixed up." Tierney assessed the situation for a moment, putting one hand on Mateo's forehead to check his injury, holding his eyelid open to check his pupils with her penlight. "He's a little shocky," she tossed over her shoulder at the other EMT. "Mateo, hey, talk to me. Why do they call this thing a paddlewheel if the paddles are called buckets? Why don't they call it a bucketwheel?"

Mateo managed a feeble smile, but no words.

She sat down on her butt, prepared to slide off the bucket and onto the crosspiece on the other side of Mateo. "Okay, Aidan. I'm going to come down to the other side of Mateo and check him out. Once I've got him, you can climb out of the way so Brad and I can slide this scoop stretcher under him. It's flexible, so we can create a chair under his butt and not have to get under his arms. It'll keep him as immobile as possible while we move him."

Aidan touched his lips to Matt's forehead. "Matty, are you awake? Did you hear what Tierney said?"

Suddenly Matt eyes flew open and he clutched at Aidan's

shoulder. "Don't go away. Please." Tears began streaming down his face. "Stay here. Don't go."

Tierney and Aidan exchanged a look of dismay over the child's head. Aidan quirked one brow, then looked up at Holly, who knelt on the stern, her expression filled with terror. His heart ached for her and for the boy. No way was he bailing now. "Can *I* work the stretcher with you?" he asked.

When Tierney hesitated, he shook his head firmly. "I'm not leaving him, Tee, so tell me exactly what to do."

Chapter Seven

HOLLY SAT NEXT to Matty's bed in the emergency room at St. Mark's Hospital near the west end of town. It was a hive of activity tonight as it usually was during town events and festivals; someone always got hurt or ate too much junk and got sick. Tonight, it was their turn apparently, as Mateo, eyes closed, lay looking small and pale in the big bed.

Nurses had been in and out several times since Tierney and Brad had wheeled him in and helped get him settled in a curtained-off alcove. Holly had stood by as they washed the green makeup off his face so the doctor would be able examine the bruise and wound that was swelling to epic proportions on the kid's forehead. His left arm was immobilized and he was probably in line for x-rays.

"Mateo, are you awake?" A perky little nurse popped her head through the curtains.

"No." Matty kept his eyes closed.

"Very cute." The nurse stepped into the cubicle, did a quick pupil check, and noted his vitals on her tablet. Then she turned to Holly. "Just do what you can to keep him awake until the doc gets here."

"I'll pinch him if I have to." Holly held two fingers up in a nipping motion and reached for Matty's uninjured arm, while he chuckled weakly.

"There's somebody pretty special out in the waiting room anxious to come back here." The nurse tapped Matty's blanket-covered foot.

"Is my mom here?" Holly looked up, surprised that Melinda would've gotten her booth packed up so quickly. They'd only been in the ER for less than thirty minutes, although Holly had sent Max and Cory back to let her mom know what had happened.

The pert nurse shook her head and lowered her voice to nearly a whisper. "No, it's *Aidan Flaherty.*" Holly must have had a blank expression on her face because the nurse's eyes widened. "You know, Pete Atwood from *LA Detectives*? He's asking to see Mateo."

"Aidan's *here*?" Holly was dazed.

Tierney Ashton, who was outside the cubicle doing paperwork, stuck her head between the curtains. "He promised Matty he'd stay with him, so he followed the ambulance here. I sent him to the waiting room, but I'm sure people are all over him out there." She raised her chin in Matty's direction. "Hey, little guy, how ya doin'? I see they got your Hulk face off."

"I'm okay." Matty's voice trembled. "Can Pete come back, Mom?"

"If you're okay with it, we are." The nurse shoved the curtain back.

"His name is Aidan." Holly chewed her lower lip for a second, eyeing Matty, then the nurse, then Tierney. "Oh, I guess it's okay."

"I'll get him." Tierney bounced out of the curtained area toward the door and was back less than a minute later with Aidan in tow.

Holly's tummy did a little flip at the sight of him, his blond hair awry and his blue eyes dark with worry. It was probably a good thing he showed up anyway since she still had his hat, his phone, and a black hoodie she figured was his since it had *LA Detectives* embroidered on the left side in white letters. The nurses had handed it to her when they'd gotten Matty into a hospital gown.

Aidan went straight to Mateo's bedside with barely a nod to the three women in the room. "Hey, dude." He touched Matty's cheek with one gentle finger. "Looks like Bruce Banner is back."

"I'm just Matt now." Matty offered a weak smile. "Thanks for saving me, Pete."

"I'm just Aidan now." Dull color washed up Aidan's neck and into his cheeks. "Here you go." He tossed Holly's scarf over the bed, eyeing her as the silky strip of fabric landed in her lap. "I didn't do anything. It was Tierney here and Brad who got you down, buddy." It wasn't an *aw shucks* kind of denial; he was sincerely dismissing his role in Matty's rescue.

Interesting and out of character for an actor.

Holly didn't want Matty turning Aidan into some kind of superhero. She knew actors—she'd grown up around them and she was aware of how easily their self-images fed on the admiration of others. She was certain Aidan Flaherty was no exception and the adoration showing in Matty's eyes made her belly clench.

Facts were, though, that Aidan *did* step up to rescue her son, and he didn't play the hero when he realized he wasn't going to be able to get the child out of the paddlewheel by himself. For that show of common sense alone, Holly would be forever grateful. She'd put her trust in him and he hadn't let his ego take charge, so she smiled at him warmly. "We do owe you thanks, Aidan. You climbed down there and kept him calm. I'm so grateful you were there."

Aidan waved away her gratitude. "Sure, no problem." He turned back to Matty, whose eyelids were drooping again. "Matt, are you supposed to be staying awake for the doc?"

Clearly struggling, Matty opened his eyes. "Why did you say you *were* Pete Atwood?"

"Did I say that?" Aidan's eyes met Holly's over the bed.

"Yeah, down on the boat. You said *were*. Aren't you still Pete Atwood?"

"I guess I'll always be Pete Atwood, kiddo." Aidan ducked his head, clearly uncomfortable with the turn the conversation had taken.

Something had happened; Holly felt it in her bones. Aidan had been home for a couple of weeks, holed up at the winery. She had no idea if that was his usual pattern when he came to town or if he walked around the streets in celebrity mode—she hadn't been living in River's Edge long enough to know. She remembered all too well how much of an attention junkie he was years ago, though. Had that changed since he'd become famous? She wanted to press him, but he so obviously didn't want to talk about *LA Detectives*, she let it go, watching as Aidan teased Matt about the stocking "muscles" that were on the chair next to the bed.

The doctor arrived, looking harried but kind as she examined Matty from head to toe, then clucked sympathetically. "You really did a number on yourself, big guy."

"I guess we're going to be here a while, huh?" Holly tried to sound chipper for Mateo's sake, even though she had a sneaking suspicion the arm was going to require surgery.

"We always admit head traumas for at least twenty-four hours." Dr. Ridgeway nodded before confirming Holly's worst fears. "I'm guessing that arm will need a surgeon. Dave Simms is the ortho on call and he's very good. I'm going to order the CT and x-rays and admit him. They should have a room for him soon. Dave will be in to talk to you shortly." As she turned to leave, the doctor glanced over her shoulder in Aidan's direction. He was lounging against the wall near the curtain, arms crossed over his chest, trying to be unobtrusive, but looking so tousled and hot that he was hard to miss. "Um, aren't you...?"

Mateo jumped in, clearly impressed that Pete Atwood was visiting him in the ER. "He's Pete Atwood. You know, from *LA Detectives*."

The doctor smiled. "I thought I recognized you. *LA Detectives* is a must-see every Friday night at our house."

Aidan offered up the smile that had set Holly's blood to tingling since she was twelve years old and just beginning to discover that boys weren't all that yucky after all. "Thanks."

Dr. Ridgeway shook her head. "My kid's never going to believe this."

"Would you like an autograph for him?"

"Would you mind? He's fourteen and an autograph from you would up my cool parent mojo by a factor of at least a thousand." She pulled a scratch pad with the name of a drug company emblazoned across the top out of her lab coat and held it out with a pen.

Aidan accepted the pad and pen. "Sure. Anything for the cool parent cause. What's his name?" He signed swiftly and then allowed Dr. Ridgeway to include him in a quick selfie.

"Are you going to stay here?" Mateo asked after the doctor left. He winced as he tried to adjust his position in the bed.

Both Aidan and Holly were at his side in seconds, each offering a hand. "Honey, be careful," Holly said, helping him shift to his side, but only slightly. "You need to lie still or—"

A commotion outside the curtain interrupted her as several ER workers tried to peer into the cubicle to get a look at Pete Atwood. Holly turned and jerked the curtain closed. She got it, she truly did. Aidan Flaherty was a star and big news wherever he went even in his hometown, although you'd think the folks here would be used to him by now.

Aidan caught her eye over the bed and quirked a brow before he laid a gentle hand on Matty's dark hair. "Dude, listen. Your grandma is down at the festival all by herself, so I'm going to head out now and help her break her booth down, okay?"

Holly tossed him a grateful smile. "He's right, honey. Grammy doesn't have any help now."

Mateo's lower lip quivered, but he nodded. "Okay. I'll see you again before you go back to California, right?"

Aidan ruffled his hair. "I'm not going anywhere anytime soon, kiddo. I'll be around. I've gotta sign your cast, right?"

Matty's eyes widened. "I'm getting a cast? Mom, am I getting a cast? Any color? Can it be green?"

Holly chuckled. "I imagine you're getting a cast and we'll see what colors they have."

"See you, champ." Aidan waved, grabbed his phone, hat, and hoodie off the chair near the bed, and slipped through the curtains.

When he got to the door of the ER, he looked through the glass, then looked all around before heading toward the ambulance bay walk-through door. Holly was right behind him. She swallowed hard before touching his shoulder. "Aidan, wait."

He stopped at the door and turned, a surprised yet expectant look in his eyes. "I'll get your mom packed up so she can join you here."

Tears stung her eyes. She'd followed Aidan's career in secret for years, erasing her internet history to hide it from Leo, so she knew he had a reputation for being one of the nicest guys in Hollywood, but she wasn't prepared for such kindness. He had idolized her dad and often attributed his success onstage and on TV to Clive's influence. Maybe that was all it was. He was being kind to her because of her dad. "How can I thank you for... for everything? Matty could've fallen and been paralyzed or even killed. You *did* save him. And now... you're going down to help Mom." She threw her hands out in a gesture of entreaty. "How will I ever repay you?"

Aidan started to say something, then caught his lower lip in his teeth. Those perfect white teeth except for a tiny chip out of one of the front ones that only added to his appeal. She'd read online about him chipping the tooth during a chase scene his first season on *LA Detectives*. Fans had found it so charming, he didn't bother to get it fixed. "You could let me take you out to dinner next week." He winked, shoved the door open with his shoulder, and walked out into the night.

"CAN I LEND a hand?" Aidan zipped his hoodie against the cool breeze off the river as he approached Melinda's booth. "I just left Holly and Mateo in the ER. Everything's under control."

Melinda looked up from the tub she was filling with un-framed, matted watercolors and smiled. "Holly called and told me you were on your way. I really appreciate your help."

"No problem." Aidan was struck at how different Holly and her mother were. Melinda was tall and curvy with gray-blond hair that was up in a twist on her head, while Holly was tiny and slight, but very female. Holly's long hair was deep mahogany with chestnut lights and her olive-tone skin was nothing like Melinda's fair complexion. That was all Clive. Her tiny frame must be a throwback to some distant ancestor. Clive had always claimed he was descended from Welsh elves and fairies.

"How's Matty?" Melinda placed a sheet of Bubble Wrap on top of the bin she was packing and secured the lid.

Aidan began taking down the framed prints on the peg-board, setting them carefully on the front counter of the booth. "Well as can be expected. The doctor ordered a CT because she suspects a concussion and, of course, an x-ray of his arm. They've called in an orthopedic surgeon for his arm—guy named Dave Simms."

Melinda glanced up from the prints she was slipping into

padded envelopes. "Surgery?"

"Yup, to set the arm." Aidan nodded, touched by the fear and concern in Mateo's grandmother's eyes. He'd never known his grandparents—all four had died before he made his first trip to Ireland during summer hiatus after the first season of *LA Detectives*.

He and Brendan had gone on an ancestor hunt in County Wexford in southeast Ireland. They'd had a grand time, found tons of aunts, uncles, and cousins on both Donal and Maggie's sides of the family, and spent two weeks driving around Ireland, drinking whiskey, and roaming old castles. Bren had taken copious photos and notes for the novel he hoped to write one day, and Aidan recalled a sweet Irish lass in a pub in Cork who'd tried to teach him to step-dance but ended up kissing his lips raw in a dark corner of the bar.

"He was in good spirits when I left. A little sleepy." Aidan set the last of the prints on the counter and then began pulling bubble sleeves from a bin and fitting them to various sized prints.

"Oh, good. Poor kid." Melinda accepted the wrapped prints from him and packed them into bins. "How was Holly? Holding it together?"

Aidan found that a curious question. However, he smiled and nodded. "She was… amazing. Calm and keeping Matt occupied."

"Yeah. Single parenting is no picnic." Melinda stacked the bins on the dim pathway and stood on her toes to begin the work of unscrewing the hinged panels that made up the actual booth.

Aidan held his hand out. "I can do that."

"Sure." Melinda placed the screwdriver in his palm and started packing the small toolbox that held... "Face paint," she explained at Aidan's puzzled expression. "I do it at every town event. It's a big draw for the little ones and even some of the bigger kids." She rinsed brushes in a bucket of water and wrapped them in a small towel before she faced him, one hand on her hip. "So, what brings you back to town for such a long stay this time, Aidan Flaherty? Generally, you're here a few days and only for some family event or holiday."

Aidan sucked in his cheeks, debating whether or not to reveal his story. He remembered Melinda as being an earth mother to all the actors in Clive's troupe—tending to injuries, listening to kids with broken hearts, offering up advice and hugs and the occasional verbal slap upside the head if any of them went off the rails. "Do you remember that time, summer before my senior year? Five of us got hammered in some little town in Kentucky one night after we did Clive's play *Dear Siggy*? We left the boat in costume—I played Freud with the old-fashioned vest and the monocle?" He smiled at her and, in character, offered a line from the play, "It is zee *responsibility* of freedom that most people fear..."

Melinda burst out laughing. "I do remember that night. All five of you down on your knees scrubbing every inch of that stage. I believe it was Jay Cochran who puked in the bucket of soapy water... or maybe it was—"

Aidan chuckled, remembering poor Jay lying on the wet stage floor trying desperately not to hurl while the others simply stepped over him, anxious to get through the punishment Melinda had meted out when she caught them sneaking back on the boat past curfew. "It *was* Jay, but man, we were all sick as dogs." He shook his head. "Was Clive ever pissed the next day. If we hadn't had three more performances, I think he would've cheerfully pitched us all overboard."

They exchanged a sentimental look over the bins of paintings, Melinda's blue eyes still gleaming with curiosity while Aidan continued to avoid her question.

"Well, not you," she said finally, giving him an affectionate grin. "You were his golden child."

A lump grew in Aidan's throat and he swallowed hard. "Melinda, I'm sorry I missed his funeral. I didn't even know he'd been sick." His voice came out raspy.

She shrugged. "It was fast and very aggressive. Holly and Mateo only got a little time with him before he went."

"Where's her husband?" The question was out before Aidan could stop it.

Melinda didn't act surprised; rather, her expression turned sour. "They're divorced and Leo's in the wind. He took her to Cincinnati to live with his grandmother when she got pregnant, but he only hung around for a few months after Matty was born. Left Holly to care for the old lady and a newborn while he was God-knows-where doing God-knows-what. Auditioning for anything he could get, I guess." Her voice grew harsher. "We begged her to come home, let us help her, but she wouldn't leave Mrs. Santos. The old lady had congestive heart failure. Died when Matty was about six, I think."

"Is that when she came home?" Aidan began taking screws out of the panels that made up the booth, trying to seem casual, even though his curiosity was piqued to steaming. Holly intrigued the hell out of him and he hadn't been intrigued by a woman for a very long time.

Melinda folded the colorful fabric that had covered the counter and set it in a tub. "Nah. She was determined to make it on her own. Clive didn't get it." She pursed her lips, silent for a long moment. "We handled things... poorly. He told her when she got pregnant that if she chose to go with Leo Santos, she was on her own, so she wasn't about to come home except on her own terms. She's a determined young woman."

"Yeah, I got that."

Melinda tossed him a sharp look, while Aidan merely smiled and continued taking the pegboards down. "Did they move back because of Clive's cancer?"

"Mostly. He could barely handle running the bar on the boat when they came back for good. Matty fell in love with the *River Queen* from the first moment he stepped aboard...

and immediately had a kinship with his grandfather." Melinda walked over and held the pegboard panel he was unscrewing, then closed it at the hinge, and laid it on the ground. "I think that's why the poor kid is so obsessed with that damn boat. He misses Clive something fierce, but he scares the hell out of Holly and me climbing all over the *Queen*. He just can't seem to stay away from it no matter how much Holly and I talk and threaten."

He gazed at her, wisps of her hair were falling out of her topknot, making her appear oddly ethereal in the lights along the River Walk. Her eyes widened in shock at his next words, although she couldn't have been more astonished than Aidan himself.

"Melinda, sell me the *River Queen*."

Chapter Eight

"MOM, WHAT IN the name of all that's holy are you doing?" Holly gazed at the boxes, files, and papers that were strewn haphazardly around the living room.

After another long day at the hospital with Matty, she was exhausted and had hoped to come home and simply fall into bed. The surgery had gone well, although he'd be in a cast and sling for six weeks since he'd broken the radius close to the elbow and had required a couple of temporary pins in order to heal correctly. Dr. Simms had even managed to put on a neon green cast, which, according to Matty, almost made up for the pain.

The concussion was another story. The doctors had decided to keep him a couple of days to watch him since he was still nauseous and occasionally dizzy when he stood up. He was crazy bored because they'd banned anything that taxed his brain, so no games on his iPad or homework or any other thinking things and only gentle physical activity. Reading in small doses, resting, walks around the hospital, and taking naps were the orders, all of which sounded like heaven to Holly, but didn't thrill a twelve-year-old boy.

He would probably be released tomorrow, so after supper, the nurses had sent Holly home to get a good night's sleep, assuring her Matty would be fine without her. Too tired to argue, she'd kissed him good-bye and left him smiling because the nurse was allowing him thirty minutes of Amy Ignotow's *The Mighty Odds*, a novel his teacher had brought him earlier in the day. After a quick stop by the tea shop to reassure herself that all was well there in her assistant manager, Carolee Millikin's, capable hands, she'd hurried to the big house on the hill overlooking the river, ready for a hot shower and bed.

Now there was this.

She walked over to the coffee table and picked up one of the file folders—something to do with the *River Queen*. "What are you doing?" she repeated.

Melinda barely looked up from where she sat cross-legged on the floor by the couch, perusing a file box intently. "I sold the *Queen*."

Holly's heart stuttered. "What? You what?"

"I sold the boat," Melinda chortled. "Becky got an earnest money check this morning, and now I can't find the damn title." She shoved the box aside, leaned back against the sofa, and heaved a disgusted sigh. "Every freaking piece of paper your father ever produced about that tub is here except for the title." She waved a handful of playbills before tossing them on the couch behind her.

Holly shook her head. "The title is with Sam, along with

the originals of your and Dad's wills and a copy of his death certificate. You gave all that to her when we closed out the estate, remember? You didn't want to lose it in all"—she waved one hand at the mess Melinda had created—"*this.*"

Melinda's face fell, then brightened immediately. "Oh, hell, that's right. Well, I'll just have to stop by Sam's in the morning."

Holly, too tired to even think, began straightening up a pile of papers before it hit her exactly what her mother had said. "Wait, you sold the boat? To who?"

Her mom dropped her head back against the couch, closed her eyes, and took a deep cleansing breath. "Whom."

"What?"

"To *whom* did I sell the boat is the question."

Holly let out a disgusted snort. "Yeah, the one that you're clearly avoiding." When Melinda didn't respond, Holly tried again. "Mom, *to whom* did you sell the *River Queen*?"

Melinda opened one eye, like a cat—something she'd always done with uncanny skill. "I got a full-price offer from Aidan Flaherty and I accepted it."

Holly's heart dropped to her socks. "Are you kidding me?"

"Nope. We're doing the deal as soon as I get my hands on the title."

Holly's stomach twisted into a knot. "Why does he want that boat?"

Damn Aidan Flaherty. He hadn't even mentioned buying the boat when he'd visited the hospital earlier that day. He'd played a cutthroat game of Uno with Matty, who sported Aidan's black fedora over his bandaged head, while Holly had taken advantage of his presence to grab a quick late lunch in the hospital cafeteria. It was too hard to be in the same room with him. Her blood sizzled every time she saw him.

At this moment, though, her blood was boiling. The last thing she needed was for Matty's latest superhero to be the new owner of the showboat. She'd never keep the kid away from it. "Mom. Aidan Flaherty does not need to buy that damn barge. Matty already idolizes him just like he did Dad. That won't get the *Queen* out of our lives."

"He says he wants to put a showboat back on the river. He thinks it's time. I agree." Melinda pulled herself up and reached for a pile of papers.

Holly's sigh rose all the way from the soles of her feet. "What about the night Dad died? It's taken us nearly two years to help Matty past that. Do we put him through all of it again when Aidan decides to go back to his real life?"

Melinda gazed at her, one brow raised. "Aren't you being just a tad dramatic?"

"No, I'm protecting my son." Holly straightened her shoulders and headed for the door.

"Where are you going?" Melinda stood up. "Holly Leigh Peterson, don't you dare mess up this deal!" Deliberately ignoring her, Holly was already down the porch steps, glancing at her phone to check the time.

Seven thirty. Someone should still be at Four Irish Brothers Winery tasting room down on the river. They'd know where she'd find Aidan.

"YOU'RE BUYING *WHAT*?" Mason's voice was loud on the speaker mode of Aidan's cell sitting on the table in front of him. Typical drama from his agent, who probably should've been an actor. "What the hell, Aidan?"

Aidan took a sip of the pinot noir he and Sean were finishing and repeated his news. "I'm buying a showboat."

"Why?"

"Because I've always wanted to own a theater and this one is a part of my history. I'm going to renovate it and produce plays and variety shows in the summers along the Ohio and maybe even the Mississippi." He held his glass up to a smiling Sean and they toasted.

"You know nothing about running a theater, let alone a freaking *showboat*." Mason's voice trembled in spite of what Aidan thought was a stellar effort at keeping his notoriously bad temper. That temper had never been turned on Aidan because he'd always been a compliant, easy client for the famous Hollywood agent. Aidan sensed he was about to get a dose of it now. He gave Sean wide eyes and his brother grinned.

"The beauty of having more money than you need, Mason, is that when you don't know how to do something, you can hire people to do it for you... or to teach you." Aidan waited for the blast of fury he was certain was coming.

Instead, Mason's voice was remarkably calm. "Aidan, what are you thinking, dude? I've got scripts for four pilots sitting in front of me here. Good offers. Plus, you seriously need to consider doing the *Hollywood Bachelor* gig. It could buy us a lot of free publicity while we're fielding other opportunities."

Aidan shook his head as he opened the Notes program on his iPad and started typing a to-do list for the next day. He and Sean had just closed up the tasting room and were enjoying wine, a plate of cheese and crackers, and an unusually warm October evening on the deck overlooking the Ohio before they left for home. "I don't want to do the *Hollywood Bachelor*. I don't want to do another cop show, and I know for a fact that's what's sitting on your desk because you've texted me endlessly telling me about them."

"Aidan, you're a television actor." Mason's voice remained reasonable. "Actors don't just leave the business."

Aidan laughed out loud. "Sure they do, Mason. Actors leave the business all the time." He googled a quick list while Sean chuckled in the background. "Audrey Hepburn, Sean Connery, Jonathan Taylor Thomas, Cameron Diaz, Gene Hackman, Rick Moranis, hell, Jack Gleeson left after he got killed off of *Game of Thrones*, and now he's working with a small theater group somewhere in Ireland, I believe. The list is endless. I can go on if you like."

Mason's sigh came through loud and clear. "I get it. Allow me to reword. *You* don't just leave the business when your career is on this kind of upward swing."

Aidan barked a rough laugh. "I just got killed off, dude. How is that upward?"

"There are four producers clamoring for you—and one's a sitcom. I'm fielding new offers every day. Please don't do this, Aidan."

"I'm doing it, Mason. So, eventually, I may need some names from you, but right now, unless you know any good carpenters, plumbers, HVAC guys, or diesel mechanics in River's Edge, Indiana, I think we're done here." Aidan hovered his finger over the End button on his phone. "I'll keep you posted."

"I'm not giving up," Mason warned as they hung up, and Aidan knew he was dead serious. Fine. If something came along that was absolutely irresistible, he'd consider it. *Maybe.* Even though experience had shown him that Mason had him pigeonholed in a little box that no longer fit comfortably. It hadn't for some time, and although being written out of *LA Detectives* was still a sore point when he probed it too frequently, he had to confess he'd been getting tired of smart-ass Pete Atwood. Apparently the writers had been too, so maybe it was best for everyone.

"Nice job, Ace." Sean tipped his glass in Aidan's direction. "Maybe this isn't such a wild-hair idea after all."

Aidan shot him a wry smile. "Thanks for the vote of confidence, bro."

"I'm behind you, little brother. Just let me know how I can help."

"Thank you." Aidan was grateful for Sean's show of support.

He was going to need it. He turned back to his iPad, adding *find new theater seats, check re: registering with the coast guard,* and *look into liquor license* to his to-do list. He would ask Melinda if she had a list of people who had worked on the boat for Clive. In the meantime, he'd help Sean close up, and then head into town to talk to Mac Mackenzie about renting Meg's old apartment above his garage. He needed to get out of Conor's basement and into his own place. Mac's garage apartment was cozy and walking distance to the *River Queen,* so he'd been delighted when Meg had mentioned it at Sunday night family dinner. "Well, as I told Mason, I need a great carpenter, a plumber, HVAC company, and a diesel mechanic."

"Hang on. I've got some names for you." Sean pulled out his phone and scrolled through his contacts.

"Can we talk?" A voice came out of the darkness near the steps of the deck.

Both Aidan and Sean spun in their seats, peering into the dim light to see who was there, although Aidan had a sneaking suspicion he recognized that sexy, husky voice.

Sure enough, it was Holly Santos who appeared at the top of the steps and walked across the deck, her heels clicking in the shadowed quiet. She stopped at the table. "Sean, do you mind giving us a few minutes?" The look of concern on her face made it clear that the only correct response to that request was *of course* and Sean's swift departure.

He gave Aidan a raised eyebrow as he collected up the plate of snacks and his own glass of wine. "Here, Holly, take my seat. Can I get you a glass of wine?" He made the offer in spite of Aidan's brief warning head shake.

"No, thank you." Holly stood still, eyeing Aidan, who had closed his iPad and was waiting, fairly sure he knew what was coming.

Holly dove in as soon as the door closed behind Sean. "Why did you offer to buy the *Queen?*"

And there it was.

He'd actually hoped his taking the *River Queen* off Melinda's hands would make Holly happy, even though in his heart of hearts, he had suspected she'd question his motives. "I—"

She released a quick breath and held up one hand. "What did you think you were doing? Rescuing me? Fix everything up for little Holly and her kid by buying the boat that's causing her so much worry?" She walked across the deck and then back to him. "When I said somebody needed to buy the boat, I didn't mean *you.*"

He raised a finger. "But—"

"Don't you see? Matty already thinks of you as Pete Atwood, superhero." Holly's voice rose slightly. "He'd walk off a cliff tomorrow if you told him to, and now you're going to own the boat I'm trying to get out of his life."

"Holly, listen." Aidan shoved his chair back and followed her as she paced to the railing. "I bought her for *me*. I didn't even think about Matt, beyond that the boat would belong to me and he wouldn't be on it by himself anymore. I bought her for the town, so we can put her back on the river where she's supposed to be. It's another draw for tourism. I bought her for every kid up there at Warner who wants to be an actor one day."

She dropped her head, then looked up, shaking her hair back off her face. "Okay, okay. Maybe that is a great idea. I don't know. But what happens to the *Queen* and this town and those kids when you go back to Hollywood?"

Her words brought him up short, since with the inspiration to buy the *River Queen*, Aidan was suddenly sure he belonged back in River's Edge. The feeling of being adrift was finally subsiding. He had a plan now. A mission. He wanted the *River Queen* more than he'd wanted anything recently. He gazed down at her. No, there was something else—someone else—he wanted just as much and she was standing less than two feet from him, so close they were practically nose to nose. "Do you imagine for a moment that I'm going to go to all the trouble and expense of fixing up that boat and then just abandon it? Do you think so little of me?" Frustration surged through him, making his tone harsher than he intended.

She backed up. "Isn't that what actors do—*leave*? A new role will come along, something you can't resist, and the *Queen* will sit empty and useless again. And my son will be here, abandoned, wondering why another man has left him."

"Are we still talking about Matty here, Holly?" Aidan peered down into her face.

Her eyes widened. "That was a crappy thing to say," she whispered. She didn't move away, though.

They were so close, her breath was warm on his face, and those amazing eyes glittered almost amethyst in the string lights above their heads. She backed up again, then was stopped by the railing. He half expected her to slip to the side, but she stood her ground, gazing up at him, her expression a curious mixture of distress and desire. All of a sudden, the urge to kiss her became nearly irresistible, and he closed his eyes for a second, hoping the sensation would go away. It didn't.

"Are you done?" he choked out, also not moving back.

"I don't know."

"Well, decide, because I'm going to kiss you."

"No, you're not."

"I'm pretty sure I am." Aidan took a step closer, pressing her against the railing with his body and set his hands on the rail on either side of her.

Her eyes closed and he felt her trembling. Or he was. He couldn't tell anymore. He was confused and aching. He lifted his hands and took one step back. "Leave, Holly, because I really, really want to kiss you, but I can't if you're not all in."

Holly eyed him with suspicion. "I'm not sure I'll ever be all in with you, Aidan Flaherty." With that she reached up and put one small hand behind his head, tugging his face down to hers. Her lips touched his, gently at first, just a whisper of a kiss. When she increased the pressure, the kiss building in urgency, Aidan wasn't confused anymore. He knew exactly what he wanted.

He pulled her into his arms, thrusting his fingers into the soft hair on the back of her head, holding her still for his mouth while she wrapped her arms around his neck. The flicker of desire that had started when she'd walked onto the deck began to burn inside him, and he slid one hand down her spine to her hip. She was so incredibly tiny, he was almost afraid to hold her.

Almost. But when she touched her seeking tongue to the seam of his lips, he opened for her, tasting coffee and butterscotch and some unique flavor that was intoxicatingly Holly.

A little moan escaped from her lips and just as suddenly as she'd seized him, she pulled away. She stepped to the side and stared out across the water, leaving Aidan aching and bewildered, his hands clenched at his sides.

"I can't do this," she muttered to the river before she turned back to him, tears shimmering in her violet eyes. "I'm sorry, Aidan. Please, just don't buy the *Queen*, okay?" She walked away.

"Holly, wait!" Aidan followed her, catching up in six long strides and taking her elbow gently to turn her toward him before she reached the stairs. "I'm buying the boat. I can't promise I can keep Matt away from it—it's part of his history just like it's part of mine... and yours."

Even though he hated the look of distrust in her gorgeous eyes, he continued, "I promise I'll do everything I can to keep him safe if he's there with me." He softened his tone even more. "Meet me for dinner tomorrow; let me tell you what I'm thinking."

Holly took a deep breath, releasing it in a long exhale before she met his eyes in the dim lights. "I don't trust you. I don't trust actors. Every actor I've ever known has disappointed me."

He shoved his fedora back on his head and grinned. "I can't help it that I'm an actor. We're not all scum, you know."

She held up one hand. "Don't waste those dimples on me, Aidan Flaherty. I'm immune."

Aidan knew different, but this wasn't the time to argue that point. "Dinner at Mac's? Tomorrow? Sevenish? I'll nab us the booth at the back."

She gazed at him, clearly wary.

"I promise to win you over with my amazing business plan and ideas for the *Queen*." He tried the smile again. "They could include you if you're interested. As I recall, you had an incredible singing voice and—"

"Whoa up there, rock star." She raised both hands to stop him. "Okay, dinner. *Only* dinner and don't expect me to participate in anything you have planned for that old tub."

It took all he had to hold back a shout of triumph. Instead, he simply smiled. "See you tomorrow night."

Chapter Nine

M AC MACKENZIE SET a pot of tea and a cup and saucer down and slid into the corner booth across from Aidan. "Do you seriously think you can get that old wreck into good enough shape in time to have a holiday party aboard it? I'm happy to help, but seriously, last time I was on the *Queen* was during one of Clive's poker games right after he dry-docked her, and things were looking pretty tired in there. The theater was dingy, the seats were all worn. We played in the bar, which was also rough as an old cob."

"I'm going to try." Aidan poured, breathing in the aroma of oolong and… "Is this oolong and jasmine?" He added a tiny amount of sugar.

"Yeah, Carly drinks tea a lot. This is one of her favorites. Bought them over at the Leaf and blended them. What do you think?"

Aidan took a sip. The tea was delicious, as was everything the chef ever made, so he tossed him a thumbs-up. "I've got a guy coming in tomorrow to talk to me about taking out the theater seats, replacing boards on the stage, and making that area behind the stage into several cubicles instead of one big communal dressing room."

Mac nodded, no longer looking so skeptical. "How many does that place hold?"

Aidan had been researching ever since he'd first mentioned buying the *River Queen* from Melinda, although he'd spent so much time on her in his youth, he'd probably seen every nook and cranny. "She's a hundred thirty-five feet from bow to stern, including the paddlewheel, and has a beam of thirty-six feet. The license from four years ago that's still hanging in the bar says she has a capacity of four hundred; but the theater won't hold that many. I counted three hundred seats, and there's the upper deck and the bar, too."

"Are you going to try to find some decent used theater seats?"

Aidan nodded. "I was, but I figured I'd just do comfortable chairs instead. That way, I can get some big round tables and have the choice to do either dinner theater or set the chairs up in rows for regular performances."

"That's a great idea!" Mac's gray eyes brightened even more at the mention of dinner theater. "Why couldn't we talk about a catering deal? I'd love to work with you on a dinner theater thing."

Swathed in a *Riverside Diner* apron over her long-sleeved checked blouse and jeans, Carly Hayes appeared from behind the counter, an affectionate smile on her face. "Oh, Graham, how fun would that be?"

Aidan had a hard time believing she was the uptight society matron that Sam always claimed she was back in Chicago, because Carly fit into the small river town like she'd been born there. She and Mac were the perfect couple and Aidan loved hearing her call the tall handsome diner owner, *Graham*—his actual first name. She was the only one who called him that, so it came out more lover-like than *darling* or *sweetheart* ever could have. Carly cocked her head to indicate Mac should move over, which he did, and she slipped in next to him.

When she immediately began waxing enthusiastic about the *Queen*, Aidan's heart swelled. "Aidan, dinner theater sounds like a fantastic idea. It would be something totally different around here. Are you thinking about professional actors or what?"

"Honestly, I'd rather use theater majors from Warner and the high school drama departments and maybe even community theater groups. Are the Starlight Players still active over at the Tivoli?"

Mac grinned. "They are and just as crazed as ever."

Carly giggled. "Oh, my Lord, their last show was *The Odd Couple*. We laughed our butts off. Noah was Oscar; nobody else in this town could have done it."

Warmth flooded Aidan's soul. How he'd missed community theater life and all the fun and camaraderie that went with it. He'd been an active part of the town's little theater group since the age of five, when he'd played Tiny Tim in their version of Dickens's *A Christmas Carol*. "I'd have paid a thousand bucks to see Noah Barker as Oscar Madison."

"You'd have gotten in for twelve and had the time of your life." Mac tossed a look over his shoulder as the bell above the door jangled. "Whoops, I think your date's here."

"Not a date." Holly sauntered toward the booth, looking incredible in a pair of skinny jeans tucked into brown boots, a soft yellow sweater, and wrapped around her neck, a knit scarf in all shades of gold, red, and brown. "A meeting."

Carly and Mac hopped up. "Hey, Holly." Carly gave her a quick hug as Mac headed for the kitchen. "Let me get you a cup for tea." She stepped behind the counter as Holly unwound the scarf from around her neck, letting it dangle as she settled into the booth across from Aidan.

She offered him a brief nod that said they were back to square one and he was going to have to figure out a way to get around her defenses again. He sure would love to talk to her about what had made her so distrustful of men—actors, in particular.

Instead, he smiled and said, "Hello. How was your day?"

She stared at him, her brow furrowed. "What?"

He shrugged. "I thought we'd start with the niceties. You know, like regular people who like each other."

She pursed her lips. "I don't dislike you."

"Well, except for about sixty seconds last night, you coulda fooled me."

"We don't know each other well enough for me to hate you."

"And now we've gone from *disliking* me to *hating* me?" Aidan kept his tone playful, difficult as it was given how matter-of-fact she was being.

The expression on Holly's face showed her effort at keeping her tone even. "I neither hate nor dislike you, Aidan. I simply don't trust you."

"Because I'm an actor?"

"That combined with your ego."

Aidan sighed. "I already said how much I appreciated you opening up early for me that day. I know it was presumptuous."

"It was the fact that it even occurred to you to ask that was arrogant." She eyed him, her expression guarded.

He smiled up at Carly, who had brought a second cup and saucer. She set it in front of Holly and poured from the teapot that held Aidan's oolong-jasmine tea.

"Tonight's special is"—she squinted over her shoulder—"whatever it was you asked him to fix, Aidan. I'm sorry I don't know. I've been at Ali's school all day helping with a Halloween party."

Holly gaped at him. "You *preordered* dinner?"

"Well, I asked him to stay open later than he usually does on Thursday night, so I thought I'd make it easy on him and just pick one meal he could make for both of us," Aidan explained. "I chose roasted chicken, butternut squash, salad, and Mac's baguette with truffle butter. Is that okay?"

"What if I'm a vegetarian?" Holly raised one brow.

Aidan bit his lower lip, then lifted a shoulder. "I know you're not because I asked Mac what you order when you eat here. However, little one, if you've suddenly decided you *are* a vegetarian, you eat the salad, squash, and bread and I'll eat the chicken."

That brought the smile he'd been waiting all day to see. "Actually, I love Mac's rotisserie chicken, although I didn't even remember he wasn't open for dinner on Thursdays." She craned her neck to see into the kitchen. "Mac, I'm sorry this brat asked you to stay open late just for us. We could've met somewhere else."

Mac waved away her protest. "Not a problem. I was going to be here anyway, teaching Carly how to make crème brûlée French toast. It's the breakfast special tomorrow."

"So, here's a perfect example of that ego I mentioned earlier, rock star." Holly took a sip of tea. "It would never occur to anyone else in this town to ask Mac to serve them on his night off."

Aidan released a frustrated breath and then resorted to the old Flaherty dimples. "Mac is family. I figured he'd help out kin."

She offered a wry smile. "But you did it because you assumed you'd be mobbed by crazed fans in any other restaurant in town. That's why you asked him, isn't it?"

"Fine. We'll stop by the River Rat after supper and try a flight of their new beers. When Bren was here last time, he said the blood-orange lager was amazing." He raised his teacup in salute.

She looked aghast. "God no, we'd be overrun with squealy little Pete Atwood fans."

Did she not see how contrary she was being? She was unquestionably one of the most exasperating yet fascinating women he'd ever met. It was as if she were baiting him, forcing him to defend himself when all he'd done was try to arrange it so they could have a peaceful dinner together. He decided to go for broke. What did he have to lose really? She was already fighting her attraction to him, so he asked the obvious question, "Why do you hate actors so much?"

She blinked, then set her teacup carefully in the saucer. "You really want to know?"

He did, so he nodded. "I really want to know."

"Because they're all about themselves. I've never met a single actor who wasn't completely self-serving." She smiled wryly. "My ex, who charmed the pant off me, literally, was gorgeous and fun and completely in love—with himself."

"What about your dad?" He tossed out the challenge even though he was probably playing with fire.

Sure enough, her violet eyes sparked. "My dad..." She rolled her lips between her teeth and bit down hard before continuing in a soft tone. "My dad was one of the most selfish bastards I ever met."

Aidan threw both hands out in a questioning gesture, almost knocking over his teacup. "I had no idea he was hard on you. He was an amazing drama professor up at Warner, a fantastic actor, a great director, and he created an opportunity for young actors to learn the craft on the showboat. I guess I never thought about what kind of father he was. What he was like at home."

Holly scoffed. "Well, there you go, from you, he got exactly what he craved—every last one of you adored him." Her expression changed, saddened. "And me? I adored him, too, and when I needed him most, he shut me out." She took a deep, trembling breath.

Aidan had no words. He remembered Clive Peterson as a generous teacher and a kind man. Of course, he didn't live with him. *Still...* He recalled what Melinda had told him, how Clive had pretty much disowned Holly when she got pregnant. He'd been floored. That didn't fit with the man he'd known, and he couldn't begin to imagine a father turning his back on his only child. His bewilderment must have shown because Holly raised one dark brow, her expression grim.

"Right to the very end, his only concern was that damn boat. He was on oxygen, barely able to hold a fork, for God's sake, and every single day, he was talking to Matty about how they were going to reopen the showboat when he got better. Not a word about his family, about his wife, about how grateful he was to be with all of us in his last days. Nope." She swiped the table with her palm and Aidan noticed how small and perfectly formed her hands were. "Every moment was spent worrying how he was going to get that boat back on the river. Do you know what happened the day he died?"

Aidan shook his head slowly, gazing at her as she wound up. He'd hit a hot button. But he didn't try to stop her. He simply listened and waited.

Holly leaned forward, her violet eyes turning dark with emotion. "He convinced Matty to help him into his coat and wheelchair. He wanted the poor kid to wheel him down to the *Queen*. Thank God I caught them on the front porch while Matty was trying to figure out whether he could get him down the ice-covered ramp by himself. It was freaking December, twenty degrees out, and snowing! He had my son out there in the dark at seven thirty in the morning because he wanted to go to the boat. No idea how he thought he was going to get up on the damn monstrosity if they'd made it there." Her lips were a grim line and her eyes flashed. "He died that night and Matty was sure that it was because he took him outside in the snow. So, thanks, Dad. Your twelve-year-old grandson believed he killed you. It's taken almost two years for Mom and me to convince him that it was the cancer."

Aidan closed his eyes for a moment. "Oh, dear Lord." When he opened them, she wasn't even looking at him anymore.

She stared at something above his head as words poured out of her. "Leo, my ex, was exactly the same way—always chasing a part. Everything was about the next audition. He drove three hundred miles to audition for a freaking shampoo commercial because his agent said he had great hair. Great hair, for God's sake! I'm at home with his two-year-old son and his dying grandmother; he's off spending our last dime on a hotel room in Chicago so he can get a part in a shampoo commercial. He's still out there somewhere, waiting tables, tending bar, trying to catch that perfect part that will rocket him to stardom. He hasn't seen Matty in eight years. Hasn't paid child support in longer than that."

Aidan reached across the table to let his fingers just barely touch hers. "Holly, I'm so sorry. I truly did not know any of this."

"Why would you?"

He didn't hear any hostility in the question, for indeed, why would he?

Her eyes met his briefly before she looked down at their hands, so close but not connected. "He hated you, you know?"

SHE COULD SEE that her words shocked him, but he didn't draw away. Instead, he grasped her fingers and laced them with his own.

"He didn't even know me." Aidan's voice was husky.

Holly looked down at their laced fingers and a tingle shot through her. His hand was big and warm and engulfed her smaller one with just their fingers clasped. "Oh, he knew you." She smiled at his puzzled expression. "You were all my dad talked about when Leo first came aboard the *Queen*. That's how I met him. He was in Dad's Showboat Summer course at Warner. I'd just turned sixteen. You were in New York by then, *working as an actor*. I was stupid, rebellious… wishing he was—"

She was just inches from saying too much. What was it about Aidan Flaherty that made her want to turn herself inside out? She didn't open up to anyone ever and she certainly never talked about Leo and their disaster of a marriage, if one could even call it a marriage. They'd spent so little time together after Matty was born, and when they were in the same room, all they did was fight.

She was relieved when he finally agreed to divorce and not at all surprised that the reason for his recalcitrance about it was that he'd have to pay child support. As it turned out, he bolted for California and never paid a dime, in spite of a warrant for his arrest in Ohio for nonpayment that was in effect to this day. He hadn't even bothered to return for his own grandmother's funeral, although he had somehow let the attorney know where he was so he could get the life insurance check. When he sold the house out from under her, Holly found an apartment and a daycare for Mateo in Cincinnati and closed the door on Leo Santos.

Aidan squeezed her fingers lightly. "Wishing he was what, Holly? Or who?"

Holly tugged her hand away, determined to get things back on a less intimate level. "Anything other than an actor."

"You know there are some very nice actors in the world." A look of disappointment crossed his handsome features when she folded her hands on the table. "Tom Hanks, George Clooney, Ellen DeGeneres."

"I've heard Amy Poehler is very nice and I had a glass of wine with Bruce Willis at a fund-raiser in Chicago once. He was charming." Carly stood at their booth with a tray and a smile. "And honestly, Aidan here is one of the nicest men I've ever met."

"Did you pay her to say that?" Holly let her tone turn teasing as she leaned back in the booth when Carly set crisp salads and a basket of warm bread in front of them.

"Any chance you could cut me some slack? Just for to-night?" Aidan's dimples nearly undid her.

She steeled herself and didn't return his cocky grin. Instead, she got serious. "Probably not. I need you to stop being Matty's hero, okay? I don't want him idolizing an actor and thinking he wants to be one, too."

"What if, without any influence from me at all, *he* decides he wants to be an actor?"

She scowled at him. "He's going to be an engineer or a teacher or a plumber or anything else! Just not an actor." Of course, she knew Matty's choice of career was his alone, but she certainly had no intention of *encouraging* him to be an actor.

Aidan raised both hands palms forward in a surrender gesture. "Okay, Mom, no acting."

Carly placed a small tray with a dish of whipped truffle butter and several different little pitchers on it between them on the table.

She pointed to the mini-pitchers. "Dressings—a balsamic, a bleu cheese, and Graham's house dressing. It's a pear vinaigrette and my personal favorite. Or I can check the fridge for anything else you might want."

Holly smiled up at her, grateful for the interruption. "The pear sounds fabulous for me. Thanks, Carly."

Aidan nodded. "I'm for the pear, too." He reached for the breadbasket, holding it out to Holly before he took a piece for himself.

They ate in a surprisingly companionable silence for a few minutes, enjoying the mix of fresh veggies in the salads and the warm truffle-buttery bread. After finishing one slice of baguette and buttering another, Holly took a deep breath and dove in.

"What are you doing here, Aidan? What happened in LA?" She nudged the breadbasket toward him. If she was going to carb up, he could, too.

He met her gaze over the food and she saw something unfamiliar in his eyes—could it actually be... uncertainty?

After a long moment, he finally said, "I got killed off."

She couldn't have been more stunned if he'd told her he'd committed murder and was on the run. "*What?* They killed off Pete Atwood? Seriously?"

His face crumpled for a moment, then he grinned at her and got very involved in pouring dressing over his salad. "Shh. It's a secret. Nobody's supposed to know until the show airs the night after Thanksgiving. So keep it quiet."

Holly's heart ached for him. He was making a good show at indifference, but his first reaction showed her his true feelings. He was hurting. "I won't tell a soul, but, why? You're the star of that show."

Aidan looked at her quizzically. "And you've just nailed the problem. *I'm* not the star of that show. I never was. Adam Paxton is, so I'm the natural choice to be offed when the ratings need a boost and the writers are bored and want some extra drama."

Reaching out to place her hand on his arm was pure instinct. "Oh, Aidan. That sucks."

"It's life in television land." His voice trembled slightly as he caught her hand in his, turned it over, and traced circles on her wrist, down to her palm. "It's okay, really. I was getting tired of old Pete. He was too predictable and—dare I say it? Too cocky for his own good."

She pulled her hand away. His light touch was sending shivers along her spine. Besides, the last thing she needed was to feel sorry for Aidan Flaherty. The man had led a charmed life so far—no reason to believe he wouldn't come out on top of this situation. "You have to be the hottest ticket in Hollywood right now. Who wouldn't want the sexiest cop on TV to be on their show? Have you gotten tons of good offers?"

Shoving his fingers through his thick blond hair, his expression turned curious, then impish. "Why, Holly, I had no idea you were such a Pete Atwood fan."

Heat scorched her cheeks. "Matty and Mom watch the show."

"You, of course, would never participate in anything as mundane as watching cop shows on television, right?" He eyed her over the last of his salad. "Because... *actors*... ugh."

She chuckled, then stuck her tongue out at him. She'd forgotten how damn charming he could be, how stinking adorable. If she wasn't careful, he'd tear down all her defenses, so she gave Carly a grateful smile when she appeared with two steaming plates and set them on the table. He'd already figured out that she was attracted to him. However she didn't want him thinking she intended to do anything about it. What she *did* want was to spend the rest of this dinner quizzing him about how long he'd be in River's Edge and exactly what he intended to do with the *River Queen*.

Chapter Ten

"WOW! THIS PLACE is huge!" Brendan's voice echoed across the vast empty theater aboard the *River Queen*. "Ace? Are you here?"

Aidan darted down the ladder he was perched on as he tried to fix the rigging that would eventually hold the scrim behind the stage. He hoped he wouldn't have to replace the whole rail system since, in the past month, he'd spent a fortune refurbishing the theater, including a rebuild of the stage. "Bren? Is that you, bro?"

The two brothers met in the center of the space, grabbing each other in an enthusiastic hug.

"God, it's good to see you!" Aidan swallowed the lump in his throat and grinned.

They hadn't seen one another since they were both back at the winery for their brothers' weekend in June, although they spoke on the phone frequently and texted almost daily. Their communication had been particularly hot and heavy in the past weeks because Brendan had agreed to help Aidan out with a special holiday project—a Christmas play to be presented at the annual Flaherty gathering on Christmas Eve.

This year, he'd convinced Conor and Sean to hold the event on the boat instead of in the winery, so he'd been scurrying to get the boat ready for guests. Pretty much everyone in town would be invited, and although most would have other events to attend on December twenty-fourth, the parents of the kids involved in the play that Brendan had written would be there, along with all the usual friends and family who attended every year. The party was a tradition started by Donal and Maggie Flaherty a few years after they opened the winery and continued by their sons. Conor and Sean assured Aidan that holding it on the dry-docked *River Queen* for one year wouldn't destroy that tradition, and he hoped they were right. Since it was a private party, he hadn't had to get a license to serve wine; the Four Irish Brothers Winery license to serve at off-premises events would work.

"Hey, look what you did to the stage!" Bren did a slow scan of the newly painted theater and rebuilt stage. "You did a"—he waved his arm—"what's this kind of stage called?"

"A thrust because it, you know, thrusts out into the house."

Bren waggled his fingers at it. "I like it. Even though you lost some seating, this is a great layout because you get audience on three sides. I think that's better."

Aidan nodded, following Bren's gaze to the new stage that Ben, the carpenter, had just finished. "I'm really going for an intimate venue and this lets the actors enter through the audience on either corner. I was in a play in a theater in Indianapolis one winter that had a thrust stage and it was a wonderful way to connect." He winked. "Plus, great storage underneath. We intend to run a tidy ship here."

"Speaking of plays, how's mine doing?" Bren's blue eyes were like his own, in spite of the difference in their sizes and the fact that his second-in-line brother more closely resembled the other two. Aidan was the only Flaherty who took after their small blonde mother. Brendan was dark-haired and brawny just like Da and Sean and Conor, but he and Aidan had always shared a special bond because Bren was a creative type, too—a writer. Not very many people knew that, since he worked in Washington, DC as an analyst. At night, though, he was a writer. He'd had several articles published in journals related to his career, but his secret passion was to write a novel—something he'd shared only with Aidan.

"I told you, bro, you're a hit!" Aidan walked him to the bar, where he had a single-serve coffeepot and an electric kettle set up, along with several gallon jugs of drinking water, a selection of teas and coffees, milk, cream, and sugar and bottled water. "Help yourself." Nodding to the coffee maker, he felt the kettle, peeked inside, and pushed the power lever down to make the water hot again.

Bren shrugged off his black puffer jacket and Irish wool cap and immediately reached for the darkest brew in the box of coffees.

Aidan shuddered. "I swear I don't know how you guys drink that stuff. I'll stick with my *lapsang souchong*, thanks very much."

"You didn't tell anyone who wrote the play, did you?"

Aidan furrowed his brows at Bren's worried tone. "No, you asked me not to, although why it matters is a mystery to me."

"I'm not a YA writer, so I'm not sure I want my first public foray into fiction to be a play written for middle schoolers."

"Well, that's dumb because the play is charming and funny and the kids are having a helluva good time with it." Aidan filled his mesh tea ball, the one that reminded him of Holly—although to be honest, nearly everything made him think of Holly these days—and plopped down on a stool at the end of the long mahogany bar.

The cleaners had been in the tiny tavern section of the boat this week, so the bar and paneling shone with the sheen of fresh beeswax, the floors had been sanded and a new coat of poly applied, while all the brass fixtures gleamed in the overhead lights that had been washed and had new LED bulbs installed.

"It wasn't too sappy?" Bren asked, his eyes hopeful in spite of his reluctance to let the world know he'd written a Christmas play for the River's Edge Middle School drama department.

Aidan snorted. "How can a Christmas play be too sappy?

It's perfect. You nailed it, Bren. Fifteen to twenty minutes running time, and somehow you managed to give every character a line or two. I stopped by rehearsals yesterday and Joanie's kids are doing an amazing job."

"Who's playing Nick?" Bren pulled out his full mug, wrapped his hands around it, and took a deep sniff, smiling in appreciation.

Aidan hesitated. Mateo Santos was playing Nick Claus in *Nick of Time*, an original one-act play by Brendan Flaherty, and Aidan's heart stuttered at the thought of Holly's reaction to that news. He'd tried to convince Matt to tell his mom and grandmother. However, the kid had been adamant about keeping it secret. Joanie Thomas, the drama teacher, was going to let the kids know today that they had to have permission slips signed by their parents in order to rehearse and perform the play off school property, so the news was going to come out if Matt wanted to continue in the lead role. And although he didn't expect Matt to be a kid who'd sign his mother's name, Aidan wasn't sure.

He *was* certain that as soon as Holly discovered that Matt was playing the lead in the Christmas play, she'd be storming up the steps of Mac's garage apartment to tear him a new one. At least he had a decent defense this time. He didn't have a thing to do with the casting of the play; that was all on Joanie. Matt was perfect though and his acting skills more than obvious. The kid had his grandfather's natural gift. Maybe even some talent from his father, although Aidan couldn't speak to Leo Santos's acting chops. He hadn't seen the guy in so much as a commercial. He did google him when he got home from his dinner with Holly right before Halloween, and the man had a few credits on his IMDb page, mostly very small parts in a couple of low-budget films.

Aidan had only seen Holly a couple of times since he'd bought the showboat. She'd been polite when he came into the tea shop; almost friendly when they'd run into each other at Mac's one morning where they discovered they both loved brie, bacon, and spinach omelets; and practically chummy the two or three times he'd been by her house to check on Matt. But she'd discouraged his attempts at a date, turning down invitations to dinner or a movie or a stroll along the River Walk with a wry smile and, "Not today, rock star, too many groupies for me."

It was a lousy excuse. He still signed the occasional autograph and now and again, he was stopped for a selfie, but River's Edge had pretty much gotten used to having Pete Atwood back in town. He was convinced she was afraid to let him—an actor—into her life and after her experience with her ex, who could blame her? Although Aidan respected her wishes—orders really—that he keep Matt away from the showboat, he made no attempt to hide his attraction to her whenever they were in the same room. How could he when those huge violet eyes looked up at him from under that adorable fringe of dark chocolate-brown hair that swept across her forehead? When he watched her walk away, dark hair shining as it fell down her back, her slim hips swaying...

"Ace?" Bren snapped his fingers in front of Aidan's face. "Where'd you go?"

Aidan blinked, shoving back the tangle of emotions that came up every single time his mind turned to Holly and Matt. "Sorry. Drifting. My to-do list is crazy long, tomorrow's Thanksgiving, and this place needs so much more work before Christmas Eve."

Brendan grinned. "That's why I took all the damn PTO I had saved up. I'm staying right here until after the New Year's Eve bash. Tell me what I can do to help you."

Aidan's heart surged in his chest. "You're *staying*?" He threw his arms around his older brother and kissed his bristly cheek heartily. "Dude, that's awesome!"

Bren returned the hug. "Gotta see how the play turns out, right? Isn't the playwright supposed to be at rehearsals?"

Aidan couldn't stop the chuckle that probably sounded a bit patronizing. "If this were Broadway, I'd say ask the director. Since it's River's Edge Middle School, I'm guessing you'd be very welcome. That is, if you get rid of that butt-ugly man bun." He tugged on the thick dark hair that Bren had bundled up on the back of his head.

The whole mass fell, tumbling down to Bren's shoulders as he shook his head vigorously. "Dammit, Ace. Do you know how long it takes me to get that thing perfect?" He grabbed the black hair elastic from Aidan's fingers.

"From the look of it, I'd say, two minutes, tops."

Bren raked his hair away from his face with his fingers and pulled it back into a knot. "Ha! Not even thirty seconds, Ace."

Aidan punched him gently on the bicep. "God, you're such a dweeb. The only thing saving you is that you've actually mastered the well-trimmed scruff."

"Coming from you, that's high praise indeed." Brendan gave him the lopsided grin that said more than words could express about brotherly love.

Once again, that old familiar lump developed in Aidan's throat and he swallowed hard. "I'm so happy you're here, Bren. Want to start by helping me fix this rigging?"

"Sure." Bren tapped the bar with one finger. "Hey, wait, you never answered my question. Who's playing Nick?"

Aidan took a deep breath, glad to finally have someone to unload on about Holly Santos. "That's a long story, dude. I'll tell you all about it while we work on the rigging."

Brendan drained his coffee, then slapped his hands once and rubbed his palms together. "Well, I'm already intrigued. Lead the way, little brother, and start talking."

HOLLY POUNDED ON the door to the apartment above Mac Mackenzie's garage. "Aidan Flaherty! Open up!" She shivered as she paced the tiny landing at the top of the stairs and tried to peer into the long narrow sidelight beside the door. She probably should've grabbed a warmer coat. The weather had turned colder over Thanksgiving weekend and her denim jacket was not cutting it, in spite of the bulky fisherman's sweater she had on underneath. The heat of her anger should have been keeping her plenty warm, but the longer she stood there, the more she shivered.

"Dammit, Aidan!" She knocked again, this time with the palm of her hand because her knuckles ached from the first go-round.

Still no answer, even though all the lights were blazing and she could hear music inside.

Where was he? He'd better not be ignoring her.

She yanked her phone out of the back pocket of her jeans and found him in her contacts, even though she'd sworn to herself that she'd never dial him when he'd put his number in her phone at the diner.

Just in case you need anything at all. And then he'd flashed those damn Flaherty dimples before he saved his number to her cell. "Well, I need something alright, you evil, arrogant, too-handsome-for-own-good, dimpled, deceitful… *actor*!"

She didn't even realize she'd said the words out loud until a voice at the bottom of the stairs startled her. "You are the only woman I know who can make the word *actor* sound like a curse."

She spun around so fast she had to grab the wooden railing that surrounded the landing on three sides to keep from plummeting down the stairs.

Aidan was up the steps and beside her in two seconds. "Are you okay?" He put an arm around her waist to help her get balanced.

"I'm fine," she mumbled as heat rose in her cheeks. "Where have you been?"

He held up a small brown bag. "Liquor store. I got a hankering for a hot buttered rum and I didn't have any rum."

"You got a *hankering*?" Holly eyed him, trying not to let the tingle that flickered through her at his touch show. He hadn't removed his arm and she couldn't step away from his embrace without falling down the stairs.

His blue eyes twinkled in the porch lights. "You don't like that word?" He was so close his warm breath caressed her cheek.

"Coming from you, it's a bit condescending." She didn't lean away even though all her better instincts were telling her to leave.

He quirked one blond brow and tightened his arm around her waist, letting his hand drift down to her hip. "Coming from me?"

"Pete Atwood would never say he has a *hankering*. That's pure Hoosier." She had no idea why she was involved in this ridiculous discussion, but his body pressed against hers made it impossible to think.

He tipped his head back and met her eyes. "That would

be a valid point, I suppose, if I were Pete Atwood. However, I'm Aidan Flaherty and, except for a wee bit o' old Eire, I'm Hoosier through and through." He touched his lips to hers so quickly at first she thought she'd imagined it. "So I can hanker after anything I want"—another quick kiss, this time on the tip of her nose—"including you." His mouth hovered over hers.

Holly couldn't tear her gaze from his. She sucked in a breath, willing herself to pull back from his full enticing lips, but her wiser nature had abandoned her, making her body unable to comply. Just one kiss and then she'd really let him have it. Surely, one kiss wouldn't dampen the anger that still burned inside her.

"Holly?" Aidan voice was husky, his breath laced with chocolate and… corn chips?

Her mom instincts kicked in for two seconds and she almost asked if that was what he'd had for supper, but when his lips came a fraction of an inch closer, the woman who'd been living like a nun for the last God-knew-how-many-years bounded to the forefront. "Aidan?"

"I'm going to kiss you. I mean, really kiss you."

"I know."

"And you're good with that?"

Why didn't he just do it already instead of giving her time to think? Her conscience nudged her. *Because he is a gentleman and he wouldn't do anything to a woman if she wasn't fully onboard—not even kiss her.* "I don't know. Let's see," she whispered.

His eyes narrowed. "Hmmm. I need *Kiss me, Aidan. I want you to kiss me. I need you to kiss me. Now...*" He gave the teasing words a sultry, sexy read, still not moving even an inch away from her mouth. His smile was the most enticing thing she'd seen... ever.

He was driving her crazy. She was so pissed at him for encouraging Matty to be in the Christmas play, but dear God almighty, if he didn't kiss her soon, she was going to explode. She slid her hand up his arm and thrust her fingers into the thick hair at the nape of his neck, sending his fedora tumbling down the steps. "Just kiss me, dammit."

He pressed her back against the rail and took her lips with a ferocity that surprised her, then set her senses ablaze. Passion and anger became jumbled as his tongue explored the seam of her lips, entreating her to open to his hunger. How could she not open for him when she was starving, too? His tongue tangled with hers and the taste of him sent shivers up her spine.

He pulled back, breathing hard. "God, you're shaking. It's damn cold out here. Let's go inside. I'll make you some hot buttered rum." His blue eyes had darkened almost to navy.

When he tugged her away from the railing, the action brought their bodies into such close contact, she could feel how much he wanted her. *This* was not why she stormed over here. She slipped to the side and rubbed her face with both hands, grasping for the anger that had sent her out into the cold night in the first place. "I don't want hot buttered rum, Aidan. I need to *talk* to you!" Her voice trembled, in spite of her determination to remain calm but firm.

His effect on her was frustrating and bewildering and... delicious. Every nerve ending was alive, and that seductive smile when he held the door open was next to impossible to resist. Okay, she'd go in, but she wasn't going to sit down and she certainly wasn't going to have a drink. She stalked past him, careful to avoid brushing against his arm, while he just grinned. "I don't want a drink," she repeated.

Had the grin turned into a smirk? *It had better not have!*

The apartment was warm and cozy and Aidan bustled to the tiny kitchen with his bottle of rum, humming as he flipped on an electric kettle, then pulled a small saucepan out of a cupboard and began collecting ingredients. In no time, the whole apartment was filled with the scent of melted butter, brown sugar, cinnamon, and nutmeg. He continued humming as he mixed the liquefied butter, brown sugar, and spices into two mugs. Suddenly, he was singing—his strong baritone ringing out the lyrics to...

Oh. My. God.

Holly pulled her jacket tighter around her and crossed her arms over her breasts. "Aidan Flaherty, are you seriously singing 'Baby, It's Cold Outside'?"

He winked as he opened the bottle of dark rum, added some to both mugs and replaced the actual lyrics with, "I am. Join in. Your part's coming up," to the tune of the old Frank Loesser song.

"Do you know how politically incorrect that song is considered these days?"

He added hot water and a cinnamon stick to both mugs and carried them to the living room. "I do. So sue me, I still love it." Smiling, he held one drink toward her. "Here you go. Get warm before you go back outside."

"You really think you're a charmer, don't you?"

Still singing his words, he replied, "No, but you do."

She did, dammit.

Wait, that isn't the point.

Closing her eyes against the sight of his handsome face smiling at her, she ignored the proffered beverage and leaned against the door. "Just stop, okay? I mean it, Aidan."

When she opened her eyes, he stopped singing and a resigned expression crossed his face. "You're here about Matt being in the Christmas play, right?"

Her ire returned, more subdued. And the steaming drink smelled amazing, so she accepted it. He extended his hand toward the sofa; she sat in the rocking chair instead. "Why did you let him audition for that part?"

Aidan dropped onto the sofa opposite her and tasted the hot buttered rum. Then he set the drink on the trunk that served as a coffee table and thrust his fingers through his hair, tousling it in such a sexy way that for a moment, he took her breath away. "I had nothing to do with the casting of the play. Joanie had a sign-up sheet, Matt signed up. She gave out parts as she saw fit."

A twinge of guilt passed through Holly's mind, and she shrugged it aside. "But *you* know how I feel about him being an actor. You could've discouraged her from giving him the *lead*, for God's sake."

"That's not my business." He looked sincere. But he *was* an actor.

"Today he brought *this* home! I knew he was helping with the play, but this is the first I've heard about him being the *lead*." She pulled a piece of paper from her jacket pocket and tossed it at him.

He caught it as it fluttered to the floor. "Ah. The permission slip for rehearsals and the performance on the boat." He offered a regretful look. "I hate to tell you this; I have to ask you to also sign a waiver for him to perform on the boat. I have insurance, but I need the waiver, too."

Tears clogged Holly's throat, so she took a sip of her drink and it warmed her all the way down to her toes.

Holy cow! How much damn rum did he put in this thing anyway?

Before she could respond, he leaned toward her, his blue eyes bright and earnest. "Holly, the kid's a natural. He's got the part cold and he's only had the script for two weeks. Plus, he's having the time of his life, in spite of the cast on his arm. He brings such light to the stage and his performance is making the rest of the kids shine. The whole cast and crew are enthused and having a blast—all because of Matt."

She bit her lower lip to keep it from trembling and stared into her drink, unable to meet his eyes. "I'm not trying to be a hard-ass. I just don't want him following in his father's footsteps. That's all. I want him to have a happy, stable life, not always chasing after the next big part—the one that will rocket him to stardom. Because we all know how that ends up, don't we? If I allow him to go down this path, he could end up—"

His voice was so soft she almost didn't hear him. "Like me?"

Chapter Eleven

Holly sat back, stunned at the pained expression on Aidan's face. "No, no." Immediately remorseful, she set the drink on the side table next to her and held up both hands, palms outward. "That's not what I meant."

Aidan shrugged and took a swallow of his drink. "No worry. It's okay if it was."

"No, *you* are an amazing actor. I can only hope for Matty's career, whatever it is, to be so successful. It's just that..." She gave him a small smile. "You were exceptionally lucky. Most actors don't go from basic obscurity to international superstardom in a matter of months."

His face told her she was simply digging herself into a deeper hole. "I'd like to think it wasn't all *luck*, that talent had a little bit to do with it."

His tone took her aback. She was so flustered, she kept saying the wrong damn thing. "Of course it did."

He scowled. "And it wasn't months. It was years. All the years of my childhood until well into college where I worked my ass off on your dad's boat, doing anything I could do right down to fixing the damn diesel engines just so I could be around actors and directors—to *learn*. Years where I went to school and studied and graduated with double degrees in drama *and* theater arts and technology, so I would know every element of the craft. Years I picked grapes and trimmed vines and hosed down cellar floors just to earn enough money for summer programs and theater camps." He leaned forward and set the glass on the table with such force that some of it splashed out. "All the years in New York where I worked days at a bookstore and long nights as a waiter or bartender so I could get to cattle calls for everything that came along. When I got the part in the revival of *Streetcar*, I was at my personal pinnacle. Sure I'd be there for as long as it ran. I wasn't looking for celebrity; I just wanted to be able to work at my craft. The craft your father taught me. To act onstage and do it well."

"And you were so incredible as Stanley that when the producers of *LA Detectives* saw you, they snapped you up and made you a rock star in no time at all. It's okay, I know the story and I'm very proud of you." She found herself using the same soothing voice she used with Matty when he was upset.

"Don't freaking patronize me, Holly." Aidan leaped up and paced the living room. "Do not!"

Aghast, Holly rose and turned toward him. "I'm not, I swear I'm not. I know how upset you must be about losing the television gig and I'm not trying to make you feel worse, but what's happening to you right now is my greatest fear for

Matty."

"Your *greatest fear*"—he air-quoted with a look of disdain—"is that Matty might be a highly successful actor with dozens of offers on his plate? An actor whose agent won't stop texting him deals for freaking TV shows? I'm not your ex, Holly. I can go back to LA tomorrow and get a new gig without so much as an audition."

The anger simmering in her when she arrived cooled in the wake of Aidan's rush of emotion. "I'm sorry. I know you're hurting."

"I'm *not* hurting!" He released a frustrated breath. "God, I'm so sick of everyone thinking I'm crushed because freaking Pete Atwood is dead. I'm *glad* he's dead, okay?"

"Okay." Short answers and just listening seemed best at this point.

He swung around. "Look, being killed off stung, only because I wasn't prepared for it. Frankly, I'd been unhappy for at least a year, maybe longer. LA was driving me crazy. I hated the perfect weather all the time. God, what's wrong with a thunderstorm or even a decent gully washer once in a while? And forget the ocean—"

She crossed her arms over her chest, debating whether to just leave or let him get it all out. "Aidan, I—"

He rode right over her, his voice growing harsher. "In spite of what you might read in *celebrity* magazines, I don't like jogging on the beach or swimming in saltwater. Give me that river out there and the River Walk any day of the week.

I hate expensive champagne. I want Da's sparkling tra-minette. I'm grateful for fans, but I love more being able to eat a meal in peace at the Riverside. And the freaking traffic! Holy crap! If you think that two hours sitting at a dead stop on the freeway every day is any better in a limo, you'd be wrong as hell. The traffic on the double M bridge from here to Kentucky is more than enough cars in a line for me." He barely paused to take a breath and his voice trembled as he continued. "I missed my brothers and the people in this town who saw me grow up, who don't have an agenda, folks who share my history. Every real friend I ever had." He glared at her, stomped into the kitchen, and picked up the bottle of rum. "So stop thinking I came home to lick my wounds or that I'm washed up as an actor because I got written out of one lousy cop show."

"I don't think those things at all."

He opened the rum, looked in the bottle, then screwed the cap back on—tight. "Okay, I'll admit when I first got home, I was unsure about what I wanted next." He paused, staring at the rum bottle. "The *Queen* has been in the back of my mind for over a year—ever since Conor and Sam's wedding. I couldn't stop thinking about her just sitting there in dry dock and how great it had been to be a part of her glory days and why couldn't she have that again. Why couldn't *I* have that again? And not just me. What if I could create a venue for young actors that would give them a stage like the one I had to learn and practice their craft on? To learn everything about being a *part* of a theater?" He took a deep breath and slowly walked to her until they were so close, she could see the sheen of perspiration on his brow. "Your dad did more for my career as an actor—as an artist— than anyone else in my life. I want to pay that forward. It's that simple."

Even though it was probably time to walk out, Holly stayed put, her heart aching at the memories he'd dredged up. She never understood the impact her father had on the actors he'd mentored. All she ever saw was Clive's obsession with the *River Queen*, how it kept him distant from her and Melinda. She stroked back the blond hair that had fallen over his brow. "Aidan, listen, I—"

His tone softened. "No, *you* listen." He gazed at her for a long moment, his eyes navy with emotion. "As much as you may hate it, your kid is an actor. I see myself at his age every time I talk to him. Now whether that turns out to be his lifelong career remains to be seen. But don't dare try to douse that flame in him. He'll never forgive you. And you'll regret it the rest of your life."

THE DEVASTATED EXPRESSION on Holly's face stopped his tirade cold, and he took her hand—the one that had just caressed his brow—and pressed a kiss into her palm. Dear God in heaven, it felt good to finally say it all out loud. It was the conversation he should have had with his brothers weeks ago, the one he should have had with Mason before he bolted LA. Holly had just stood there and let him dump on her, and although he believed with his whole being the truth of what he'd told her about Matty, he'd had no real right.

"Wow." She crossed her arms over her slim middle. "Now it's my turn to say I had no idea. From back here, your success seems like a fairy tale. Magical." She stared at him, her expression bewildered yet tender. "It wasn't so magical with Leo. It's hard to trust again when the person you give your heart to shoves it aside on his way out the door."

"I imagine." He reached for her hand again and kissed the soft skin of her wrist. "And honestly, that wasn't all meant for you." He smiled at her quirked brow. "Okay, so some of it was. I've needed to get it off my chest and somehow you hit my hot button. We seem to keep doing that to each other, don't we? In response to your actual reason for coming over here, I do need to make the point that *I* had nothing to do with Matt being in the Christmas play. Plus, I've told him he has to stay away from the *Queen* because she's a construction zone at the moment and I could be in trouble if he comes aboard."

Visible relief showed on Holly's face. "Thank you. I wondered why he was spending so much time closed up in his room. Apparently, he's minding you… and rehearsing. I get what you're saying, but as his mother, I guess I just don't want him following in his father's footsteps. It scares me, Aidan."

He offered his best beseeching smile. "Come on, Mom. It's a middle school play. It's not going to transform his life. Let him have some fun."

After a long moment of simply gazing at him, her shoulders drooped tiredly and she threw up her hands in a gesture of defeat. "Okay, I'll sign all the permission slips and waivers. But I'm *not* going to encourage this acting thing. He's already got too much of Leo in him. Stubborn. Sometimes sneaky when he doesn't get what he wants."

"I think that's universal to all kids, not just Leo Santos's son."

She gave him a wry smile. "Like you know anything at all about kids." She was still standing close enough he could see the fluttering pulse just above the rolled collar of her heavy sweater.

"Fair enough." Experimentally, he slid one hand down her arm and then around her waist, tugging her to him. She didn't object or pull away when he touched her cheek, letting his finger explore her lovely bone structure and her perfectly shaped ear. "Where'd you get those cheekbones, gorgeous?"

She ducked her head shyly, staring down at their bodies, so close he could feel the heat coming off her. "From my grandmother. Dad's mom was a full-blooded Chippewa from Michigan. The rest of me is all Welsh and English."

That was interesting news. "Native American? Really? I didn't know that."

"I didn't know her. She died very young." She rested her forehead on his chest and heat radiated from that spot to all his nerve endings. "Besides, why would you know that? I'm guessing you weren't very interested in Clive's family when you were working on the *Queen*."

"Probably best where you were concerned. You were so young, I'd have been arrested." Dear Lord, he wanted this beautiful, complicated, edgy woman—more than he'd ever wanted any woman. And she wanted him, too, even though she was fighting her attraction. "Now that I think about it, I remember Native American features on Clive's face."

She nodded. "My grandmother was fifteen when she got pregnant with Dad." She tipped her head back and gave him a wry smile. "Apple doesn't fall far from the tree, rock star. Never diss genetics."

"I don't think you got pregnant as a teenager because your grandmother was a teen mom." Aidan ran his fingers through her thick shiny hair.

"No, I got pregnant because I was young and stupid, but Matty is my whole life. I'd do it all again exactly the same way if I knew he'd be the end result." Her voice quavered. She was so small and seemed so vulnerable, Aidan just wanted to tuck her in his pocket and keep her safe forever. She rubbed her cheek on his flannel shirt. "It's late. I need to go. I have to be up to open the tearoom in the morning."

He sifted her hair through his fingers, fascinated at the way the dark strands appeared almost purple in the light from the living room lamps. "Just a few more minutes?" He touched his lips to her forehead. "Let me…" When he pulled back slightly, her eyes were closed, so he kissed each lid, the tip of her straight nose, then each peachy cheek before slanting his mouth over hers.

She breathed a sigh into the kiss—a sigh that Aidan interpreted as surrender as he held her face between his palms and sought entry to her sweet mouth. Her tongue met his with a ferocity that startled him, but he didn't stop. Instead, he slid one hand around to tunnel his fingers into her hair, while the other slipped down to her waist, then to her slim hip. He pressed her to him, allowing her to feel the effect she was having.

She wound her arms around his neck, pulling away for a heartbeat, then coming back in for another passionate kiss. Her hands found the hem of his flannel shirt before burrowing under the bottom of the waffle-knit henley beneath it. When she touched bare skin on his back, he shivered, more from the sheer sensuality of it than from her chilly fingers.

She moaned. "God, you're so warm."

"Your fingers are like ice, sweetheart." Aidan grasped them and brought them around, under his shirts, to his belly, where he held them flat against him for a moment, trying to warm her with his own heat. The ache for her grew to nearly unbearable proportions when her fingers gently kneaded his stomach. He groaned and found her lips again as he yanked his hands from hers and fumbled for the edge of her heavy knit sweater.

She had layers on, at least two more.

"Holy crap, Holly, it's like unwrapping a mummy to find you under all these clothes." She breathed a soft laugh as he tugged her blouse and then her tank top out of her jeans. When he ran his hands up her spine, he was delighted to discover that she was braless. He brought one hand around to cup warm rounded flesh for a moment, enjoying her sudden intake of breath. God, she was perfect. She fit perfectly in his hand and her little hum of pleasure caused every one of his muscles to tighten.

The urge to sweep her up into his arms and carry her to his bedroom was so intense he had to pull away or... He dropped his hands from her body and took one step back.

When he did, she jerked her hands out from under his shirt, her violet eyes clouded with confusion. "What's wrong?"

"No, Holly."

"No?" She blinked and shook her head slightly.

Aidan rubbed his face with both hands, inanely noting that his scruff of beard was getting too long. He'd either have to make the choice to grow one or shave soon.

He offered a wry smile. "I want you so bad I ache from the top of my head right down to my toes and all parts in between, but I don't want to do this if all we're doing is scratching an itch."

She dropped her head back and looked at him through half-closed eyes. "What's wrong with scratching an itch? I thought you rock stars did that all the time—I mean with all those groupies?"

He turned away, taking a few steps toward the front door. "*I* don't. And besides, *you're* no groupie." He opened the door. "You better go."

She raked her eyes over his body as he looked over her head, unwilling to meet that bold stare. "We can do it. I mean… if you want to," she whispered, but she was still standing a good ten feet away. When he didn't respond immediately, she took a step closer.

He stared up at the ceiling for a second trying to calm his racing pulse. "Oh, I want to. Trust me, I want to! Just not tonight. Not yet."

Her brow furrowed. "I'm not looking for a relationship, Aidan."

He shrugged. "And I'm not looking for a one-night stand or a frenemy with benefits. Let me woo you, little one. Let me show I'm not like all the other actors you seem to hate so much. I'm home to stay. We have all the time in the world because I'm not going anywhere."

Silently she eyed him for what seemed like ages to Aidan, even though it couldn't have been more than a few seconds. "I want to believe that."

"That's a start." With a sigh, he opened the door. "Good night, Holly."

Chapter Twelve

"YOU CAVED, HOLS, and I totally don't blame you." Melinda yanked damp towels from the washing machine, shook each one, and shoved them into the dryer as Holly leaned against the laundry room doorjamb. "That man's a hottie for sure. If I weren't old enough to be his mother… hell, if I hadn't been *friends* with his mother and stepmother, I'd have taken a crack at him myself."

"I didn't cave, Mom." She stepped into the compact space, grabbed a basket full of Matty's freshly laundered jeans and shirts, and carried it to the living room. "The decision to be okay with Matty having the lead in the Christmas play has nothing whatsoever to do with Aidan Flaherty. It's about Matty having a little fun. That's all." She dumped the clothes on the sofa. "And by the way, ewww! You are way too old for him!"

Melinda, hot on her heels, gave a little hip shake and a wink before plopping down on the couch. "I've still got it, baby. The boy might need a little older woman experience."

"Mom, seriously, stop or I'm going to need brain bleach. The point is, I'm worried about Matty and his fascination with all things riverboat and Aidan Flaherty." Even though she'd declared this was the winter Matty was going to learn to do his own laundry, Holly began folding jeans, noting that another pair had a hole in the knee. She held it up, shrugged and simply folded them and added them to the stack. Oh, well. Matty loved shredded pants—the more holes the better as far as he was concerned. She bit her lower lip. Torn pants reminded her of Aidan and the sexy low-slung jeans he wore the other night when she was at his apartment above Mac's garage. Soft washed, faded almost white with a hint of tanned thigh showing through a hole in the pant leg.

"*Is* that your worry?" Melinda reached for a long-sleeved *Star Wars* T-shirt and folded it neatly. "You're sure we're talking about *Matty's* fascination?"

Holly raked her hair off her face, then flipped her hand tiredly. "Okay. Mine, too. He's making it really hard to resist him. Sometimes I feel like that dumb kid who had the terrible crush so many years ago. I just want to hurl myself at him. Hell, I practically did the other night."

"What stopped you?"

Holly groaned. "I'd like to tell you it was common sense, but truth is, he did." She held a still-warm folded sweatshirt against her chest and shivered, still feeling the effect of Aidan's kisses and touches. "I think he wants a relationship, Mom."

"And you just want sex?" Melinda's frank question didn't

surprise her at all.

She and her mother had grown into a very open rapport since Holly had returned to River's Edge. Conversations after Clive's death had frequently gone on late into the night, both of them talking with brutal honesty about their marriages, Holly's childhood, and how Melinda felt she'd failed as a mother. Time had been both a cruel and a gracious mentor; Holly knew from her own experience as a parent that sometimes feeling like a failure was part of the game. She was just very happy she and Melinda had finally connected.

Folding another shirt, she gave the question serious thought. She'd set those urges aside long before Leo left. There was too much to do raising a child all alone, trying to keep food on the table and a roof over their heads and Matty in new shoes every six months while she went to school part-time and worked full-time. But nights, all alone her bed, the loneliness would creep over her and she'd think... okay, she'd fantasize about the teenaged actor who'd stolen her heart so long ago. Now he was here, all grown up and wanting her, and she had no clue how to respond. She'd spent so many years with her head down that she wasn't sure she knew how to open herself up anymore.

"What if I fall in love and he leaves?" Just saying the words aloud caused a chill around Holly's heart.

"What if he doesn't?" When she looked up, Melinda's smile was full of affection.

Holly grimaced. "He's an actor, Mom."

Melinda nodded. "He is and he will probably go away sometimes. Opportunities will come up, and you and he will have to talk each one through." Her expression grew serious. "Honey, Aidan isn't Leo. Aidan isn't your father. Aidan isn't even *me*." She met Holly's eyes over the pile of laundry. "I know you've felt abandoned by everyone you've ever loved—"

Holly reached for Melinda's hand. "Mom, you don't have to—"

Melinda shook her head. "Let me get through this, okay? I *did* abandon you when I didn't fight your dad over you going with Leo. I didn't protect you and I should have." She put one hand over her heart and Holly's throat tightened at the guilt in her mother's eyes. "I'm your mother. Protecting you should have been my first priority. I'm sorry it wasn't. I'm so terribly sorry. I love you so much."

Tears stung Holly's eyelids. "It's okay, Mom," she whispered. "It's okay."

Ignoring the stack of folded clothes, Melinda pulled her into her arms and held her for a long moment. "It's not okay because I contributed to all your fears about falling in love and about protecting Matty and I hate that you can't just have joy. That you've built this... this wall around yourself that Aidan and Matty both have to try to conquer. Aidan from one side and Matty from the other."

Holly's whole body softened and she relaxed into her mother's embrace, laying her head on that strong shoulder.

She allowed herself the luxury of the moment. "I love you, Mom."

Melinda gave her another squeeze, then sat back and grinned, even though tears tracked down her cheeks. "So, what are you going to do about these actors?"

Holly contemplated the question. "Maybe release one of them just a little bit and grab the other one and hold on tight?"

Melinda chuckled. "Are you asking me? Because if the first is Matty and the second is Aidan, then I say go for it."

Holly eyed her mother over the pile of folded shirts and sweatshirts. "You think it's that simple?"

Melinda laughed out loud. "Of course not, you idiot! However, the man of your dreams has just walked back into your life. Don't you think that deserves a small step out in faith? Hell, child, it's Saturday night and you're folding laundry! Live a little."

Holly's heart lightened even more, and the knot in her stomach loosened just a little. "Do you truly think Aidan Flaherty is the man of my dreams?"

It was Melinda's turn for an eye roll. "Are you kidding? You've been in love with that guy since you first laid eyes on him. You were eleven or twelve when he strutted onto the *Queen* the very first time. Your jaw literally dropped." Melinda chuckled. "You looked like one of those cartoon characters whose eyes bug out with hearts. You followed him around like a puppy for years. Then he went to college and

Leo turned up." She screwed up her face like she'd just taken a bite of a sour apple.

Holly shuddered. "God, was I *that* obvious?"

Melinda took off her glasses and rubbed her eyes. "You were to me—then... and now. Go for it, sweets. What have you got to lose?" She plopped the glasses on top of her head. "Even if it doesn't work out, how many women get to say they did the nasty with Pete Atwood?"

Holly gave her mother a withering look. "You're just an incurable old romantic, aren't you?"

"Yup. It's what kept me from murdering your father for thirty years." Melinda hauled her lithe body off the sofa. "It's late, kiddo. I'm going to bed." She ruffled Holly's already tousled hair. "Alone... and you know, that's the hardest part of losing your dad." Her face grew serious and Holly's stomach tightened. "Clive could be selfish and so often we took second place to that damn barge out there, but you know... when he cuddled me close at night and it was just the two of us... Well, that part made everything seem possible."

Holly reached a hand up to her mother when Melinda dropped a kiss on the top of her head. "I love you, Mom."

"I love you, too, baby girl." Melinda winked.

Holly shook her head as Melinda headed toward the stairs. "Oh, Mom, remember we have our mammograms next week. We're meeting the gang at the breast center Thursday at eight thirty, so make sure it's in your calendar."

With one foot on the bottom step, Melinda gazed back over her shoulder and held up her cell. "Got it. Don't you just love how Paula made a party out of mammos? You're going to have fun with this, I promise. Have you heard how many are going to be there this year?"

"Paula told me this morning that we're an even half dozen." Holly grinned. This was her first ever mammogram, and although at twenty-eight, she was young for the screening, her family history made early detection mandatory. Melinda's grandmother, mother, aunt, and sister had all died young of breast cancer. A mammogram party with a group of River's Edge women—an event that Paula Meadows had started some ten years earlier and named the Main Squeeze—would make a daunting experience bearable.

Melinda executed a graceful pirouette on the step. "And you know Mac will have an amazing brunch waiting for us at the Riverside when we're all done."

Holly nodded. "That's the whole reason I signed on. Well that and breast health, of course."

"I'm very glad you're doing this with us, Hols." Melinda's voice diminished as she disappeared up the stairs.

Holly folded the rest of the clothes pensively, her thoughts once again turning to Aidan Flaherty. Her mother was right. Aidan had always been her go-to fantasy—always. Wasn't it safer to simply leave him in that zone? If she got involved, two hearts could get broken—hers and Matty's. On the other hand, her mother was right, Aidan *wasn't* Leo.

And he could still set her pulse to racing just by tossing that dimpled smile her direction, something no other man had ever been able to do. God almighty, she practically salivated every time she was in the same room with him. She wanted him with every fiber of her being, even when he infuriated her.

She chewed her lower lip, then plucked her phone from the coffee table and opened her messaging app. Quickly, before she chickened out, she found Aidan in her contacts, tapped on his name, thumbed a text, and hit Send.

"MAN, I'VE MISSED this!" Brendan pulled his long dark hair back up into the man bun that his brothers couldn't stop kidding him about and boosted himself up onto an oak barrel in the wine cellar.

From his perch on a high stool next to a tall fermenting tank that held Four Irish Brothers Winery's newest vintage of chambourcin, Aidan had to agree. He and Bren had spent the whole day helping Sean and Conor down in the cellar and also up in the tasting room pouring tastings and selling wine. It had been a good day of brotherly camaraderie, hard work, and sweet memories of Da. Now, after restocking the racks upstairs for the next day's usual Sunday rush, the four of them lounged around the cellar, sharing bread and cheese and a bottle of pinot noir while remembering their days working the winery as kids.

For Aidan, the day had started out on a positive note for an entirely different reason, with a pot of tea and a delicious bran muffin at the Tea Leaf. Holly had surprised him by coming out of the kitchen to deliver a small beehive-shaped pot of local lavender honey and sitting down across from him for a few minutes. When he said good morning, she'd merely canted her head and gazed at him, a peculiar light in her violet eyes. Her expression was so intriguing, so sensual Aidan nearly dropped the dipper that was dripping delicately scented lavender honey onto his muffin.

"What?" he'd asked finally when she didn't speak.

She shrugged. "Just astounded that I'm sitting across from *you* here at the tea shop I run in River's Edge, Indiana. It's surreal." She took the dipper from him, swiped some honey from it, and licked her finger.

Aidan had grinned, too aware of the effect the unconsciously sexy gesture had on him, also very aware of his own effect on her. It showed in the blush of pink in her cheeks, the slight tremor in her hand when she'd given him the honey. "Not all that astounding really, sweetheart. I live here, I love tea, and I'm so damn attracted to you that just looking at you in this moment is making me... Well, let's just say it would be best if I stay seated for now."

The light in her eyes darkened from violet to deep purple while her face flushed even rosier. "Aidan, what am I going to do with you?"

At least fifty different suggestions came to mind, but circumspection had kept him from listing them one by one, although he had leaned across the small round table to run his thumb across her soft, full, honey-coated lower lip. "If this wasn't your place of business, you could let me kiss that honey off your lips."

Her tongue slipping out again to lick the honey away sent a spasm of heat straight through him. How had the skinny little kid he'd barely acknowledged all those years ago turned into such a beautiful and tempting woman? He wanted to know her better, find out her whole history, to know what drove her, the good and bad of being a single mom, what she thought about everything from climate change to pizza toppings.

"You're killing me here, little one." His voice had come out husky with longing.

She'd given him a wide-eyed look. "Back at you," she'd whispered, then set both palms on the table and shoved up out of her chair. "I-I have to think about this."

He'd closed his eyes, willing away the hunger for her without much success. "Don't think. Just give me a chance, Holly. That's all I'm asking for—a chance. What we have… This"—he'd waved his hand between them unable to find the words—"this… *connection* doesn't come along every day. Trust me."

She'd gazed at him for a moment. "Trust. Ah, and there's the rub, rock star…"

Before he could respond, she was gone and he'd spent the entire day with Hamlet's soliloquy earworming in his brain.

"Don't you think, Ace?" Conor's voice interrupted his musings and brought him back to the present with a start.

Aidan blinked, absolutely clueless as to what his brother was asking him to agree to, and debated whether to simply agree or confess that he'd been about five miles down the road in town instead of here in the cellar with his family. "Um…"

Bren chortled. "I told you. He's definitely not here."

Aidan blinked again. "I'm here."

Sean held up the bottle of pinot. "More wine? We're thinking about opening a bottle of Da's chambourcin next. Have another glass and tell us why you're not here with us even though you're physically present."

Conor reached for the bottle, adding some to his tumbler before holding it over Aidan's glass with a question on his face. Looking into his brother's eyes was like looking into a mirror in spite of how different they were in nearly every other way. "Problems with the boat?"

Aidan put his hand over his glass and shook his head, smiling at the thought of the *Queen* and how wonderfully she was turning out. "No, not at all. It's going great. I can't believe how fast work gets done around here. In LA, it took six weeks for my landlord to even call me back about fixing the pool heater. I finally ended up fixing it myself and of course, the landlord got pissy about me messing with it. Two weeks later, a pool guy shows up, checks the damn thing out, and he's like *there's nothing wrong with it*. Duh, I know, dude. *I* fixed it two weeks ago."

Bren cracked up. "Honest to God, sometimes you sound like such a California kid. All you need is little more tan and a surfboard... *dude*!" He gave the last word a Valley boy reading.

Sean joined in the laughter. "You missing LA, little brother? Maybe we could convince Mac to put a plastic pool down in his yard. Meg might even ask the town council to add a few fake palm trees and *like* some sand to the River Walk for ya... *dude*." His Valley boy wasn't much better than Bren's.

Aidan took the good-natured teasing in stride. It was a brother thing and nobody did brotherliness like the Flahertys. He'd missed this fellowship every single day he'd lived in California. "You guys can't know the suffering that happens in LA when a pool heater goes kaput. There's weeping and gnashing of teeth."

Conor rummaged in the stack of wine cartons by the office. "And I'm sure only the Hoosier kid would think to get out tools and fix it himself. Aha!" He turned, holding up a bottle with a triumphant grin. "The golden ticket—Da's chambourcin." He got busy with a corkscrew.

"What did they do on the *Queen* today?" Sean held his tumbler out for Conor.

Aidan thought for a moment. "Installed the *Floating Stage* sign above the theater entrance and hung the new house curtain. The carpet's down, thank heaven, because the tables and chairs I bought at that restaurant auction in Louisville are supposed to show up on Monday." Aidan had refinished the theater floors, then had commercial-grade carpet laid over the wooden surface to muffle noise during performances. "We're going to be good to go on Christmas Eve."

Sean, Conor, and Brendan raised their glasses to him. His brothers' obvious pleasure delighted him, but also gave him a moment's pause. "Are you guys *sure* you're okay having our annual Christmas Eve bash on the boat? It's tradition to have it up here."

Conor's dark brows furrowed. "We told you, Ace. It's great! It's cool that we can invite more people than this old place holds. Joanie was in today bragging on her kids and the play, so we're all anxious to see it."

Aidan caught the sapphire light in Bren's eyes at the mention of *Nick of Time* and almost spilled the beans about who the playwright was until Bren's slight head shake stopped him. The play was amazing. Aidan had stopped in rehearsals last week to watch from the rear of the classroom. Mateo Santos's portrayal of Nick, the lead character, was spot-on. The kid had natural talent.

"It'll be a blast." Sean waved his questions away and took a sip of wine. "Did you figure out the electricity thing?"

"Yeah, the power company came out Thursday and got us all set up. Put a bigger service in the ticket hut and ran a line to the boat that can be used whenever we're in dry dock, so we'll be able to open year-round if things work out the way I hope they will. New HVAC is in—all electric. Water will still be coming from the holding tank below, but I just had it filled, so we have plenty for the party."

Bren pulled an end off the loaf of French bread that sat on the keg next to him. "The restrooms are done and so is the galley behind the bar. Conny, you said you're cooking the ham at home, so I'm thinking we won't be cooking anyway, just doing coffee, tea, and hot chocolate along with wine and bottles of water. We're going to need a place for all the potluck food, though. Did you buy rectangle tables too or just round ones?"

"I got a dozen eight-foot conference tables online. They'll be here next week, so we're"—Aidan's pocket vibrated and he paused to pull his phone out—"all good."

He caught his breath at the name on the screen—Holly had texted him. He swiped and the message appeared.

"Will you show me the boat? Now?"

His expression must have been really peculiar, because all three brothers stopped chatting to gape at him. He glanced at his watch—ten thirty—and thumbed back, *"Fifteen minutes?"* Then he hopped off the stool, emptied the dregs of his glass, and set it in the sink. "Gotta go. Catch you guys tomorrow. Am I working in town or up here?"

Sean's eyes narrowed. "What was that text?"

"Nothing important." Aidan kept his tone as casual in spite of the fact that he was about to fly out of his skin. "I just remembered something I need to check on the *Queen*."

Bren scowled, suspicion lacing his pointed stare. "What? It's all good down there. I closed everything up after Ben and his guys left."

As Aidan inched toward the door, his phone lit up. "I'm going to go take a look."

Bren was on him in a heartbeat, snatching the phone and zipping across the cellar. "Oh. My. God!" he exclaimed when he swiped the screen. "It's a booty call!"

Aidan sprinted over to him, tackled him, and rescued his phone. Shoving it into his jacket pocket, he headed for the door. "*Not* a booty call, you douche." He stopped to grab a bottle of sparkling traminette from the small wine fridge in Conor and Sean's cellar office and drop a twenty on the desk. At the door, he turned, and amidst his brothers' hoots and catcalls, said quietly, "A date."

Chapter Thirteen

AIDAN STOOD ON the tarmac, gazing up at the glorious sight of the *River Queen* decked out in Christmas lights with garland festooning the top deck railing and colorful red bows every few feet. Always before, the riverboat had been tucked away for the winter, so for the first time ever, she was dressed for the season and his heart swelled when a car slowed down to check out his and Bren's handiwork. He grinned and turned to wave. The whole town was getting a big kick out of seeing her decorated and lit up with holiday cheer.

Inside, he flipped on the wall sconces in the big theater, where the piney scent of the Christmas tree mixed with fresh paint and new carpet made the old place feel brand new. Even in the dimness, soft ivory walls made the empty space feel larger and more airy. The new stage jutted out into the room and he imagined tables full of people, eating, laughing, enjoying a performance. Perhaps the first public one would be a variety show—old vaudeville with a couple of skits and singing and dancing. Bing Crosby and Danny Kaye all the way. He'd missed doing musical theater.

His heart was old, he knew that. He'd always wanted to dance like Gene Kelly, sing like Frank Sinatra, and have the acting chops of Spencer Tracy or Cary Grant. He'd watched old movies from the time he was big enough to turn on the VCR himself, spending long Saturday afternoons watching classic black-and-white movies when he probably should have been down in the vineyard. Da once told him he was an old soul. Maybe that was true, because even though he'd won an Emmy for the role, Pete Atwood never really fit into his skin.

Bren's Bluetooth speaker sat on the edge of the stage, so Aidan switched it on and connected it to his phone, finding his favorite Pandora station full of old and new love songs and ballads—the ones he played guitar to and sang along with back in LA when the longing for home grew so over-whelming, he ached. Sam Phillips's "Reflecting Light" was up—one of his favorites—and the music filled the hall. It sounded great—even from that small speaker. He'd forgotten how good the acoustics were on the old tub.

A sound near the door spun him around. Holly stood in the opening, the outside lights illuminating her slim body and giving her dark hair a purple cast. He stood still, but crooked one finger at her. He wanted her to come to him, for her to *want* to come to him. It was subtle and deliberate on his part. He was asking her to be his—maybe not for a lifetime, but for tonight and tomorrow and beyond that, who knew?

She moved into the room and their eyes met. She walked toward him, slowly, almost cautiously, dropping her light-weight winter jacket, gloves, and woolen scarf on the new carpet in a forgotten heap. He could tell she didn't even notice all the renovations he'd done to her father's showboat because her entire focus was on him. When she was an arm's length away, she hesitated, then without a word, she took his hand and allowed him to pull her into his arms.

They danced with her hand clasped in his and his arm around her waist as he led her across the floor. Waltzing the old-fashioned way he remembered from watching Ma and Da dance in the living room when he was a kid, they were in perfect sync. She fit in his arms and they move together effortlessly. He pressed his face against her head, letting his breath stir the hair over her ear while she rested her cheek on his shoulder.

When the next song came on, they slipped right into the rhythm of the music, moving as if they'd been dancing together forever, as if this wasn't the very first time. The fact that *she'd* texted *him* to meet her left him rather befuddled. Her contacting him was… unexpected. She'd been running like a frightened deer from day one. He got it. Her experience with men was limited and what little she'd had had pretty much sucked. Somehow, he'd have to convince her that he was different—that *they* could be different. Show her that just because he was an actor didn't mean they couldn't have a long and fulfilling relationship.

He kissed her ear and whispered, "Paul Newman and Joanne Woodward."

She didn't respond, so he tried again. "Hume Cronyn and Jessica Tandy. Tom Hanks and Rita Wilson. Ozzy and Sharon Osbourne. David and Victoria Beckham. Ronald and Nancy Reagan."

Holly tipped her head back, a look of confusion in her eyes. "*What?*"

Aidan smiled down in to her bewildered face. "Celebrity couples who've been together forever."

Her brow furrowed. "Your point?"

He brought their clasped hands up between them and held them to his heart. "It can be done. It's done all the time. Just because I'm an actor doesn't mean I have no staying power."

She tugged her hand from his and placed it on his face—such a gentle touch if he hadn't leaned into it, he might never have felt it. "I believe you, I-I just don't know how to"—she ran her thumb over his lower lip, sending a tremor of pleasure through him—"how to be with you."

Unsure what she meant, he pressed a kiss into her palm and touched his forehead to hers. "Just the normal way, I think. A man. A woman. There's no trick to it. I'm not asking for forever, little one… not yet. But don't close the door before we even get a chance to see if this thing can work." He kissed her temple and pulled her closer as the song ended. "Tell me about your life in Cincinnati. What are you longing for? Let's discover each other." He swung her around, dipping her mildly as the next song began. "Ask me anything."

She shivered. "Are we going to make love tonight?"

That question set him back on his heels and he cleared his throat, not sure how to answer. He hadn't come prepared for sex—not that there weren't plenty of other ways to love her. Heat shimmered through him at the thought of touching her, learning every curve, every inch of smooth skin on her body. He gazed down into her amazing expressive eyes, but found only a question. In spite of Bren's insinuations, he hadn't believed her text was a simple booty call; now he wasn't so sure. "Is that why you texted me?"

She leaned back. "Isn't that what you want... *too*?"

Aidan slid his hand from her waist to her hip, pressing her into his body to show her that it most definitely *was* what he wanted. But not just a one-night stand. "We've got time, Holly. Talk to me."

So she did. They danced and she talked. Cool, zipped-up Holly Peterson Santos emptied her soul into his hands, sharing her years of loneliness and despair with a matter-of-factness that left his own heart sore and aching. She told him about being all alone when Matty was born because Leo had driven their beat-up car to Nashville for an audition and his grandmother was too sick to come to the hospital with her. "I took a taxi. Gran gave me some money. I came home the next day because we didn't have health insurance and he still wasn't back. That was the moment that I knew." She rested her head on Aidan's chest.

He stroked her hair. "Knew?"

When she looked up tears shone in her eyes. "That I was alone. That I would be raising this child on my own. He'd make grand promises and break them the same day. He'd work construction for a week, then quit to go audition. That cycle was my life until he left for good."

Aidan didn't know what to say, although if Leo Santos had suddenly walked onto the *Queen*, he'd have beaten the crap out of him, tossed him in the river, and done it all with a smile. His own family was so close, he couldn't even imagine a man abandoning his wife under any circumstance, let alone when she was about to have his child. He remembered Conor's agony when Alannah was born; how his brother had struggled with the joy of being a father and the pain of knowing he was losing his wife to cancer and how they'd all surrounded him with love and care. Birth was supposed to be the jubilant occasion like it was when Sam had little Griffin and the waiting room was crowded with family and friends. It was never ever something a woman should have to do all alone.

So he held her closer and pressed a kiss to the top of her head, inhaling the sweet apple-vanilla scent of her hair as she continued to pour out the story of Leo's grandmother dying and how he'd been absent for that as well.

"He took her life insurance money, sold the house, and

bolted," Holly finished abruptly, pulling away, putting a few inches between them. "Left Matty and me homeless, without a dime, and his grandmother's grave unmarked in a public cemetery in Kentucky. I found an apartment and daycare for Matty while I worked days. I joined a program at the local college where I could get my GED and an associate's degree in restaurant management. Got a job in a tearoom in Newport and worked my way up to manager. That was about the time Dad got sick and Mom asked me to come home."

"Is that when you moved back here?"

"No, it was a couple more years before I could make myself come back." She worried her lower lip with her teeth. "I came for visits, helped out when I could. I had so much resentment built up though; I didn't want to share Matty with them."

"I can understand that." Aidan couldn't really, but he could imagine how painful it had to have been for her parents to reject her. If Da had disowned him when he opted out of the winery and gone to New York, he'd have been devastated.

Holly chuckled grimly. "No, you can't, but I appreciate the sympathy." When he furrowed his brow at her, she touched his scruffy cheek. "Your family is amazing. They're always right there for each other."

He couldn't deny it. No matter what happened, the Flahertys stuck together. Look at how Bren was taking all his vacation time to stay through the holidays and help him with the *Queen*. How Conor and Sean had readily agreed to hold Christmas Eve on the showboat and let it become a town event. How Megan and Sam and Mac and Carly were all pitching in to make his opening night a huge success. He couldn't imagine them *not* being right on the spot to help him, just as he couldn't fathom not being right there for any one of them. "You and your mom seem good now." It was a simplistic observation on a complicated relationship, but he was certain that she wasn't looking for *poor, baby* as she told him her story.

She smiled—a real smile, not one that hid sadness. "We are good. She and Matty are quite the team and Mom keeps me"—she closed her eyes for a moment—"she helps me find the joy I so often miss because I'm too busy trying to survive."

He grinned down at her. "Do I have Melinda to thank for being able to hold you in my arms tonight?"

"Maybe. A little." Holly tucked her body closer to his and sighed.

He wasn't sure how to interpret the long whoosh of air. Fear? Uncertainty? Frustration? "What was that sigh about?"

"Contentment," she said softly. "This is perfect."

HOLLY SNUGGLED INTO his muscled body—relishing the feeling of being in the arms of a strong, good man.

And Aidan Flaherty *was* a good man... for an actor. She scolded herself inwardly for the automatic addition of the caveat. That was unfair. He was showing her in every way possible that actors were no worse or better than any other people. Her prejudice had started when she was just a kid, spending time on the showboat, seeing the drive and single-mindedness of the student actors her father worked with every summer and her father's devotion to the craft. After her miserable marriage to Leo, she hadn't bothered to rethink lumping all actors into the same category. Aidan Flaherty was messing with her preconceived notions, and maybe it was okay to let him send all her carefully constructed walls tumbling down.

She kissed his chest, his neck, then rising on tiptoe, pressed her lips to his chin, to the scruff of whiskers on his cheek before sliding to his warm mouth. His response was immediate as he opened his lips to her seeking tongue and released her hand to put both of his on her hips. She loved that she fit so perfectly in his palms, loved when he lifted her with no effort so she could wrap her legs around his waist as he carried her past the bar to the kitchen. She barely had time to notice the shining new galley features when he set her on the prep table in the center of the small space.

The cold stainless-steel surface chilled her right through her jeans and she shivered, although whether the tremor was actually from the cold or Aidan's warm seeking fingers under her sweatshirt was up for debate. He found the skin of her belly and moved upward to cup and caress her while their mouths remained fused. Holly wanted him so bad, she moaned into the kiss and fumbled with the buttons on his plaid flannel shirt.

He pulled back and slipped his hands out from under her shirt, grasped her fingers in his. Gazing into her eyes, he kissed each finger—all ten—sucking the last one into his mouth, scraping it softly with his teeth in a gesture so sensual, it took her breath away. "No. Let me," he whispered. He grabbed his wool jacket off the counter next to him and spread it on the prep table behind her.

At her questioning look, he kissed her, put one hand on the center of her chest, and with a gentle pressure, pushed her to her back, leaving her legs dangling over the edge of the table.

"Aidan?" Her voice came out low and hoarse when he stood between her legs, crossed her wrists above her head with one hand, and tugged her sweatshirt up with the other.

"Shh." The chilly air raised gooseflesh on her bare skin and then it was his hands, his mouth, his tongue that caused the bumps. He kissed and licked and nibbled his way over her whole trembling torso, before yanking off her boots and socks to lavish attention on her bare feet. Holly had no idea the arch of her foot was an erogenous zone until Aidan made her toes curl. Desire like she'd never known, ever, eddied through her when he unzipped her jeans and sent her crashing over the edge of the world into mindlessness.

As she floated back to earth, back to the reality of lying half-dressed on the prep table in the kitchen of the *River Queen*, he hopped up beside her and gathered her into his arms. At some point in the long moments he'd been loving her—and there was no other word for what he'd just done—he'd unbuttoned his flannel shirt. He opened it, pulled her into his chest so that her bare skin touched the waffle knit of his henley, and held her as her shivers subsided. Tucked under his chin, close in his arms, she felt safer than she had in years.

She slid one hand between them but never reached her goal because he stopped her, bringing her fingers to his lips. "Tonight is all about you, love."

"But I want you. I lo—" She snapped her lips shut. The words were nearly out there, her hunger for him overwhelming her, coming from a place inside her soul that had fallen in love with Aidan Flaherty years ago.

He lifted her chin to gaze into her face, longing evident in his eyes that had turned navy with emotion. "God, how you've bewitched me, little one. It's been so very easy falling in love with you." His voice trembled. "But we've got time... all the time in the world. Let's take it slow."

She'd thought it was impossible to want him more, but with each word, each gesture, each touch, he was teaching her how very wrong she'd been about him. "What about you?" She ducked her head, suddenly shy, in spite of how she'd responded to his ravaging mouth and hands on her just moments ago.

"Oh, my time's coming, sweetheart, trust me." His smart watch buzzed against her back and they both grinned at the irony of it.

She sat up. "Do you need to answer that? It's late enough, I'm guessing that's someone in California."

He didn't even peek at it, just ran one warm, calloused hand up her bare back. "Nope."

She leaned into the touch, savoring, yearning, aching for more, but when she saw the clock above the sink, she moved away from him, landing barefoot on the cold tile floor of the galley. "God, it's two thirty! I need to get back. I told Matty I'd take him to Cincy to Christmas shop tomorrow."

Aidan released her with a look of regret. "I'd ask to join you, but I'm on duty at the winery tomorrow. The holidays are always crazy. Sam, Meg, and Liz are doing gift baskets, so I'm going to have to pour tastings and run the cash register. We don't open until noon though, so how about breakfast at Mac's before you go? I'd like to see Matt. I haven't seen him since he got his cast off."

Holly's heart surged, then bumped happily at his words. He *wanted* to spend time with her and Matty. "Sure. Nine o'clock?"

He hopped down, suddenly sweeping her back up into his arms and onto the table again. "Perfect." He scooped up her socks and boots, brushed the bottom of each foot in spite of the spotlessly clean tile floor, and got her back into her footgear, lingering over the process with sexy calf and ankle caresses and more fervent kisses that Holly responded to with shameless pleasure. How was it possible that dressing her was just as hot as him undressing her had been earlier?

At last he set her, fully buttoned and zipped, back on her feet while she clung to him for one more kiss. "I thought you said you had to go." A teasing smile played on his kiss-swollen lips, hunger so evident in his eyes, she almost swooned. "Look what you're leaving me to deal with." He glanced down between them.

What had happened to the smart, cool, doesn't-get-ruffled woman who'd greeted him with such disdain two months ago, she wondered as she stroked his scruff of beard and rose up for another passionate kiss. "You're the one who wants to take it slow, rock star."

"I'm not prepared to do it any other way tonight, little one, and I want our first time to be someplace warm with maybe at least a week's worth of food and wine handy so we won't even have to leave the bed to nourish ourselves. Did you walk here?" When she nodded, his sexy smile made her insides quiver and he hitched his chin in the direction of the door. "Come on, I'll take you home." He turned her around and nudged her to the theater where he spent too much time zipping her into her winter jacket and wrapping her scarf around her neck before slipping into his own coat.

He started to flip the switch to turn off the wall sconces, but instead tossed her a look of studied indifference that his next words contradicted. "What do you think of the theater?"

It was only then that Holly realized they hadn't even talked about the renovation of the *River Queen*, about what that meant to both of them. Holly scanned the big space, barely recognizable from the last time she'd been on the showboat not long after her dad had died. Her answer would affect their future, how they progressed from here—of that she was certain. "I love it, Aidan. It looks amazing."

His huff of breath and smile of pleasure told her she'd said exactly the right thing. What surprised her most was that she meant it. She meant it with her whole heart. When he hit the switch, the theater fell dark.

But he simply said, "Thanks," as he dropped a quick kiss on her head and led her to the exit.

Chapter Fourteen

MATEO BOOSTED HIMSELF up onto the long counter in the kitchen of the Tea Leaf, far enough away that he wasn't in danger of getting himself covered in the flour that Holly was sprinkling over a lump of raw Christmas cookie dough. "Mom, are you and Pete going to get married?"

Holly gave him wide eyes and brandished the rolling pin she had just set on the cold dough. "First of all, his name is Aidan. Pete is a fictitious character who is dead. Aidan is an actor and a showboat producer who is very much alive."

Matty held up both hands in a gesture of surrender and leaned away from her.

She applied the rolling pin to the dough with a bit more vigor than necessary. Matty's question had thrown her for a loop. "Second, where would you get an idea like that?"

"Well, when we went to Sam and Conor's for the watch-Pete-get-killed party, you and he were snuggling in that big chair, and I saw him kiss you out in the kitchen last night after supper. Plus, you're not mad because I'm in the play and I think *he* convinced you it's okay." He shrugged, completely unaware that his twelve-year-old logic wasn't far off the mark.

Truth was, Holly didn't know where she and Aidan were headed, although it was clear that in Aidan's mind, they were headed somewhere, and his open and generous heart *had* contributed to her softening her attitude about almost everything. Even her memories of Clive were somehow sweeter when they were filtered through Aidan's recollections of his days on the showboat. As for Leo, well, she was beginning to believe that Leo was simply a bad person and that his lack of responsibility toward his son had nothing to do with his chosen profession.

She smiled as she rolled out dough and cut Christmas cookies into shapes, thinking about how Aidan had been including her in all his plans for the showboat. He simply assumed she'd be hosting the Christmas Eve party with his family and they'd already included her and Matty as if they'd always been a part of the Flaherty clan. He kept sharing excited plans with her for the Showboat Summer course he was crafting—schedules, stops along the river, his meetings with the dean of the school of performing arts and the chairs of the theater, art, and music departments at Warner College. His delight in their enthusiastic response elated her. His pleasure was her pleasure, a sensation she'd never shared with a man before.

They had talked and planned for hours, curled up on the sofa in his apartment above Mac's garage or snuggled under the sheets of his big bed, exhausted and satiated, or as they worked together hanging white twinkle lights and cedar garland around the outside of the bay window at the Tea Leaf. Aidan was one of the sunniest people she'd ever met; his natural optimism was infectious and when he sang Christmas songs as they decorated, his lusty baritone rang out across the street, bringing smiles from the other shop owners who were also trimming their stores for the holidays.

One night, while they decorated the Fraser fir he'd set up in his apartment, he crooned Joni Mitchell's "River," and unable to resist, she joined in, her soft contralto blending perfectly with his deep voice. After they sang the last bars, he'd hung a strand of lights around her neck, touched his nose to hers, and whispered, "You have a gorgeous voice, Holly. Sing it with me on Christmas Eve. Just you, me, and my guitar."

She hadn't agreed yet, but he'd been working on her. Oh, how he'd been working on her.

Matty snapped his fingers near her face, bringing her back to the present. "And there's also that really dopey look you get whenever anyone mentions his name—like now. And the totally smashed way he looks at you. He's in lu-uh-uh-uve."

She shook her head and childishly stuck out her tongue at his impish grin. "Smashed?"

"You know"—he affected a dreamy expression—"seriously, Mom, the guy's falling for you. I'm glad. I like him a lot!" He shared a grin with her, then sobered. "I think he's made you not be so mad at Grampy anymore."

Holly opened her mouth to refute his observation that she'd been unhappy with her father, but that would be lying and she made a conscious effort to always tell her son the truth. "I think Aidan has helped me see Grampy in a new way. I was a kid and I could only see how much the *River Queen* took him away from me, not how he served so many young actors and performers. It's hard to share your parent with their jobs, even though the jobs are what keeps food on the table and a roof over your head and"—she nodded to Mateo's iPad on the opposite counter—"toys in your hands."

Matty offered an indignant huff. "That's *not* a toy. It's for school!"

She raised one brow. "Point being, *I* paid for it." She flipped a little flour his direction. "Besides, that thing gets just as much use outside of school as it does in your class-room."

He had the grace to look sheepish before hopping down from the counter. "I'm going to take the trash to the dump-ster and finish decorating that scrawny tree out there while you finish cutting out cookies. Then I'll come back and help you decorate them. Did you make that icing that gets hard?" He waited for her answer, doing a little soft-shoe across the kitchen.

She held up four piping bags filled with royal icing in Christmas colors. "Yup. You can do the Santa faces again this year." She watched him dancing—easy and with such natural grace, her throat swelled. "Where'd you learn that?" she asked even though she knew the answer.

"Aidan. He showed me the other night after we watched *White Christmas*." He demonstrated the moves again. "See? Just like Bing and Danny. Want to try it with me?"

"I'd love to." She grinned and turned to reach for a towel. Suddenly, her cell phone rang and she peered at the screen, helpless to answer it with flour-covered fingers. It was a local number she didn't recognize. "Honey, get that for me, will you?" She went to the sink to rinse her hands while Matty swiped the screen and let the caller know she'd be right with them, then scooted out to take care of his chores.

"Hello?" Holly held the phone between her shoulder and cheek as she toweled her hands dry. "Yes, this is Holly Santos."

The voice on the other end of the line was chipper, even though the news was anything but. Her mammogram had shown a small mass of irregular cells and they needed her to come back in for a second test.

Holly dropped to the edge of the desk at the back of the kitchen, keeping her voice hushed as she scribbled an appointment time on the back of an envelope. Due to her family history, she'd had the BRCA testing done several years ago in Cincinnati, and she didn't have the gene mutation, so she'd always felt somewhat protected from the disease that had taken her grandmother and other family members. Plus, Melinda had never had a bad mammo. Did breast cancer skip a generation?

The calm person calling from the breast center assured it this was not an unusual occurrence and that it was too early to worry. The nurse's brisk words didn't reassure Holly much, especially given that her new appointment was only two days away. If it was nothing significant, why were they rushing her in? Christmas was in less than two weeks. Couldn't it wait until after the holidays? No, best to get it looked at as soon as possible.

Holly was shaking as she ended the call, panic blooming in her belly. Automatically, her right hand went to her left breast, fingers pressing and probing. She couldn't feel anything there. She ran her fingers along the outside, then under, and then over the top of the mound of flesh. Nothing. Her breasts were on the small side—*a perfect handful* was how Aidan had described them just last night as he'd thoroughly explored her body. Surely if there was a lump, he would have noticed it. Wrapping her arms around her middle to stop the trembling, she dropped her head and closed her eyes.

The sound of Matty's scurrying tread brought her upright immediately and she blinked back the tears that threatened as he appeared in the doorway, holding up a Santa-drinking-tea ornament. "Mom, how do you hang this one? There's no—" He stepped into the kitchen. "What's wrong? Is it Grammy?"

She hurried to him. "No, Grammy's fine. Everything's

fine. I was just… just thinking about Grampy. I miss him at the holidays. Remember his old St. Nick costume with the long red coat and the long beard?" A twinge of guilt made her tone too sprightly. She didn't lie to Matty, but she also only told him as much as his tween mind and emotions could handle.

"Yeah?" Suspicion laced Matty's tone.

"I wonder if it's still around somewhere." She took the ornament from him, picked up a random paper clip from the desk, bent it into a hook, and attached it to the loop on the top of Santa's hat. "Here you go, kiddo."

Matty accepted the ornament, still eyeing her warily. "Do you think the St. Nick suit would fit me? It would be fun to wear it for the little kids after the play on Christmas Eve."

Holly ruffled his dark hair, already tousled from the knitted cap he wore outside in the chilly December weather. "Hmmm. I dunno. Let's see if we can find it when we get home. It'll probably be too big, but you're taller and broader than most kids your age, so maybe Grammy can hem the coat so it won't drag." She followed him out to the tearoom to admire the tree they'd placed in the bay window. The multicolored lights twinkled in the late afternoon dimness and Matty had done a great job with the decorations, which were all tea-related. She watched as he placed the Santa front-and-center on a high branch.

"How long do you suppose it took Aunt Susan to find all

those tea ornaments?" she wondered aloud, although her head was spinning with visions of x-rays and chemo treatments and surgery. *Cancer!* Her heart lurched in her chest and her knees went weak. She clutched the curved wooden back of a chair at the table nearest her. *Oh, dear God, no! Not now.* Not when she had Matty to raise. She was the only parent he had. Not when she and Aidan had just discovered one another. Not when he—*they*—found such pleasure. No, please, not now.

Matty, focused on the tree, wasn't facing her, thank God, when he said, "I'll bet her customers just kept bringing them to her. Or she could've found an online store that sells Christmas tea stuff. I'll bet there is one." When he did turn around, she'd composed her expression into a neutral smile. "I could google it right now *if I had a phone.*"

Holly grinned. Safe territory. Something she could handle even though her entire world had just turned upside down. "Oh, the tragic life of young Mateo Santos, ladies and gentlemen. How awful that his evil mom won't buy him a phone. How does he bear up under the utter misery of it all?" She gave it her best melodramatic read, including the back of her hand pressed to her forehead.

Matty rolled his eyes. "And people think *I'm* the actor in the family? Yeesh, Mom."

Holly wandered over to check that the front door was securely locked before hitting the switch, leaving only the Christmas tree lights to illuminate the tearoom. Taking a deep breath, she composed her features and was able to give her son a bright smile as she led him back to the kitchen. "Come on, you poor deprived child. Let's decorate those cookies and then go home and see if we can find that costume."

BRENDAN SET THE last of the cases of wine down behind the bar. "When did Conor start using these sideways cases?" He hitched his chin toward the cardboard container he'd just placed under the bar. "Setting the bottles on their sides in the case is an awesome idea."

Aidan looked up from where he knelt, stashing bottles of sparkling traminette into the new wine cooler. "I'm not sure. It's a great idea, though." His watch vibrated with a text that he tossed a glance to, then ignored.

But Brendan picked up Aidan's phone from the bar. "It's your agent again. Maybe you should answer him. He's sent you six texts in the last thirty minutes."

Aidan scowled. "He just wants to tell me about another damn cop show or something else I'm not interested in. No thanks." He jerked his head toward the cases Bren had set down. "Can you load some of that pinot and zin into the wine racks up there and down here?" He pointed to a wooden rack under the bar and one above the sink on the back wall. "Maybe a case of each?"

Bren began placing bottles, label-side up, of course, in the racks. Aidan couldn't help smiling as he realized how Da's influence showed up in the smallest details of each of their lives. None of the Flaherty brothers would dream of setting wine bottles into a rack any other way than label-side up.

He rose and stretched his back, shoving the sleeves of his henley up and swiping one arm across his forehead. It was definitely getting warmer in the showboat, which meant the new furnace was doing its job, thank God. It had cost a fat fortune to go total electric, but so worth it when he'd considered what it would've taken to get the old boiler he'd had removed from below working again. He peered at the digital thermostat next to the kitchen door when his phone and watch clamored for attention once more, this time with a phone call.

Bren plucked the phone from the bar, smirking as he swiped the screen. "World-famous actor, dancer, singer, and Emmy-winner Aidan Flaherty's phone. This is his annoying brother. How may I help you?"

"Dammit, Bren…" Aidan swallowed the words as Brendan held out his phone.

"It's Mason. He says he *really* needs to talk to you."

Aidan gave his brother the stink eye and grabbed the phone. "Mason? What's up?"

"About damn time you decided to grant me an audience." His agent's voice sounded even raspier than it had last time they'd talked about a month ago. Smoking those damn black cigars was going to kill Mason Riverton one day.

"I'm staying on long enough to tell you, no thanks." Aidan leaned against the bar, crossed his ankles and continued to glare at Brendan, who merely grinned and kept filling the wine racks.

"You need to get your ass back here, kid." Mason's tone fairly sizzled with excitement. "I got a call from Dick Leonard. 3Guns is branching into films and your name has been bandied about for the first one."

"Give me one good reason why I'd ever want to work with Dick Leonard again." In spite of pretty much being over Pete's demise, Aidan *did* still smart from Dick's betrayal when the writers had killed off his character—Dick could have at least warned him. The man Aidan thought was his friend as well as his director, a guy who couldn't keep a secret for longer than sixty seconds, hadn't said a word to him about what was going to happen. That stung.

"Two words, pumpkin. *Stanley Kowalski.*"

Aidan drew in a quick breath, momentarily speechless. His expression must have changed dramatically because Bren had stopped smirking and was gaping at him. "*What?*" he stage-whispered.

Aidan held up one hand and shook his head, too stunned to form a sentence. 3Guns Studios was remaking *Streetcar*? No way. And Dick Leonard was directing? No *freaking* way.

"You still there?" Mason asked.

Aidan blinked. "Yes. Yes, I'm still here. Are you serious?"

"As a heart attack, kid. They want a meeting the day after Christmas. I've already reserved you a first-class ticket on the red-eye from Louisville and a suite at One West, where the producers are staying and where we'll be meeting," Mason chortled.

Knees weak, Aidan boosted himself up onto the counter behind the bar. "Wait. Wait a minute." He took several deep breaths. "Is this another one of Dick's made-for-TV projects that gets started and never gets done?"

Mason's booming laugh was so loud Aidan held the phone away from his ear. "Nope. It's a serious remake of *A Streetcar Named Desire*—a theatrical film that will open in movie theaters all over the world Christmas after next. Apparently, it's been on Dick's mind ever since he saw you as Stanley on Broadway. He's got some new backers, 3Guns is onboard, and he wants *you*. You and I need to talk about what it's going to take for them to have you."

Aidan's heart pounded. A chance to play Stanley again, this time on film! Years ago, when he'd studied Brando's 1951 film performance before playing the part in a college production, he'd longed for a time machine so he could have been in the audience at the Ethel Barrymore Theater on November twenty-fourth, 1947, when Brando opened the play on Broadway. When Aidan reprised the role seven years ago on that very stage, he'd been honored, delighted, and terrified to follow in the great actor's footsteps, and even more honored when audiences and critics alike had praised his performance as *enthralling, inspired*, and *the best Stanley since Brando*.

His hands trembled so hard, the phone nearly shook out of his grasp as Mason gave him details of who was backing the project, how they wanted to film it on location in New Orleans, and the biggest surprise of all—they wanted Janine Garcia for the part of Stella. Dick had loved their chemistry on *LA Detectives*, especially on Aidan's last day of filming when Janine had wept real tears as Pete lay dying in the street on 3Guns's Burbank backlot. The rest of the cast was still up for grabs, although Dick had mentioned several top actors under consideration for the part of Blanche du Bois. "Like I said, the first meeting is December twenty-sixth at two p.m. Hope to start preproduction January second. Eight weeks of filming in June."

"Mason, why haven't I heard anything about this before now? Usually, word about a new film concept comes out long before the first preproduction meeting even gets scheduled. How's this been kept secret?" Aidan's antennae were up. Dick Leonard thrived on publicity. He couldn't keep projects a secret if his life depended on it.

"Dick said 3Guns wouldn't agree unless he could find some other backers, so he's been out selling it like mad to anyone with an open wallet for the last two years and keeping it quiet so he could present a fait accompli to 3Guns. He did it and he did it with *you*, kid. Two of the backers are in only if you agree to play Stanley." Mason chuckled and then started hacking. When the storm of coughing was over, he said, "I thought it was pretty ballsy of him to assume you'd jump at this after what happened, but Dick's never hesitated to use whatever's necessary to get what he wants."

Bren opened a bottle of pinot and poured two servings into a couple of the wine stems they'd unpacked, washed, and stacked behind the bar several days earlier. He accepted one gratefully and took a deep sip, holding the wine in his mouth for a few seconds before swallowing.

"Come on, kid, talk to me." Mason's voice took on the smarmy, beseeching tone that had always annoyed Aidan, particularly lately, when all his agent had offered him was more of the same thing he'd just left.

This was different. This was his chance to play one of the greatest roles in American theater for the second time in his life. To reprise his Stanley Kowalski on film. If anyone had asked him what remake would send him back to LA in a heartbeat, this one would have been at the top of his short list.

His mind raced. How could he get the showboat on the water this summer and be gone for June and July filming? There was so much to do between now and his tentative opening date in mid-June. So many arrangements needed to be finalized, music and plays chosen, sets to be built, students to interview and audition. The list was long and growing longer each day. This was his mission—reviving the *River Queen*.

But it wouldn't hurt to take a meeting, would it? He hadn't signed a contract or agreed to anything. He could go and just see what was planned. Who knew if Dick Leonard could even direct a film version of *Streetcar Named Desire*? He wouldn't be surprised if the dude decided to rewrite the play or do the whole film as an animated feature. Anything was possible. He took another drink, chewed his lower lip for a long moment, and then took the plunge. "Okay, I'll take the meeting. Listen to me, though; coming to hear Dick out doesn't mean I'll accept the part."

"Sure, kid, I hear ya." Aidan heard Mason's grin over two thousand miles of satellites and cell towers.

"I mean it, Mason."

"I know you do, kid, I know you do." Mason's tone reeked of victory. "I'll send a car for you at LAX. You land at six thirty in the morning on the day after Christmas."

Aidan ended the call with a tap on the screen and dropped his phone on the bar. He pressed both hands to the center of his chest, which was aching from his heart pounding so hard. He shoved his fingers through his hair and dropped his face into his palms, taking a deep shaky breath as Bren poured more wine into his glass.

"What is it?" Bren's eyes were alight with curiosity. "What's the part?"

Aidan didn't even realize he'd been holding his breath

until it all came out in a giant exhale. "Dick Leonard's doing a remake of *Streetcar*. He wants me for Stanley."

Bren's eyes widened and his jaw fell open before he blew out a long blast of air. "Oh, daay–umm."

Aidan shook his head. "Yeah, exactly."

Chapter Fifteen

AIDAN BURST INTO the Tea Leaf, his handsome face aglow with cold and something else Holly couldn't identify. "Hey, gorgeous."

Holly smiled. "Funny, I was just going to say the same thing to you." She tapped the screen of the register to close out the day and zipped bills and coins into a canvas bank bag before scooting around the counter to allow him to scoop her into his arms.

"Man, I've missed you! We've both been so busy, we've barely had a moment together in a week!" Aidan scanned the café, and then pressed a hungry kiss to her eager lips as his fingers traced the knobs of her spine. "Awful quiet in here. Where is everybody?"

"They're here." A resounding crash, then a burst of laughter put truth to her words, and she turned in his arms. "Everything okay back there?"

Fran's voice drifted out from the kitchen. "We're good. Dropped a stack of baking pans. Nothing serious."

Holly rolled her eyes. "If they were clean, they're going to have to be rewashed."

"They weren't," Layla called. "I dropped them as I was setting them up on the counter to rinse."

"What's the rest of your day?" Aidan nuzzled her neck, his scruff of beard tickling the sensitive skin behind her ear. "Want to go to my place?"

Holly wanted that more than anything, but she'd promised Matty they'd go up to Target to find a pair of black pants to wear under Clive's St. Nick coat. Melinda had altered the costume to fit a twelve-year-old. She'd even bleached and refreshed the old beard and tightened the inside of the red cap. Matty was going to look fabulous as St. Nicholas on Christmas Eve.

She had another reason not to go back to Aidan's apartment—the small bandage covering the sore biopsy spot on her left breast. He'd find it immediately and she hadn't yet mentioned the second mammogram or the additional testing she'd undergone. It had all happened so fast, she'd hardly had a chance to process it herself—two bad mammos, the positive needle biopsy, and surgery scheduled for the day after Christmas. According to her doctor, she was most likely dealing with a lumpectomy and because of her family history, a round of radiation.

She'd been holding back until she knew for sure what she was facing, but now, she was glad Aidan had appeared because she needed to let him know what was going on with her body, let his natural optimism reassure her that all would be well. More than anything else, she needed to know that whatever happened, nothing would alter the intimacy they shared. She remembered all too well how Leo had drawn away from her after her pregnancy had started to show. How he'd teased her about being fat and made crude, cruel comments about her thickening waist and engorged breasts.

Holly had been holding onto the stories her friends had shared as well as Melinda's assurances that everything would be fine. Last night at a wine-and-cheese girls' night out at Paula's, several women from the Main Squeeze mammo event had related their own callback stories. Mae Boyles and Paula had said they'd had the exact same mammogram result and it turned out to be nothing for both of them. Melinda had hugged her tight, reminding her several times that she didn't carry the gene. The knot in her stomach had eased ever so slightly with all the support, and she had even sung Christmas carols the next night as she and Matty and Melinda had decorated their tree and watched *White Christmas* for what seemed like the hundredth time since Matty had seen it with Aidan.

"Hey?" Aidan's breath in her ear sent a shiver through her. "Where are you, little one?"

"I'm right here." She pulled off his knit cap, thrust her fingers into his blond hair, and brought his head down for another passionate kiss that left both of them breathless. "I can't, Aidan, I'm sorry. I've got to hit the bank and then take Matty to Target."

"Really?" Aidan's disappointment was clear, as was his

longing for her when he pressed her into his body and let his hands roam over her hips. "Melinda can't take him?"

Holly shook her head. "Nope. Melinda's doing face painting at the nursery school this afternoon." She leaned back in his arms. "I do have something I need to talk to you about, though."

His eyes widened. "Yeah? As it happens *I* have something I want to talk to *you* about. You go first." He was clearly excited and she hoped his news was that all the tables and chairs had arrived on the showboat. Christmas Eve was just a week away and the delivery delay had been worrying him.

"No, *you* first. What's up, handsome?" She tugged him over to a table near the front window.

He plopped into a chair and reached for her hands, his blue eyes shining, but his first words sent her heart right to her socks. "My agent called this morning."

Holly sat still in her seat, literally bracing herself for what was coming next—what she was certain was coming next. She pinned on a smile. "Really? Something other than another cop show, apparently?"

Aidan chuckled. "Oh, yeah, sweetheart. A film." His next words were the ones she dreaded most in the world. "The role of a lifetime." He gripped her fingers. "Dick Leonard is remaking *Streetcar* and he wants me for Stanley."

Holly kept the smile in place as she looked into his face, which was as eager as Matty's when he talked about Christmas morning. Honestly, she didn't blame him for being thrilled. Stanley Kowalski *was* the role of his lifetime—any actor's actually, but definitely Aidan's. It was the one that began his rise to stardom. Of course he was delighted. She pushed her way through the heaviness in her heart, trying to think of an intelligent question to ask so she wouldn't cry out, *no! no! no!* "Does he want you to audition soon?"

He kept his hold on her hands, even though she was very subtly trying to pull away. "That's the incredible bit. I've got the part if I want it. Two of his backers are only in if *I'm* playing Stanley, so he *needs* me." He gave her a wry smile. "Irony at its best, don't you think?"

Holly gently tugged her hands away, leaned one elbow on the table, and rested her chin in her palm. This scenario was all-too-familiar. Same words—*the role of a lifetime*—different day, different actor. The scene she'd been anticipating since the first time she'd kissed Aidan Flaherty was happening and for some odd reason, all she felt was numb.

Part of her—the part that loved him without a moment's question or hesitation—was happy. Aidan deserved to play the lead role in this remake. He knew Stanley Kowalski inside out. He would play the beer-stained T-shirt off that character. She wanted to throw her arms around him, tell him how proud she was of him, but somehow, she couldn't muster anything more than a strained smile as he waxed lyrical about the role, the plans for filming on location in New Orleans, and how he was meeting with the producers and director the day after Christmas.

Her heart stuttered. He would be gone on the day of her surgery. Hadn't she braced herself for news like this when they first began? Common sense had warned her the very first time she'd reached for his kiss, but she'd ignored that little voice because she wanted him so much. Well, here it was. Reality was kicking her butt again and all she could do was swallow hard and try not to let him see how devastated she was. "Aidan, how wonderful. That's your dream role," she finally managed when he took a breath. The words sounded false even to her.

Tiny frown lines appeared between his brows as he eyed her. "Yes, it is." He folded his arms over his chest, one blond brow quirked. "Your enthusiasm is underwhelming me here, Holly."

The remark smacked her like a wet rag in the face and she tried to swallow the harsh words that first came to mind. She failed. "Gee, rock star, so sorry I'm not up doing a happy dance for you, but you just told me you've got a part in a new movie and all I heard was *good-bye.*"

He slapped his palms down, making the tiny wooden table rock on its pedestal. "Dammit, Holly, of course this isn't good-bye. You're being silly. This is what I do. I'm an actor."

"Yup, you sure are." This time she quirked a brow at him and did a rather admirable job of impersonation. "'I'm not going anywhere, Holly. I'm home to stay, Holly.'"

He fell back, clearly wounded, before coaxing softly,

"Look, I'll only be gone for eight weeks—eight weeks, then we wrap and I'm back here"—he turned on the dimples and sent a shiver though her, damn him—"doing a soft-shoe with Matty onstage on the showboat. We're practicing 'Did You Ever?' for opening night, but if I'm on location, maybe we'll just do it as the finale at the end of September instead. He's doing Sinatra's part."

Holly rolled her eyes, numbness heating to anger. "What about the showboat? Who's going to be keeping the *Queen* on the water while you're in *N'awlins* feasting on beignets and crayfish and playing the *role of lifetime?*" She hated how bitchy she sounded, but she couldn't stop the words. "You said you were done, Aidan. That you wanted to be here, to restore the *Queen* to her former glory, to mentor young actors... kids like *my son*. That dream is out the window the first time your agent calls with a plum role?"

He held up one hand, palm forward. "First of all, I *never* said I was done. I *do* want to live here, I *am* restoring the *River Queen*, and I fully intend to be on her for at least some of the summer. I haven't figured out exactly how I'll do that and be on location for *Streetcar*, but I will make it work."

"Because you're the big star who can make anything happen, right?"

He huffed a frustrated breath, but remained unruffled, speaking to her the way he'd explain something to a small child. The calmer he was, the madder she got. "I'll have the people from Warner onboard and I intend to hire teachers for the summer to help out, too. Les Janssen from the theater department at Warner has agreed to stage manage the shows—she's the best. I'll have people to run the lights and soundboards. Even someone to be up in the wheelhouse steering us down the river. I'll start interviewing pilots this spring and a crew to help keep things moving below." His eyes sparked even as his tone was reasonable and controlled. "And, hey, don't use Matt against me in this, Holly. He will understand that this is my job."

"Don't *you* assume you know my son better than I do, Aidan Flaherty! Matty's had enough men abandon him in his life. He doesn't need another one jumping ship." She blinked back the angry tears that were stinging behind her eyelids. The last thing she wanted was to cry, for heaven's sake. When she raked her fingers through her bangs, her arm brushed her left breast near where she'd had the biopsy a few days earlier. Another man, leaving when she needed him most. The tiny sore spot suddenly ached and she resisted the urge to rub the bandaged place under her sweater.

Aidan scowled. "I'm not Leo, Holly."

"But you'll be gone all the same." She stared at him, challenging him to argue that point, which was the *real* point, after all, wasn't it?

He massaged his temples. "Not immediately and not forever. When I do go to work, *I* will be back." His watch must have vibrated because he glanced at his wrist. "Dammit, Bren needs me to come over to the kids' dress rehearsal. The ERS isn't working. Can we finish this later?" He reached for his knit cap sitting on table between them and rose. Zipping his winter jacket, he leaned down and dropped a kiss on the top of her head. "Oh, you said you had something you wanted to talk about. What was it?"

She let the tingle at the touch of his lips ease the despondency that had dissolved her anger. Wasn't this her life? Men leaving. But he was here for now and she ached for him in a way she'd never wanted any other man before. This might be all there would ever be—this toe-curling hunger, but she wanted him… desperately, so she turned her face up to him. "Nothing important."

He caressed her cheek. "Don't do that. Tell me."

Not a snowball's chance in hell now, she thought, but she said, "I just wanted to ask you if you minded Matty dressing up as St. Nicholas for the kids on Christmas Eve. Mom is altering Dad's old costume for him."

Aidan gave her a probing look and then his grin lit up the room even more than the late afternoon sun streaming through the front window. "He already asked me. I love it! We're going to do presents for every kid, so Meg and Sam and Carly are busy wrapping little generic gifts for old St. Nick's bag as we speak." He kissed her soundly and started to walk away. Suddenly he backed up to where she sat and tugged her up and into his arms for another kiss that left her stunned with its intensity. When he released her, he winked and gave his good-bye a Bogart read. "See ya later, sweetheart."

Always the actor.

A single plump tear crept over her bottom eyelid before trickling onto her cheek as she watched him push the door open with his shoulder and stride down the street.

Chapter Sixteen

"WE COME BEARING sustenance for weary thespians." Conor's deep voice boomed across the theater where Bren and Aidan were onstage, setting up the scenery that the high school art students had provided for the Christmas Eve show coming in just two days.

Ali's little voice chimed in. "He means we brought you chicken, Uncle Aidan."

"And biscuits and slaw and cheesecake," Sean added as he appeared in the doorway with Carly, Mac, Meg, Sam, and baby Griff bringing up the rear. "Mac's disgusted with us for going up on the highway for food, but we thought he deserved to actually be *off* on his night off, so this is dinner."

Grinning, Mac sauntered over to the first round table, yanked the crisp white tablecloth off, and folded it. "You bunch o' Irish peasants don't know fine cuisine from greasy spoon fare anyway."

Aidan laughed, delighted to see his whole family together on the showboat for the first time since he'd bought her. Only their beloved stepmom, Char, and her new husband Myles were missing. They were celebrating Christmas in

Florida with his family this year. How comforting it was to have all the Flahertys and Mackenzies in one room with only a few days left before Christmas. Da would've loved it and been right in the thick of things. "You may be a gourmet French chef, Mackenzie"—Aidan gave it his best Irish brogue—"but a Scotsman givin' an Irishman crap about fine cuisine is a little nervy, don't ye agree, lads?"

His brothers all nodded and Mac chuckled. "You've got me there, kid. Wow, this place looks amazing!"

Prideful as it might have been, Aidan had to agree as he looked around the vast space. The old tub had come together exactly as he'd pictured it and in only a few weeks. He was still amazed at how quickly the work happened here. In LA, it would have taken months to accomplish what the workers had gotten done on the *Queen* in what seemed like no time at all. There were still repairs and painting to be finished on the upstairs decks and her hull to get her river-worthy for summer shows. Inside, though, she gleamed like a bright new penny.

Ali rushed up on the stage and Bren swept her into a hug, then onto his shoulders for a ride down the steps to the back of the theater where Sean and Sam were setting out food while the others wandered around oohing and aahing over the changes he'd made. Aidan followed Bren and Ali, turning around when he got to the bottom of the steps to give the stage setup one more approving smile. Everything was ready for Christmas Eve—the boat, the theater, the stage, the kids, and the party.

As he followed the aroma of fried chicken, he saw Megan drop onto a chair next to the table where they were setting up supper. She looked rather unwell. Come to think of it, she hadn't been around as much as Sam and his brothers; he'd just assumed she was busy with town holiday events. But when he stooped down in front of her and peered more closely at the smudges under her eyes and her pale face, he became concerned.

"You okay, Meg?"

She managed a wan smile, before looking up at Sean, who appeared behind her with a bottle of water and a packet of saltines. "We may as well tell them. They're all here."

Sean grinned. "If you keep turning green every time you see food, they're going to figure it out without a word from us, my love." He pressed a kiss to her temple, then cleared his throat theatrically. "Everyone gather 'round. Announcement time."

Aidan rose, excitement bubbling inside him, certain of what Sean and Meg were about to reveal. He was going to be an uncle for the third time.

"Meg and I are pregnant." When everyone cheered and applauded, Sean bowed elegantly from the waist and gave them a coy smile. "It was my pleasure, everyone, I assure you."

As the laughter subsided, Meg filled in the rest of their news. "The baby is due around the first of July, so I'll be finishing up my term as mayor round as a beach ball. And I've been sick as a dog, not just in the morning. Every time I see or smell food."

Mac rushed to her side. "Oh, sweetheart, your mom was the same way. Puked for three solid months." He smiled encouragingly. "But suddenly it stopped and she was great for the rest of her time."

Meg closed her eyes and leaned her head back against Sean. "Swell. If genetics hold, I've only got three more weeks to go."

Sean patted her shoulder. "Here, babe, let's get you away from this table full of food and see if you can hold down some crackers and water." He led her to the bar and settled her on a high stool.

Ali followed them and boosted her small self up onto the stool next to Meg's. "I'm sorry the baby is making you feel bad, Aunt Meg. Do you want me to find you a puke bucket?"

Aidan hustled behind the bar and offered up an ice bucket. "Think this'll work, Ali?"

"It's perfect." She set it next to Megan. "And a damp rag, Uncle Aidan. Sam always brings me a cool damp rag when I'm sick. And she sits with me and sings. I can sit here with you and I'll sing while I eat, okay?"

Megan stroked Ali's dark hair and tweaked her braid. "Thanks. I'm good for now, honey. Go eat with the others and I'll sit here with my crackers." She exchanged a sweetly tolerant look with Aidan.

Ali had one of the best hearts of any kid he'd ever known. A lump developed in his throat as he thought about how lucky kids were to grow up in a small town, surrounded by loving family and friends. Sean and Meg's child would have all those advantages, too. He'd met some bodaciously arrogant little brats in LA—kids with too much time, too much money, and not enough supervision. A lot of them were entitled and annoying. Ali, on the other hand, was a smart, charming, interesting kid—a lot like Matt. If he'd had a biological clock, he'd wonder if it was ticking, given how envious he was of his brothers right now. He and Holly were still young and they had time, but as Ali scampered away, he couldn't help thinking what a great big brother Matt would be.

SUPPER WAS DONE, and Sam and Megan and the kids were on their way back up to the ridge where warm baths and cozy beds awaited. Mac and Carly took their leave as well, somehow sensing that the four brothers needed some time alone together. Sean, Conor, Brendan, and Aidan sat around the round table where they'd all shared their impromptu meal. An open bottle of pinot stood between them and Sean topped off all four glasses before holding his up.

"To Da, to the holidays, to our growing family. *Slàinte.*"

They all clinked glasses and drank.

Aidan looked askance at Sean. "Are you sure you shouldn't have gone with your poor hurling wife?"

Sean waved his concern away. "She's probably thrilled to be alone. Last night she accused me of hovering like a helicopter parent. I'm guessing I'll find her asleep on the sofa with that annoying pregnancy book Sam gave her when I get home."

"Speaking of growing families," Conor said, "what's going on with you and Holly? You seem pretty hot and heavy."

Aidan stared at the stage, not sure how to answer that question. A day ago, he would've said he and Holly were doing great. He was truly madly in love and he was pretty sure she shared the feeling. But he hadn't heard from her since he'd told her about *Streetcar*. She hadn't answered his phone calls, had only responded to several texts with a short, "*Busy. I'll call you later.*" And the Tea Leaf was closed up tight when he'd wandered by there before he met the table-and-chair delivery guys here at the boat earlier.

He and Bren had spent the afternoon setting the dinner theater up, sorting the load of chairs to find the ones in the best shape because, of course, the auction house had sent every last chair, even the broken ones. *Sheesh*. But now they had seating for the hundred or so guests who had RSVP'd to the invitations he'd sent out for the Christmas Eve party. He imagined the event would be a lot like the church pitch-ins he used to attend as a kid at St. Agnes church with his brothers and Da and Ma. Lots of homemade food like tuna hot dish and green bean casseroles as well as yummy desserts. He really hoped Teresa Ashton would bring her baked spaghetti and Mae Boyle that seven-layer salad she was famous for around River's Edge. He'd missed them both in LA.

Except for the spotlight, which turned out to be user error—Nate Ashton had accidentally switched off the breaker—the kids' dress rehearsal went pretty close to perfect. A few flubbed lines, but Joanie had schooled them well and the young actors had covered for one another with such panache that only Bren and Aidan were able to tell where cues had been missed. Aidan was bursting with pride at Matt's smooth, flawless performance. Even Bren said the boy was a natural and brought his character Nick to life.

Sean rapped his knuckles on the table, bringing Aidan out of his reverie. "Already got trouble in paradise, Ace? You look… worried."

Aidan frowned and shook his head. "No… maybe… I-I don't know." He took another sip of wine. "I told her about *Streetcar* and she sorta lost her stuff about it—couldn't even begin to see how I could make it work. I admit, I don't know what I'm going to do about the shooting schedule, which is right in the beginning of the *Queen*'s maiden voyage, but I'll figure it out and—"

Bren raised his hand. "I think I have an answer to that."

Aidan, Conor, and Sean all turned his way. "What?" Aidan asked.

"So, Sean sorta took over the spotlight tonight and I'll grant you, a baby is way more exciting than my news, which I *thought* I would share tonight since Ace here was in the spotlight last night at dinner with his movie news."

Conor shook his head. "Poor little middle children. We rarely get center stage, do we, bro?" He reached over and patted Bren's head, dislodging the man bun to the hilarity of all four of them. "I feel ya, buddy. What's your news?"

Bren yanked the elastic from the ends of his long dark hair and shook the shining mass out of his face. "I'm taking a leave of absence from my job—eighteen months, maybe two years and it started retroactively to when I arrived here a couple of weeks ago."

"Spies get sabbatical, Bond?" Sean ducked as Bren shot his hair elastic at him.

Conor high-fived Sean and said, "*Bond!* We've finally got the perfect nickname for him."

Bren scowled. "I'm seriously considering having a T-shirt made that says *Not a Spy... I'm an Analyst* plastered across the front. And, please, can we let go of calling me *Bond* before it turns into a name I can't escape? You know how bad this family is about nicknames. Two or three times, and it's stuck for life." He got up, rescued his hair tie, and pulled his hair back into a ponytail.

Aidan chuckled along with Sean and Conor, but gave Bren a brotherly shoulder nudge when he sat back down.

"We love you, dude, no matter what kind of secret shenanigans are going on back there in Washington. What's the sabbatical about?"

Bren rolled his eyes as color rose to his cheeks. "It's not a sabbatical. We don't get sabbaticals. It's a leave and I'm going to fix up the old log cabin on the back of the north vineyard and write my novel."

"Bren, that's great! About freakin' time." Aidan cheered while Sean and Conor looked on in surprise.

"You've got a novel?" Sean's dark brows furrowed.

Conor's eyes widened, too. "Really? You're writing a novel?"

Bren nodded. "I'm about a third into it. I need a change. I want to write and well, mostly, I just want to be home for a while." He turned his gaze to Aidan. "So, Ace, I can fill in for you here while you're on location. Just leave me a plan. You and I can work together this winter and get everything ready to launch before you go. She'll be in the water long before you leave. I can take over for the few weeks you're shooting."

Aidan's heart lifted. If anyone could handle the *Queen* while he was away, it was Brendan. By then, the show would be set, profs from Warner would be lined up with Les Janssen ready to call the show from backstage and manage the actors, students would be assigned to lighting, sound, stage crew, costumes, and makeup, and the performers would be ready to go. Bren was unnaturally organized. He could handle the day-to-day work of running the showboat with no problem. And if he had any issues, Aidan would only be a text away.

He threw an arm around his brother and gave him a smacking kiss on his bristly cheek. "You are the best, Bond!" Now he could go to Holly with a solid plan, make her see that he wasn't leaving forever, and that *they* had a future.

Chapter Seventeen

"OUR BOY IS amazing." Aidan slipped into the seat next to Holly, his words a breath in her ear.

A shiver went through her at his words *our boy* even as she shushed him, elbowing him gently in the chest. She wanted to remain focused on Matty's performance, which was nearly over. Aidan was right; *her* kid was amazing—as comfortable onstage as if he'd been acting his whole life. In the span of twenty minutes, he'd held the audience in the palm of his hand, sending them into stitches, then into tears as he played disaster-prone Nick Claus with humor and pathos. The other kids were wonderful as well, but Matty shone like a star on a clear Indiana winter night.

The final scene closed with Matty and the entire troupe onstage for Nick's heartfelt speech, praising his little elves and a blushing Mrs. Claus, for helping him save Christmas. Holly was first on her feet as applause and cheers filled the small venue, tears stinging her eyes as she gazed around to see others hopping up as well to give the kids a standing ovation. Sure, it was parents and grandparents and friends of the players who were clapping and whistling, but the kids' performances were worthy of more than mere polite recognition.

Next to her, Aidan grinned with pride, clearly delighted with the first play to be presented on the *Queen*'s new stage. He pulled her into a hug, pressed a quick kiss to her lips, and headed for the stage, not rushing up the stairs. Joanie stepped out from stage left to extend her arm toward the group of actors, encouraging them to take another bow and then another. Finally, Aidan went up, looking celebrity-handsome in jeans, a black T-shirt that probably cost more than her car payment, and a camel-colored sport coat. His blond hair was carefully mussed, his grin was as infectious as ever, and his blue, blue eyes sparkled in the stage lights. Gathering the cast around him, he accepted a wireless mic from one of the high school kids who'd served as stagehands for the play, and settled the audience back into their seats with a sweeping gesture. He tossed an arm around Matty's shoulders, sending another tremor through Holly. They looked so natural together.

Like father and son.

Immediately, she banished that dangerous thought. Aidan Flaherty was not Matty's father, nor would he ever be. Aidan was leaving. She swallowed the lump in her throat, her heart aching as she saw Matty's eyes widen in adoration at Aidan's casual touch. The kid had been so excited to hear Aidan got a film, hurrying to Clive's shelf of plays to see if he could find the Tennessee Williams classic. She'd allowed him to read it and, although he was too young to grasp the mature nature of the work, he recognized what a meaty role was there for his hero. He'd been thrilled for Aidan, asking millions of questions about being on location and the filmmaking process, but never once questioning whether Aidan would return. Matty's assumption was exactly what Aidan had told her—he'd be home when he was done shooting the film.

Why couldn't *she* believe him?

Simple. Because she'd lived through this before. Long, lonely days working her ass off and wondering when and if Leo would return. Difficult nights, trying to be a buffer when he did come back, longing for a real marriage, but also wishing he'd just go and never come back. *It wouldn't be that way with Aidan*, her conscience nudged her. The heat between them, the connection, so tangible that sometimes she thought she could reach out and touch the threads of emotion that held them together, might hold up under an actor's chaotic schedule. The real issue was that she wasn't sure she was prepared to give it a try. Being apart was too painful and she'd never been good at good-byes. She blinked back tears and settled into her chair as Aidan began to speak.

"Folks, it's so great to have everyone here this afternoon. Thank you so much. I know it's a busy day to ask you to come out, but between this amazing potluck lunch and our troupe of future stars, I hope you've found it well worth spending the afternoon on the *River Queen* with us."

That brought a round of vigorous applause and even another standing ovation as Aidan gestured broadly to the group of delighted kids surrounding him.

"There are so many people to thank for making this event a success, I hardly know how to—"

"You've had plenty of practice, Mr. Golden Globe. Go for it!" Noah Barker called from his table near the center of theater. Laughter rumbled through the audience.

Holly had to smile. *Gotta love a small town.* Even though River's Edge was justifiably proud of their superstar, they sure weren't going to let his success go to his head. Aidan Flaherty was just Donal and Maggie's youngest boy, whom everyone remembered sweaty from picking grapes or racing down the River Walk on his bike with his friends. They'd watched him perform onstage at the high school and here on the *Queen* as a teenager. He was the kid who'd made it big out in the world, while never really leaving his hometown. Now he was back and the whole town was pleased he'd returned, none more than her.

Another round of applause brought Holly back to the present with a start. She must have missed something Aidan had said because his brother Brendan was standing at his table at the front of the theater, smiling and blushing.

She nudged Melinda, sitting on her right. "What? I missed what Aidan said."

"Brendan Flaherty wrote the play." She frowned at Holly. "Where are you, kiddo? For pity's sake, pay attention.

That's our boy up there."

Our boy.

Holly bit her tongue to keep from asking her mother which boy she meant—the young actor she'd be tucking into bed tonight or the older one, who was leaving for LA in less than two days? With difficulty, she focused on the stage.

Aidan was continuing to thank people involved in making the party a success—Joanie, his brothers, all the kids in the play, right down to the scenery painters and the stagehands, calling each kid by name and bringing them up to the front. How did he remember every child's name?

Oh yeah, actor. Great memory.

"Right now, our Nick Claus needs to go do a quick costume change, so while he's doing that, I want to invite someone else up to the stage." Aidan's gaze was focused on her as Joanie suddenly appeared at his side with his guitar. "Holly? Will you join me?"

Everyone in the place turned in her direction and Holly flushed with heat, certain a red blush was spreading up her neck and into her face. She narrowed her eyes at Aidan. Surely he wasn't asking her to sing "River" with him.

As he fingered the opening notes and struck a chord, she realized that was exactly what he wanted. She grimaced, but he merely smiled that Flaherty dimpled smile. "Looks like Holly's a little shy, so let's give her some encouragement, okay?" He led the crowd in a round of applause, and glancing around at all the beloved and expectant faces, she figured she'd either have to go up or make a scene. She didn't want to do that to Matty, not after his huge success in the play.

Damn you, Aidan Flaherty.

He crooked his finger, his blue gaze fixed on her face, and she rose, moving slowly among the tables toward the set of steps stage left among the loud clapping of audience members. She heard her own mother's loud whistle and a "You go, Hols!" from Sam Flaherty.

Aidan took her hand as she approached him, offering her, no, not the celebrity grin, rather a smile so intimate, so persuasive, she felt it all the way down to her toes. Holding the mic down at his side, he whispered, "Let's do this, babe. It'll be fun." He brought the mic up and stuck it onto a stand that Joanie had thoughtfully brought from backstage while Holly was coming up. "This is a song that my mom used to sing to my brothers and me at Christmastime and it's been a favorite of mine for years. Joni Mitchell's 'River.'"

The crowd hushed as he strummed his guitar and nodded to her as they began the enchanting old ballad. She kept her eyes locked with his, knowing she'd lose her nerve if she looked out into the audience. His delicious baritone was easy to harmonize with and, as they sang, she moved closer to him, so their heads were almost touching over the mic, his breath warming her lips with each word of the song. When they finished, an awed silence hung over the theater before the audience burst into raucous applause and cheers. He leaned down and touched his lips to hers in a sweet kiss that brought an *aawwww* from the people at the tables below.

The kiss warmed her to her very center and she was hungry for more. Unfortunately, they were center stage in front of over a hundred townsfolk, so instead she touched his cheek. He looked over the top of her head, stage right and when she turned around, she saw Matty dressed as St. Nicholas, with a big red bag tossed over his shoulder and a long staff in one hand. He played it up with waves and smiles as he hobbled across the stage, becoming the aged saint with every step. If tonight had shown Holly nothing else, it was that her son *was* a gifted actor. The realization wasn't as horrifying as she'd always believed it would be, mostly because she'd never seen Matty so happy.

Aidan handed his guitar off to Joanie in the wings before returning to tug on Matty's snow-white beard. "Got a ho-ho-ho for us, St. Nick?"

Matty looked askance, placed the back of one hand next to his lips, and said to the crowd *sotto voce*, "Obviously this punk doesn't know his Santa from his saints."

The crowd chortled.

Aidan gave him an exaggerated frown that made Holly suspect he and Matty had rehearsed this routine. "Okay, wise guy, why don't you tell us all about how *Saint* Nicholas became Santa Claus."

Matty set his bag down, tapped his long crooked staff on the stage floor, cleared his throat and did exactly as Aidan suggested, delivering the tale of St. Nicholas with a confidence that belied his twelve years. He ended it with, "Even though I love being dressed up as St. Nick and sharing his story of generosity with you all, I'm going to pass this bag off to the real Santa Claus because it's filled with gifts for every child here."

Aidan's startled look told her that he had no idea what Matty had arranged, but indeed, as "Santa Claus is Coming to Town" suddenly echoed through the speakers, the old elf himself dressed in a traditional red suit hopped up the steps stage right, his nose and cheeks rosy above his white beard. The costume was so authentic, Holly had no idea who'd been pressed into service. Whoever it was tap-danced across the stage to grin at them. She looked out across the audience who laughed and applauded as Santa continued his impromptu dance, and still, she couldn't figure out who was missing from the crowd. The guy sure had some serious tap-dancing chops.

AIDAN KEPT ONE arm around Holly and one hand on Matty's shoulder as Santa ended his dance routine with a final set of paradiddles and a stamp, his arms outstretched to the house crowd. He was baffled as to who was playing the jolly old man because he couldn't place any of the features showing between the white beard and the white wig and red velvet hat. The eyes were even camouflaged behind a pair of small wire-rim half-glasses. Who was this guy?

Whoever he was, he held out one hand to Aidan and gave him a quirked white brow. "Care to join me?" The disguised deep voice wasn't familiar, either.

Aidan grinned and turned to Matt, whose eyes were wide with wonder. "Whaddya say, Nick? Want to get in on this?"

Matty nodded vigorously while Holly caught her breath as he and Matt stepped away from her and joined Santa in a short elementary tap routine, ending in a slightly awkward kick line that had the audience rolling. They clasped hands as they took a bow and that was the moment Aidan recognized a distinctive onyx signet ring on Santa's right hand.

Holy Toledo! Mac Mackenzie is Santa Claus!

Not only that, Mac could tap dance! Who knew? Aidan grinned and winked at his old friend, his mind already abuzz planning an act that would feature the dancing gourmet chef for the showboat's summer variety show. He gazed out at the crowd, wondering how many of them had talents he never knew about. His heart swelled as he scanned the sea of dear faces—each one holding a memory, both new and old. Without question, this little town was home, no matter where else his career took him.

Aidan took one more bow with Mac and Matt and then grabbed the mic off the stand. "Can we raise the house lights?" The theater lights flickered on. "Thank you, Nate. Will you all join us in singing 'We Wish You a Merry Christmas'? As we sing, Santa and his helpers will be coming down to pass out gifts to all the kids." He inclined his head toward Mac, Matt, and the troupe of actors, dressed as elves, who'd appeared from backstage. "Thank you all for being here. Merry Christmas!" With a smile, he reached for Holly's hand and started the old Christmas classic; soon the whole theater was filled with the sound of a hundred voices raised in holiday celebration.

As the last notes faded and the cast took their final bows, Aidan tugged Holly backstage. "Come with me."

She allowed him to pull her past a storage area filled with old props from Clive's days—a wooden horse, an old Amish buggy, Juliet's balcony, a barrel full of masks and feathered hats—and then along the row of new dressing rooms. "Where are we going?"

"Someplace where I can be alone with you for ten minutes." He slipped into one of the cubicle-sized dressing rooms, closed the door firmly, and pressed her up against it. "God, I've missed you." He kissed her with all the desire that had been overwhelming him for the past few days, hoping she was as hungry as he was.

He was aware of how fragile they'd become since he told her about the film. He had no idea how to make her trust him, except to show her both privately and publicly that he was all in. It was one of the reasons he'd called her up to sing with him, deliberately forcing her to acknowledge him as her person, *them* as a couple. "Merry Christmas, little one," he whispered when he raised his mouth from hers.

Her voice was husky. "Merry Christmas, rock star." The nickname that had started as a slur when he first hit town had now become a caress on her lips. She wrapped her arms around his neck and leaned back, her smile slightly tremulous. "What time do you leave tomorrow?"

"Late. Can I see you before I go to the airport?" Her supple body surged against his and a wave of longing washed over him. "Even better, come with me to LA. We can hit the beach after my meeting or go for a drive into the hills or just spend the whole time in my hotel room."

She rubbed her cheek on his shoulder and kissed the scruff on his cheek. "You know I can't do that. I'm not going to leave Matty on Christmas night and besides, I've got—" She stopped on a quick intake of breath.

"What?" He lifted his wandering hands from her body.

"N-nothing. Nothing important." An expression he couldn't identify crossed her face. It almost looked like sadness.

"What is it, love?" He touched his forehead to hers. "Why won't you come with me? It's only a couple of days."

She gave him a sharp look, then slipped away from him, pacing the tiny dressing room, two steps across, two steps back. "I'm not going to follow you around like a groupie, rock star. I've got obligations here—Matty, the Leaf, Mom. I can't just take off on a moment's notice."

Suddenly the nickname sounded like a curse again. Aidan turned around, leaned against the door, and held his hands up in supplication. "Hey, truce, okay? I don't want to fight with you on Christmas, especially since it looks like we're only going to get these few minutes together for me to give you your gift."

She closed her eyes for a second, looking a little abashed. "I'm sorry. I'm trying here, I really am. I want to believe that you and I are different, but no matter how I try to rewrite my story with you in it, it always ends up the same way. You're gone and I'm alone."

He gazed deep into those violet eyes shimmering with tears. Swam in them. Drowned in them. How did he convince her? "Stop writing our story, Holly. Just let it happen."

"I don't know how to do that. Not when Matty's in the story, too." She stood before him, looking so small and vulnerable. In spite of that, he also knew all too well how tough she was, how fierce she could be when she was protecting her cub.

He shook his head. "I can't promise I'll never go away, Holly. But I will promise you this. I'll be back. I'll always be back." She opened her mouth to speak, but he crossed the two steps to her and put his finger against her lips. "And I promise to love you... and Matt, with all my heart."

Her lips trembled against his finger, so he replaced it with his mouth, kissing her tenderly with just their lips touching. Although she smiled when he pulled back, it was as if something was trapped behind her eyes that he couldn't reach, so he dug in his jeans pocket and pulled out a light blue box and handed it to her.

"Merry Christmas, little one."

Chapter Eighteen

HOLLY LET THE box rest in the palm of her hand. It wasn't a ring box, thank God, rather it was a square flat box. The light blue color could only mean that it was from Tiffany—one of the most expensive jewelers in the world. "Oh, Aidan. What have you done? I thought we agreed no gifts."

He kissed her—another soft tender touch of his lips to hers. "Well, I found something that seemed like the perfect way to remind you every day that I'm all in." He nodded at the box. "Open it."

She untied the ribbon, anticipation building as she lifted the lid. Inside lay a silver necklace with a small key-shaped pendant hanging from it. The top of the key was in the shape of a fleur-de-lis and in each curl of the fleur-de-lis gleamed a sapphire—three stones the exact color of Aidan's eyes.

Tears stung her eyes. "It's gorgeous, Aidan. Thank you. I love silver."

He smiled. "It's platinum, actually, so you never have to take it off. It's the key to my heart, little one, which has been yours since the day you grabbed me and kissed me on the deck of the tasting room. That was the hottest thing that's ever happened to me. You had me from that moment." Carefully, he lifted the necklace from the box. "Let's put it on you."

Holly dropped her head down and tugged her hair around to grant him access to her nape. He secured the clasp, pressed a kiss to her neck, then turned her to face him. "I'm giving you my heart, Holly, and I'm asking you to trust me with yours. Can you do that?"

Her heart pounded and her voice trembled. "I want to. I want to so much." She took a deep breath. "We're a fantasy, Aidan. One that I've dreamed of since I was a little girl. This isn't real. Celebrities like you don't leave their rich golden lifestyles, come home to their small town, and fall in love with the girl next door. That just doesn't happen, except maybe in Hallmark movies."

His face tightened and his hands balled into fists at his side. "Apparently it does, 'cause here I am, home and falling madly in love with *you*. This is real. *We* are real. Do you think I'm not just as amazed that *you* could want *me*? I'm no prize, little one. I'm an arrogant, smart-assed attention junkie. I joke around too much and I don't have an ounce of fashion sense. I have no idea how to be a parent. You're such a terrific mom, so I'm scared to death of screwing up with Matt. I've been accused of having a short attention span; but that's *not* true. When I'm in, I'm *all* in. I'll get this old tub back on the water and make a success of her. As for you and me? Well, we just have to see how we work. But I stick. Why else would I have stayed with *LA Detectives* for so long when I hated Pete Atwood?" Clearly agitated, he raked his fingers through his thick blond hair and yet it still looked perfectly tousled.

Inanely, she thought, *how does he do that?*

His expression softened and his voice came out deep and hoarse. "I love being an actor. It's what I do. But it's a job, Holly. It's how I make my living, not who I am. I work hard at my craft and I've been successful, you know? Just the same, nothing changes the fact that I'm still that scrawny kid from River's Edge who spent his childhood picking grapes and hosing down the wine cellar floor." He took her hands, holding them between their bodies and a rush of emotions overwhelmed her—hunger, passion, love, exhilaration, and yes, the huge one, fear.

This devilishly handsome Irishman drew her like a vat of full-fat butter pecan ice cream and yet also brought out her fiercest protective instincts. She gazed at their linked fingers. Her heart yearned to give in, but how could she be sure she wouldn't end up in the same mess she was in years ago with Leo? As adrift as she often felt on her own, maybe too much was at stake to tether her whole self to another actor.

A hint of vulnerability appeared on Aidan's face and he kissed her. "Just don't take the necklace off, okay? Keep it next to your heart. Let it work for me. Promise?"

She nodded, mesmerized by the fervor of his words. "I promise." She would keep it on. That much she could do.

MELINDA BLEW A frustrated breath into her bangs. "Honey, you *have* to take it off. It's the hospital rules."

Holly fingered the key pendant and scowled at her mother. She was aware of how stubborn and childish she was being, but Aidan had asked her not to remove the necklace when he'd placed it around her neck two days ago. Somehow, taking it off so soon, even for surgery, seemed wrong. "Can't we tape it up under my hair?"

The surgery nurse standing at a computer behind Melinda shook her head. "No, I'm sorry. Surgery rule is the patient removes all jewelry and there are lots of valid reasons for it. It could get caught in some tubing or wires and choke you or it could fall off and get lost. Besides, metal conducts electricity. It's just too dangerous to leave it on."

Holly's throat clogged with tears. "Even platinum conducts?"

The nurse, a sweet motherly woman named Sarah, nodded. "Especially platinum, sweetie."

Melinda pulled the light blue box out of her capacious handbag. "I'm going to take it off you now. I brought the box. I'll put it in here and keep it safe, I promise."

Sarah grinned. "Tiffany, eh? Somebody must really love

you."

Melina chuckled. "Someone does indeed."

A tear trickled down Holly's cheek as Melinda reached behind her to unclasp the chain and bring the ends around. Holly kept her grip on the key for a few seconds before releasing it. "I promised him I wouldn't take it off," she whispered.

"See?" Melinda made a show of tucking the necklace in the box and then the box into a zipper compartment in her purse. "It's safe. Aidan will understand, honey. We can call him right now if you like and he'll tell you so."

Holly's heart stuttered. "No!" She shook her head vigorously. "He... he's in a meeting. Please don't interrupt him. Don't contact him. I-I'll call him when this is done."

Melinda gave her a curious look, then held up one hand. "Okay. Okay."

Sarah's eyes narrowed and suddenly she snapped her fingers. "*That's* how I know you! I saw you singing with Aidan Flaherty on the showboat, Christmas Eve. My granddaughter, Maisey, was one of the elves in the play."

Holly managed a weak smile through her tears.

"You're a lucky lady if you're dating Aidan Flaherty." Sarah smacked her lips as she snapped on a pair of latex gloves and began swabbing Holly's arm, preparing to insert an IV. "He's yummy."

Melinda stepped to the other side of the bed and pressed her cool cheek to Holly's warm one. "I'm going to head out to the waiting room to check on Matty, okay?"

Holly was embarrassed at how much she longed to cling to her mother's hand and beg her to stay. She quashed the urge because the surgeon appeared in the doorway, and Melinda stayed anyway to hear what the doctor had to say, keeping Holly's hand tucked in hers.

"Hi, Holly." Dr. Michelle Troutman, dressed in green scrubs, stood at the end of the bed. "How are you this afternoon?"

Holly saw no point in diplomacy. "Terrified."

"I'm sure. That's natural." Michelle's smile only reassured Holly slightly. "I'm sorry we had to move you back. We had an emergency and they had to use our OR this morning. We're all good now, though. They're getting set up in there, so we should be starting in the next hour. I just have some things I need to go over with you, okay?"

Holly tried to focus as Dr. Troutman, once again, went through the hows and whys of the lumpectomy or breast-conserving surgery she was about to undergo. Even though her mind was numbed with fear, she understood it all—the surgery, overnight in the hospital, six weeks of radiation therapy afterward, and the chance that Dr. Troutman might find more cancer cells than she expected to during the surgery. Holly had already signed consent for a more invasive procedure if the pathology on the cells turned out differently than expected, although at this point, the surgeon was pretty certain that wouldn't be the case. She seemed confident that she would remove the offending cells and a margin of healthy tissue and that Holly, although high risk, would be fine after treatment.

Dr. Troutman finished her explanation, asked a few essential questions, outlined the significant place on Holly's left breast with marker, patted her shoulder, and left with a *see you inside* and a jaunty wave.

Holly squeezed Melinda's hand. "Mom, make sure Matty gets some lunch. It's already two thirty and he only had cereal for breakfast."

Melinda kissed her one more time. "I'll get him some food while you're in surgery. Do you want him to come in before you go back?"

Holly considered for a few seconds. "No. I'll only cry and upset him. We already had our hugs earlier. We're good."

Melinda nodded. "Okay. I love you, baby girl." She stooped down to kiss Holly's forehead and rub noses with her. "It's all going to be fine."

"I know."

As Melinda left, Holly blinked back the ever-present tears and wished with all her heart that Aidan was there. Her foolish pride and fear prevented the one person she was longing for most from being with her. What a stupid wish. He was in LA talking to important people about the role of his lifetime. Although he'd deny it with his last breath, he'd have resented her forever if he'd had to give this part up because of her. Her heart ached. Rolling over to her right side, she buried her face in the rough hospital pillow and wept.

THE HOTEL SUITE gleamed all clean lines and warm earthy colors in the California morning sun. Aidan sipped his tea and gazed out the floor-to-ceiling windows at the Hollywood hills. The suite was lavish with a wet bar, deep comfy sofas, and a Jacuzzi tub. No, not the penthouse—Mason hadn't gone that far—but he'd booked a luxurious room with an amazing view. Aidan was sure that wasn't dumb luck. No question his agent was wooing him back to LA. If this deal fell through, Mason was sure to have others in his back pocket.

According to Mason, Dick Leonard was romancing the hell out of these backers and Aidan would be on exhibit shortly, where he'd be expected to wow them as well. He couldn't deny being extremely curious about the moneymen who were only backing the film if Aidan Flaherty played the part of Stanley Kowalski. They had to have seen him on Broadway, but that was years ago. How would they remember that performance and like it enough to put up the cash to make *Streetcar* with 3Guns Studios? And even more interesting, how did Dick find them?

His phone chimed in the pocket of his sleep pants. Mason, making sure he was awake, even though he'd only gotten a few hours of sleep after taking the red-eye from Louisville. He smiled as he skipped the text and flipped to his photos—the latest were of Matt and Holly taken on the upper deck of the *Queen* on Christmas Eve. All bundled up in winter jackets, scarves, and knit caps, they were standing in front of the Christmas tree he'd set up outside, making goofy faces for his camera. Holly's hair shone with mahogany and chestnut lights in the late afternoon sun, while Matt gave her bunny ears and crossed his eyes. The kid was already as tall as his mom.

Aidan chuffed a laugh remembering Matt's incredible performance in Brendan's play. No doubt about it, Mateo Santos was an actor. Mason could probably get him a guest spot on any teenaged sitcom tomorrow, not that Holly would allow it. He'd work on her. That was something for the future.

He'd texted her when he landed and gotten back a sleepy-face emoji and a heart before he fell into bed. She and Matt were having a family movie day today since the Tea Leaf would be on holiday through New Year's Day. He couldn't wait to get back to River's Edge so he could spend some of Holly's time off with her and Matt. Maybe they'd drive up to Indy to see the children's museum. He'd always loved that place as a kid. They could stay at the Westin and maybe even take in a show. He'd check and see what was playing at IRT or one of the other local theaters.

He scrolled his camera roll and wished he'd gotten a chance to see Matt and Melinda before he left. He'd have loved to have been there when they opened the gifts he'd left under their tree for them. Matt's was a pair of tap shoes, a top hat, and a cane. He'd included a certificate for tap dance classes that would begin mid-January at Warner College School of Dance. The kid sure loved to dance, so Aidan thought it was the perfect gift. Matty must have agreed; Holly said he'd whooped, plopped the hat on his head, and jumped up to do a quick soft-shoe, he was so delighted.

Melinda had texted him to thank him effusively for the all-expenses-paid New York weekend for her and a friend, that included a deluxe double room at the luxurious art-deco Chatwal hotel, a day at the Elizabeth Arden spa located in the hotel, dinner at the Greek restaurant, Nerai, and tickets to *Hamilton*. Melinda and Mateo had been easy. Planning their gifts had brought him as much joy as had shopping for his own family. He always overdid it and never apologized for being extravagant. What was the point of making lots of money if you couldn't spend it on the people you loved most in the world?

Holly's necklace had been a tougher choice because what he'd picked out originally was a ring—an elegant yet simple diamond solitaire in a platinum setting. Then he'd abandoned the idea. It was too soon. She'd never have accepted it and would have immediately refused the proposal that he'd intended would go with it.

He'd cruised Tiffany's website, certain her gift would be jewelry, just not sure what to choose if he couldn't ask her to marry him… yet. When he came upon the fleur-de-lis key pendant, he was drawn to it immediately. Not flashy, but a lovely statement piece with the three shimmering sapphires. When he looked up the meaning of the blue stones—faithfulness and sincerity, he ordered the necklace immediately.

Another text from Mason yanked him out of his reverie, so he drained his tea and hurried into the bedroom to take a shower and get dressed. The meeting was due to start soon and he needed to put on his celebrity persona—one he hadn't tried on in a while.

Mason's gaze raked over him when he opened the door to the penthouse suite at Aidan's brisk knock. The sounds of conversations and laughter drifted out into the small foyer and, when Aidan peered around Mason's broad shoulder, he recognized Dick Leonard's leonine white hair among the people gathered around a table inside.

"Get in here, kid," Mason whispered and brushed at the lapel of Aidan's camel's hair sport coat. "You're late."

Aidan shoved Mason's fidgety hand away and glanced at his watch. "I'm exactly on time. Chill out."

"Remember, these folks already want you, so be cool, but not too cool."

"I'm an adult, Mason. I know how to behave in a business meeting."

Mason managed a slightly chagrined smile. "I know, I know. See the man and woman on the window side of the table?" He hitched his chin toward the large wooden table where a graying middle-aged man and a very attractive blonde of around the same age sat, their heads together over a portfolio on the table in front of them. "They're your backers."

Aidan nodded, noting the other three men in the room, whom he vaguely recognized as suits from 3Guns.

Mason straightened his tie and strode into the big open penthouse, which was decorated in the same earth tones as Aidan's suite a couple of floors below. "Here he is, folks, our Stanley."

Introductions all around followed for several minutes, with the couple, Harry and Sandy Watts, greeting him effusively. Sandy patted the chair next to her. "Come sit by us, Aidan. We're so excited to be a part of this venture." Her voice was warm and her eyes kind, not at all a typical LA mogul type.

Harry leaned around her, his brown eyes shining behind a pair of wire-frame glasses. "We saw you in *Streetcar* in New York several years ago and your performance just overwhelmed us both. We came back three times and you were amazing each time. We love the theater and support it any way we can back in New Canaan—that's where we live. My family has a textile mill there."

Aidan smiled. Ah, no wonder they didn't seem like LA

types, they were New Englanders. Apparently New Englanders with a lot of money because New Canaan, Connecticut, was one of the wealthiest places in America.

Mason, sitting in the leather chair next to Aidan, scribbled something on the pad provided at each place and casually nudged it toward Aidan. He'd written *Watts & Shaw Woolen Corp.* and Aidan struggled to keep his eyes from widening. Thanks to Philomena's vast knowledge of fashion, he did recognize the company as one of the largest manufacturers of fine wool and cashmere fabrics in the world. The jacket he had on was tailored from a camel's hair wool that came from Watts & Shaw. *Holy cow!*

Sandy took up their story, telling about how Harry golfed with Dick's brother and when Ray Leonard mentioned Dick was trying to find backers for *Streetcar*, she and Harry immediately thought of Aidan's stellar performance onstage at the Ethel Barrymore Theater. "I mentioned to Harry how wonderful it would be to see you as Stanley on the big screen, didn't I, darling?"

Harry's grin lit up the room. "You did, m'love, and I agreed wholeheartedly. We had some extra money to invest, so Ray put us in touch with Dick and 3Guns and here we are."

Sandy put one hand on Aidan's arm. "Someone told us you'd left the business. That you went back to your hometown. Is that true?"

Aidan smiled at their touching and infectious enthusiasm. "Thank you so much. No, I haven't left the business, just LA. Frankly, I got written out of *LA Detectives*"—Aiden leaned away from Mason's elbow in his ribs—"and I needed a break, so I went back to River's Edge, Indiana, where I was born and raised."

Harry's booming laugh filled the room. "Ah, a small-town boy. Me too! I was born in Old Saybrook. We still have a cottage there."

If the Watts had enough money laying around to invest in a feature film, Aidan could just imagine what their "cottage" looked like—probably one of those forty-room mansions like he'd seen in Newport, Rhode Island, a couple of summers ago. What an intriguing couple. He gave Harry a smile and a nod—this wasn't a hail-fellow-well-met kind of acknowledgment on the older man's part. He seemed genuinely pleased to learn of Aidan's roots.

Just as Dick cleared his throat and said, "Shall we get started?" Aidan's smart watch buzzed on his wrist. He glanced down and saw he had a text from Holly. Why was she texting him? She knew what time his meeting was. Unless maybe she forgot the three-hour time difference. Unlikely. Something had to be wrong.

He put his wrist down in his lap and tapped the screen, then caught his breath.

Hey, it's me, Matt! Update: We're still at the hospital. They started Mom's surgery late, so they just wheeled her back.

Aidan's heart rose to his throat. *Hospital? Surgery?* What the hell was Matt talking about?

Chapter Nineteen

AIDAN PUT A hand on the table and shoved his chair out. "Please excuse me for one minute. I think I've got a... a family emergency going on." He hurried toward the foyer. "I'll be right back."

The panic in his voice must have been more than evident, because everyone else at the table stood, too, and he heard Mason reassuring them that he'd see what was happening.

Aidan's hand shook as he dug his cell phone out of his pocket and tapped Holly's number.

Mason appeared just as it began to ring Holly. "What's going on?"

Aidan was sure his concern had nothing to do with whatever was happening in River's Edge, so he just pointed at him and shook his head.

Matty's pleased voice came through loud and clear. "Aidan! Hi! Is your meeting over already? Does that mean you got the part?"

"Hey, buddy." Aidan fought to keep his voice calm, but failed miserably. "What's up back there? Why is Mom in surgery? Is she hurt? What happened?"

Silence on the other end of the line made his heart sink even deeper. Suddenly Melinda came on. "Hi, Aidan. It's Melinda."

"What's going on, Melinda?"

Melinda's frustrated huff of breath made him want to gnash his teeth. "Dammit. I thought she'd told you."

"Apparently she didn't. What. Is. Going. On?" His heart was pounding and sweat began to trickle down his ribs under his espresso-brown T-shirt.

"Now, Aidan, everything's okay." Melinda's words did nothing to reassure him, so he bit his tongue and let her continue. "She had a bad mammogram. They did some other testing and discovered a small mass, so she's having a lumpectomy today."

"Cancer?" Aidan's knees went weak and he reached behind him for the linen-covered wall, trying to find something to keep him from sinking to the floor. "Holly has breast cancer?"

Next to him, Mason's eyes grew larger.

"Aidan, calm down. It's encapsulated, so they're taking the mass and a healthy margin. A round of radiation and she'll be all good." Melinda's tone was firm. "I truly thought she'd talked to you about this. I'm guessing she didn't want to worry you when you had this meeting coming up."

"God." Aidan breathed, emotion tumbling through him. "She didn't tell me because she keeps confusing me with Leo freaking Santos. *Dammit.*" He straightened. "I'm on my way, Melinda."

"Aidan, you don't need—"

"I'm on my way," he repeated. "Put Matt back on, would you?"

Melinda sighed. "Sure."

"Aidan?" Matt said timorously. "I'm sorry, man. I thought Mom had talked to you."

"Dude, it's fine. Don't worry. I-I just wanted to tell you... I love you." The words came out before Aidan even had a chance to think, and they felt so right, so natural, he repeated them. "I love you, Matty. I'll be home in a few hours."

Matt sniffed. "I love you, too, Aidan. See you soon."

Aidan hit End and took a shaky breath. It was as though something was pressing down hard on his windpipe. He started to open his mouth, but panic settled in his chest. At last, he managed to say, "I've got to go, Mason. I'm sorry." He headed into the airy penthouse without giving Mason a chance to say a word as he approached the tableful of curious expressions. "I-I'm so sorry, everyone. I just found out my... my... the woman I love is in the hospital back home. She's in surgery. I-I didn't know. I've got to get to the airport and get a flight out of here."

Dick Leonard slapped a hand on the table. "Wait just a damn minute, Aidan. *We* brought you out here for this meeting. Harry and Sandy flew all the way across the country on the day after freaking Christmas. You can't just—"

"Of course he can, Dick," Sandy Watts declared and rushed to Aidan's side. "Didn't you hear him? *The woman he loves.*" She put one hand on Aidan's arm. "Honey, you're going to be stuck in LA traffic forever and God only knows how quick you can get a flight back to… where did you say you're flying to?"

"Louisville." She was right, even though Aidan was pulling up his Lyft app to get a ride to LAX as he answered her.

Harry snorted. "Hell, boy, you'll be hanging around that damn airport for hours." He pulled his phone out of his inside jacket pocket as he strode across the room. "I've got a Gulfstream out at John Wayne that'll get you to Louisville in three-and-a-half hours, and a charter helicopter on call to pick us up on the helipad on the roof after this meeting." He tapped his screen with what looked like a solid gold stylus. "Let me call those guys. They can be here by the time you're packed. Hold tight now."

Aidan's head was spinning. "Mr. Watts, that's unbelievably kind of you, but I can't—"

Sandy patted his arm. "Of course you can. Harry, darling, make this happen."

"I'm on it, sweetheart." And he was, pacing as he spoke terse instructions into his phone.

"You're walking out?" Dick Leonard's voice boomed. "Seriously? You're walking out on this project?"

Aidan turned to his former director, whose already florid

face was flushed with anger, and then looked at Mason. All the color had drained from his agent's dismayed visage and he looked deflated. "No, Dick. I'm leaving *this* meeting because I have an emergency. I'm sorry. I want to do this project and, honestly, I believe with all my heart that I'm the right person to play Stanley. Thing is, this... *she* is more important. I've got to go." He shrugged and offered them a brief, apologetic smile. "I hope you find another Stanley soon."

Harry got off the phone and jabbed one finger at Dick and the other producers who were murmuring among themselves. "*I* don't want another Stanley. I want this guy!" He tossed a beefy arm around Aidan's shoulders and nearly knocked him over. "We'll wait for you, son. Take whatever time you need to get your young lady back on her feet. You can tell us all about her on the ride to Louisville."

Dick looked aghast. "What? You're leaving, too?"

Harry waved him away as if he were nothing more than an annoying fly. "No need for us to hang around now. You know what we want. Make it happen."

Apparently, Harry and Sandy were *make-it-happen* people. Aidan was too stunned, too touched, too dazed by the Watts's incredible generosity to speak. Besides, if he opened his mouth, he was scared as hell he'd start blubbering.

Harry and Sandy marched to the table, picked up their packets, and shook hands all around. "We'll be in touch," Harry said. "In the meantime, get the rest of your cast together. Find a decent cinematographer. Get someone to write the score—whatever the hell it is you guys do to get ready for a movie. We're still onboard as long as Aidan is our Stanley. When he's able to do the picture, gentlemen, that's when we do the picture." He nodded as he shepherded Aidan and Sandy to the door. "Mason, I'll call you."

Aidan couldn't stop trembling as they rode down on the elevator with him. Sandy gave him a little push. "Go get packed. We'll get our stuff and meet you up on the helipad. There's a door at the far end of the top floor. Use your room key to access it. We'll be in the waiting area." She nudged him toward the open elevator doors. "Go on now."

He stepped off, turning to watch as the doors shut. Holy Mary, they were seriously taking him home to Holly on their private jet. He was still enough of that kid from River's Edge to be flabbergasted at how easily money could buy convenience. In disbelief, he dropped his head back and cast his eyes heavenward. "Da, if you're behind this, I'm listening. I got the message. I know where I belong and I'm heading home to her right now."

"Oh, for the love of all that's holy, you have truly lost your mind." Mason's breathless voice right next him made him start.

Aidan peered at him in the dim light from the hallway sconces. "Where did you come from?"

Mason huffed and put one hand against the wall between the two elevators. "The stairs. I think I'm having a heart attack."

Aidan watched him for a moment. The guy *was* breathing heavily and sweat beaded on his brow. "Does your chest hurt?"

Mason shook his head.

"Pressure? Pain in your arm or shoulder or jaw?"

"No." His breathing became more even.

"Then you're fine." Aidan headed for his suite with Mason hot on his heels.

"Kid, you're going to have over three hours with these folks, so for God's sake, keep them interested."

Aidan whirled around, his key card in his hand. "How do you suggest I do that, Mason? A quick Hugh Jackson-style song-and-dance routine in the aisle of the plane? Recite Hamlet's soliloquy while we're flying over the Rockies. Or maybe I should just offer either one of them my body in exchange for keeping their checkbook warmed up." He shoved the key card in the door and waited impatiently for the light, before storming into the suite.

"You know what I mean."

Aidan shoved his belongings into the small duffel he'd brought with him, placed the film packet that included a copy of the screenplay in his messenger bag, and checked that he had his phone, wallet, ID, and iPad. He made a quick perusal of the suite to verify he'd left nothing behind, and nearly ran into Mason as he turned toward the door. "Dammit, Mason, move. I'm trying to get out of here."

Mason put one hand on Aidan's chest. "Look, kid, I'm merely suggesting you make certain they realize that this thing is just a little glitch. A temporary delay. That you'll be back and ready to go in a couple of weeks. We can't screw up this deal over some piece of—"

Aidan clamped his hand on Mason's wrist and held his arm away from him. "Do *not* even go there. Holly is the woman I intend to marry, so just… just *don't*, okay? And as far as Harry and Sandy are concerned, they're simply being kind to me. I realize that's a foreign concept to you, but that's all this is, so I won't be spending this flight schmoozing them to keep them interested in me and this film. Got it?" He dropped Mason's wrist, wrenched the door open, then pivoted and offered a regretful smile. "I'm leaving. Please apologize again to Dick and the suits for me. I'm really sorry, but this is my life now. *She* is my life now."

IN THE END, Aidan spent the three-and-a-half-hour plane ride reading everything he could find online about breast cancer, encapsulated tumors, surgery to remove them, and radiation treatments. Website after website gave him more details than his brain could comprehend to the point that, terrified, he finally leaned back in the luxurious seat and closed his eyes.

Sandy reached for his iPad and shut it. "Honey, stop

now. You need to breathe and rest so you'll be good for her when you get there. All you need to know is that she needs you."

"What if she doesn't *want* me there?" Aidan hated the quiver in his voice. "What if she didn't tell me because she simply doesn't want me that deep into her life?"

Sandy gazed at him, sympathy and something warmly maternal in her eyes that Aidan hadn't seen since the last time he'd been with his stepmother, Charlotte. "Does she love you?"

"She wants to." It was an odd response. But he wasn't sure how else to answer. He shook his head and gave Sandy a tired smile. "I think she loves me, but she's scared because I'm an actor and she's kind of mistrustful of us as a breed."

"All you've got to do is show her how much you love her." Sandy nodded firmly. "I think rushing to her side is a pretty good demonstration of that."

"I hope you're right."

She smiled broader. "I've only known you for a few hours, Aidan, and my sense is you've got a good heart. Show it to her."

"Aidan, where can we land a helicopter in River's Edge?" Harry had his iPad open and was looking at a map of the Ohio River.

Aidan rubbed both hands over his face as Harry's question sank in. "Harry, you don't have to get me a helicopter. You've already done too much. Besides, my car's at the airport."

Harry chuffed and waved away Aidan's protests. "Nonsense. We've gotta get you to the hospital right now. Google Maps says that drive takes over an hour, plus you're in no shape to drive. You can get your car back another day. I've got this charter service on the line here, but they won't land on the hospital helipad because it's just for medical emergencies. So tell me where they can set you down."

Aidan bit his lower lip. The field behind the winery was pretty big, although he had no idea how many acres. "Hang on. Let me call my brother and check."

Conor picked up on the first ring. "Ace! How'd it go? Is *Streetcar* gonna happen?"

Aidan choked at the sound of a dear and familiar voice, and he swallowed hard. "I don't know, Con. I had to leave the meeting because I found out that Holly's at St. Mark's having surgery for breast cancer." His voice broke and he swallowed again. "So a-a friend"—he caught Harry's firm nod out of the corner of his eye—"brought me to Louisville on his jet and we've just landed. He's getting me a helicopter to River's Edge. It's a long story, I'll tell you later. I just need to know if there's enough space behind the winery for a helicopter to land."

Conor gasped and was quiet for a moment. "Um… sure, the field where we do summer concerts is plenty big enough. You could probably even land in the parking lot except that customers are parked in it right now. Use the field and I'll come down in the gator to get you."

"Thanks, brother." Aidan looked out the window as the Gulfstream taxied past the terminal to a private area of the tarmac. "And may I borrow your car? Mine's in long-term parking here at the airport and I'm trying to get to the hospital as fast as I can."

"How did you *not* know about this?" Conor's voice was husky with concern.

"She deliberately didn't tell me. Did *you* know?" It occurred to Aidan that perhaps Holly had talked to Sam or Meg when she'd gotten the news.

"No, I didn't have a clue." Conor must have read his mind because he added, "I'm sure Sam would have told me if Holly had spoken to her about it. God, Ace. I'm speechless."

"I think she kept it a secret from everyone, especially me, because she knew how much this film means to me." His voice cracked again. "But nothing means more than her... and Matt. How do I make her see that?"

"I think she's going to realize it when she sees you."

Aidan released a long breath. "We've stopped and there's a car here waiting to take us to the heliport. I want you to meet these amazing people who've helped me get home, but that's going to have to wait for another time."

"I'll be down in the field waiting." Conor's worried tone gentled. "Hey, it's all going to be okay. See you soon."

The plane came to a stop as Aidan tapped his phone, stuffed his iPad in his bag, and unbuckled his seat belt while

Harry grabbed the duffel out of the overhead. They descended the stairs to the black SUV waiting near the plane and Aidan turned to the couple who'd so graciously rescued him. "Harry, Sandy, I have no words. How can I ever thank you?"

Harry grinned. "Tell you what you do, boy. You get that girl of yours healthy and strong and then you marry her and bring her and her son out to our cottage this summer for a visit." He paused and side-eyed Sandy before he continued. "Oh, and if you could see your way to shipping us a case or two of wine from that winery of your family's that Dick couldn't quit talking about last night, that'd be nice, too."

For the first time in five hours Aidan felt a genuine smile forming on his lips. "It would be my pleasure, Harry! What do you like, red or white?"

Sandy enveloped him in a hug. "Send us a variety. We love to try new wines. And sweetie, make sure you text and let us know how Holly is. You've got our numbers. We'll keep her… and you in our prayers."

Aidan returned the hug, clinging just a little longer than he meant to, but Sandy didn't seem to mind as she patted his cheek and passed him off to Harry, who threw his arms around him in a giant bear hug and said gruffly, "Stay in touch now. Let's get you on that whirlybird."

Chapter Twenty

HOLLY FLOATED, HALF-AWAKE, half-asleep, trying desperately to hold onto the dream that was fading away. Aidan, with his too-sexy smile and those knock-your-socks-off dimples, stood on the River Walk with Matty, calling over his shoulder for her to hurry up. They were late. But it seemed as if she were slogging through wet sand and the harder she tried to reach them, the farther away they drifted. She was frantic to get to them, to tell them both how much she loved them.

Matty's voice came from far away. "Show me again. I've almost got it."

And then Aidan's. "Okay, now... dubba, dubba, dub. Imagine you're dancing in sand. That's right. Now step in place with your left foot, draw back with your right. Good. Now again, step in place with your left foot; this time shuffle forward with your right. The beat is ba-Da-ba-da-Da..."

Holly opened her eyes, squinting even though the hospital room lights were dimmed, and turned her head. She wasn't dreaming. There they were. Matty and Aidan in an open area near the draped window, their shoulders swinging back and forth as they danced a soft-shoe together in perfect rhythm. No music, just the sound of their feet shuffling on the tile floor and Aidan singing softly and stage-whispering directions. She watched, bewildered, as they finished big with a silent clap, a turn, and a final step shuffle with their arms extended.

Aidan ruffled Matty's dark hair. "Nice work, dude." He glanced up and caught her eye. "Hey, gorgeous." He sauntered over to the bed. "I hope we didn't wake you."

Matty followed, practicing his soft-shoe shuffles along the way before edging in next to Aidan. "Hi, Mom!"

The haze in Holly's brain was lifting somewhat. She remembered the recovery room, what seemed like twelve different nurses asking her to open her eyes, and Dr. Troutman coming to tell her they got everything with healthy margins and after some preventive radiation therapy, she'd be good. High risk, but good. She vaguely recalled Melinda and Matty walking alongside her bed as the CNA wheeled her down the hallway to her room. He'd offered cool water for her dry throat when they got there. But Aidan? He was supposed to be in LA.

She peered at them. "What are you doing?" Her voice came out raspy.

Matty grinned. "Frank and Bing for our summer show. I finally got that last bit. Watch!" He demonstrated, ending with a flamboyant *cha*, and received an enthusiastic high five from Aidan.

She blinked, managed a weak smile and thumbs-up for Matty, before she turned her eyes on Aidan. "Why are *you* here?"

His blue eyes were full of tenderness. "Because this is where I belong?" He reached for the pitcher of water on the side table. "Here, you want a drink?"

She nodded, accepting the glass and taking a deep sip. She shifted uncomfortably in the wide support bra that bound her chest and pressed on the bandaged place just to the left of her heart. Hadn't the nurse placed a remote for the room next to her head? She felt under her pillow, gasping at the shaft of pain that shot through her when she moved her left arm.

Aidan gently took her wrist and lowered it to her side. "Let me." He found the remote. "What do you want?"

"Sit up?" Holly had no idea why she couldn't seem to form a coherent sentence, except that she was so dumbfounded to see Aidan at her bedside. She tried again. "Why aren't you in LA?"

Aidan looked up from the remote. "Is that comfortable? Do you want me to fix those pillows? They're kinda crunched up."

Matty stepped around the bed to her other side. "I've got them. Mom, lean forward a little." He straightened the pillows behind her while Holly, still dazed, tipped forward, then dropped back, exhausted by just that simple process.

Her mind raced, jumbled with questions, so she reached

for Aidan and repeated the one closest at hand. "Why aren't you in LA?"

He regarded her, his eyes narrowing, then he dug in his pocket and pulled out his wallet—a leather money-clip style with credit cards on one side and cash under a metal holder on the other. Yanking a twenty from the clip, he handed it to Matty. "Hey, Matt, you must be starving. Why don't you go down to the café and grab some supper? It's only eight and I think they're open until ten."

Matty tossed Aidan a knowing smile. "In other words, get lost for a while because you need to talk to Mom alone?"

Aidan chuckled. "Yeah, pretty much." He twined his fingers with Holly's as Matty headed for the door, looking so grown-up and confident, Holly's heart twisted in her chest.

She resisted the urge to remind him not to talk to strangers. Instead, she said, "Bring me one of those orange-cranberry muffins, honey. Please?"

"Sure." He stopped at the doorway. "You want anything, Aidan? Tea? A muffin?"

Aidan squeezed Holly's hand. "Tea would be amazing, kiddo, and grab a muffin for me, too."

"You got it." Matty backed out the room on a soft-shoe step and a toothy grin.

"Scooch over." Aidan hitched his chin toward her, lowered the head of the bed a little, and kicked off his loafers.

"Hold on." She scooted to the side of the narrow bed slowly, being very protective of her sore breast, while Aidan handled the tangle of IV tubing attached to her left arm, the oximeter on her index finger, and the annoying blood pressure cuff. "Are you allowed on the bed with me?"

Once she was comfortable, he settled next to her, pulling her into the crook of his arm to hold her close, while his fingers traced the length of her hip. "I'd say that's your call, and you didn't stop me."

It hadn't even occurred to her to stop him because she needed his warm body next to her like she needed air to breathe. She inhaled the scent of his throat, the clean, woodsy, citrus, and musk fragrance that was Aidan. His brown T-shirt was some super-soft cotton that felt like cashmere when she laid her cheek on his chest. She should've been asking questions because there were so many. For now though, the utter contentment, the rightness of his arms around her was enough.

He held her, pressing his lips to her hair, caressing her back and hip, finding her bare skin under the rough fabric of the hospital gown. He leaned over and unsnapped the left shoulder of the wretched thing and pulled it down.

"Where?" he whispered.

She raised her arm slightly. "Here. You can't see it, though, it's all covered up with bandages and this industrial bra thing."

He lowered his head to touch his lips to the place where she pointed, then he kissed her forehead, each closed eye, her nose, and finally her mouth. A sweet, tender kiss that sent an arc of longing through her. Damn the man for making her so hungry when she was dopey from surgery and lying in a hospital bed. She quelled the urges he was arousing. At least he was here next to her.

Because he is a kind, gentle man. A man of integrity. He's not Leo.

"Holly?" Aidan's breath stirred the hair over her ear. "You should've told me. This isn't going to work if we don't talk to each other."

"I know." She swallowed, trying to find more words, the right words.

She *should* have told him about the cancer, but she knew him. He would've turned down the film to stay with her and she didn't want to be responsible for ruining his dreams. Didn't want that between them, because when he realized what he'd given up, he'd resent her forever. He'd leave and never return and her heart would be broken again. All those pieces would have to be gathered up—again. Put back together—again, and what if she couldn't get them in the right places? What if she let him have her heart and he broke it and she was never able to love again?

He's not Leo.

Would Leo have climbed down the back of the *River Queen* to rescue a boy he didn't even know? Leo would never have gone back to the River Walk to help that child's grandmother take down her booth or arranged a first date— and yes, it was a date—in a place where they could eat without being bothered by fans. Leo would've soaked up the attention and demanded more. Would Leo have spent hours teaching Matty the soft-shoe? Leo would never have spent time nurturing a young boy's dreams. Not even his son's.

He's not Leo.

"What happened in LA?" She didn't want to ask, but she had to know.

A gurgle of laughter rumbled in his chest. "I pissed off a roomful of suits by walking out before the meeting even got started. Matty texted me on your phone. Apparently, he thought I knew and was just updating me."

"You came back for me?" Holly's heart skipped one beat and then another. "You gave up the part... for *me*?"

Dear Lord in heaven, he is not *Leo.*

"Of course I did." Aidan put one finger under her chin and lifted her face to his. "I love you. Nothing—no part, no film, no TV show, no Broadway play—*nothing* is more important to me than you... and Matt." He smiled and pressed a quick kiss to her lips. "Although in the interest of full disclosure, I may still have the part if I want it. The backers really want me to play Stanley."

Again, she didn't want to ask, but she had to know. "Do you want to?"

He gazed into her eyes. "To be honest, yes, I *do* want to. Fact is, though, I want you, too, and if I have to make a choice..." He shrugged. "Well, there is no choice really. It's you every time, little one."

"You should do it."

He shook his head. "I should be here with you. Melinda says you have six weeks of treatment ahead of you."

"But shooting doesn't start until June." She was testing him and she was sure he was aware of that fact.

He released a long breath and tucked her head against his chest, resting his chin on her hair. "Listen to me. I'll be here to take you to every doctor's appointment and every treatment, I'll hold your hair if the radiation makes you puke, serve you tea and soup and crackers, shovel your snow, help Matt with his homework, and do anything else you need. Just try and get rid of me."

Holly put her arm around him and snuggled closer, enjoying the even *thump, thump* of his heartbeat beneath her cheek. She exhaled, certain of what she needed to say to demonstrate that she trusted him completely. "I'm sorry I didn't tell you about the cancer. I should have, you're right. I want us, Aidan—more than I've ever wanted anything since Matty was born. I want *us!*" She emphasized her words with a fervent kiss. "And, you must do this film. No one else in the world could play Stanley like you." She smiled as he stroked her cheek with one finger. "Okay, maybe Brando, but you own that role now. That's why they want you so badly."

"Babe, stop." He brought her hand up to his lips. "If it's meant to be, it'll work out. I'm home to stay, although you know, *home to stay* doesn't mean I'm never going to go out on location again, never be in front of a camera again. I'm not even saying I'm not going to do *this* film, but you come first. You and Matt. The most important thing is we're all together and nothing's going to change that. We'll figure out the rest as we go along." He gently tugged her hair so he could kiss her, a deep, delectable kiss, full of promise. When he pulled away, his eyes shone with anticipation and purpose.

"He's not Leo." She didn't realize she'd said the words that had been roiling in her brain out loud until Aidan threw his head back and laughed.

"Damn straight I'm not Leo. I'm Aidan Flaherty and"— he brushed her lips with his—"I am *all* in, Holly Peterson Santos. Are you?"

She trembled as joy surged through her. He *wasn't* Leo. He was her kind, steady, loving, delicious Aidan. She stared into his clear sapphire eyes, so like the stones in the necklace that Melinda was keeping safe for her, and saw only the purest light of love. "I love you, Aidan Flaherty, and yes, yes, I *am* all in."

His eyes twinkled and he gave her a raised brow. "Even though I'm, gasp, an *actor?*"

She kissed him, putting all the love and passion she could muster from a hospital bed into the caress. "Actually, rock star, I kinda think that's one of your finer qualities."

Chapter Twenty-One

Six months later…

"YOU'VE GOT A packed house, Ace! Just about everyone's onboard. And you're not going to believe who's here!" Brendan's face appeared in the mirror behind Aidan, who was patting his own face with a sponge tinged with light powder. Conor and Sean peered over Bren's shoulders, making him look, for all the world, like a three-headed brother-monster.

"You do have a capacity crowd out there, man," Conor exclaimed. "Opening night is a smash already."

Sean patted Aidan's shoulder. "I gotta tell you, Ace, I had a misgiving or two when you started this harebrained scheme, but obviously, folks were ready for a showboat on the Ohio again. Bravo, brother."

"I couldn't have done it without you guys." Aidan swallowed to keep from getting choked up and sappy. "How can I ever thank you for all you've done?"

"Accolades, dude." Bren gave a small bow. "I'm the playwright. I expect to be onstage at the end of the night, receiving accolades for my brilliant little one-act melodrama."

Conor nodded, edging into the small space. "Yeah, and we should get accolades, too, 'cause we provided the wine for tonight's festivities. No wine, no joy, you know?" He lifted his chin in Sean's direction. "Right, bro?"

Sean grinned. "Absolutely." His gaze raked over Aidan, pride overtaking the teasing glint in his eyes. "By the way, Ace, stroke of genius on your part, making the *River Queen*'s first season a salute to Cole Porter. You're introducing a whole new generation to his songs. The 'rents would be so proud."

Aidan's heart swelled. The choice to use Cole Porter's catalog of music as the theme for the *Queen*'s first summer back on the Ohio came after several meetings with the Warner College performing arts department and River's Edge High School drama department way back in snowy January. "It was either Porter or Lennon and McCartney. Porter was my first choice—"

Brendan smirked. "Because you were somehow born in the wrong era, little brother. Remember all the Sunday afternoons we spent watching old black-and-white movies with this guy?"

Conor and Sean chuckled while Aidan simply shook his head. He snapped his fingers and pointed to Brendan. "Hey, you said someone was out in the house. Who?"

"Oh yeah!" He chortled. "*Entertainment This Week* is out there with a camera guy and that cute little reporter, Marie…

something."

Aidan couldn't help chortling, too. "Marie Mills? Fantastic!"

Sean's brow furrowed. "How'd you pull *that* off, Ace?"

Aidan managed a modest smile even though in his heart, fireworks were going off. "Pays to keep your publicist close, even if you're not in LA anymore. I've been keeping her updated and she said she was going to try to get the press back here to cover opening night. Looks like she did it." He took his white dress shirt off a hanger on the door and slipped into it. "Hey, I'm going to run down, say hello, make sure she's got a great seat. You know, schmooze."

Just then Jason Oleson, the musical director at Warner College, tapped on the door. "Aidan? We've got everyone backstage ready for the opening number. Do you know where Matt Santos is?"

"He should be in cube three with the other kids." Aidan had cordoned off the front of the upper deck and added more dressing rooms and extra restrooms to accommodate all the performers in the show.

Jason shook his head. "Not there. I checked."

Aidan snapped on his cummerbund, grabbed his tux jacket, and stuffed his tie in the pocket. Taking up his phone, he called Holly. "Do you have Matt?" he asked as soon as she answered. His heart still beat faster whenever he heard her voice. He could hear the sounds of the crowd in the background, so he figured she was somewhere out in the house or backstage. "Where are you?"

"I'm backstage, helping Mom with last-minute costume adjustments. I thought he was with you."

"No, he was supposed to be up here with the rest of the boys, but Jason can't find him." He heard her quick intake of breath. "Don't worry, little one, he's around. I'll find him. The guys are here. We'll go look." He shoved the phone into the inside pocket of his jacket.

Brendan turned toward the door. "We'll find him, Ace. You go schmooze."

Aidan clamped his lips shut in a tight line for a second. "No, *I* need to do this. Bren, can you go down, find Marie, make sure she's got a great seat? Get her a glass of wine? Tell her I'll see her after the show."

Bren's blue eyes lit up with delight. "You betcha." And he was gone.

Sean and Conor scooted out too, both heading in different directions. Aidan moved toward the stern, tying his bow tie as he hurried across the deck, hoping Matt was just getting some air before their big opening number.

The two of them had Cole Porter's "Did You Ever" down pat, complete with a soft-shoe routine that they'd choreographed with the help of Debby Myers, one of the dance teachers at Warner. Matt was a natural performer—confident and comfortable onstage—exactly like his grandfather. Several singers and dancers from the college's show choir would join them onstage. The number was the perfect way to open the first season of the Showboat Summer course on the newly renovated *River Queen*.

He scanned the crowd on the upper deck. No sign of Matt, so he pelted down the circular metal stairs and slipped through the door that led to the deck behind the paddlewheel, which was turning, splashing river water along its wide buckets. Dan Shafer, who had returned to pilot the *Queen* as he had years before, blew the whistle from the wheelhouse, preparing to leave the dock. Aidan heard the sound of the gangplank being lowered and pulled back under the dock—an innovation of Brendan's when they had the dock redone a few weeks ago.

Suddenly a figure moved in the shadows.

"Matt?" Aiden peered into the dimness. "Is that you, son?"

"Aidan?" The boy's voice broke and when he stepped into the light above the door, it was obvious he'd been crying.

Aidan held out his arms and after a second or two of hesitation, Mateo rushed into them, sobbing. "Matty, what is it, kiddo?" He held Matt in his arms, stroking his hair and murmuring soft words of comfort. After a minute, he set the boy back and handed him a napkin he had in his tux jacket pocket from drinks after dress rehearsal a couple of days earlier. "Here, wipe your eyes and blow."

Matt sniffled and blew his nose obediently. However, he still looked like he could burst into tears any second.

Aidan brushed the kid's dark hair off his forehead. "Tell me what's wrong."

Matt's lower lip trembled. "You'll laugh."

"Never."

Matt held up his black tie. "I can't tie my bow tie." The words came out on a sob. "All the other guys are older than me and they could do it... you know, like... like real professionals. I tried, but I couldn't do it. I'm too stupid."

Aidan struggled to keep a straight face. *This* was the kid's problem? He'd been prepared for an emotional breakdown because Matt missed his grandfather or a terrible case of stage fright. He'd been practicing his dad skills for months, never sure he'd say the right words when he needed them. This? A bow tie? This was cake.

"Dude. You are *not* stupid. It took me years to learn how to tie a bow tie. Heck, first time I was nominated for an Emmy, I had to have my personal assistant, a *girl*, do my tie for me." He held out his hand. "Here, turn around and face the door." He positioned the two of them so they could both see their reflections in the window of the door. "Okay, here we go. Watch and learn, little buddy."

Mateo watched closely as Aidan tied the tie, giving instructions with each step. When they were finished, Matt smiled tremulously. "How come all those college guys know how to do it so well?"

Aidan shrugged. "Practice, I guess. They wear those tuxes every time they perform."

The floor beneath them shuddered and Aidan grinned. "We're under way! Time to get up there, kid. Let's go have some fun!" He tousled Matt's hair and then smoothed it again. "You look amazing."

Matt reached out and straightened Aidan's tie. "So do you." He yanked the door open, grabbed Aidan's hand, and dragged him to the stage door. They took their positions center stage where two folding chairs and a table awaited. The table held a Four Irish Brothers Winery sparkling wine bottle, which had been emptied and refilled with ginger ale, and two glasses ready for their number.

Matt side-eyed him. "Hey, Aidan?"

"Yeah?"

"Thanks… for all of this, for everything." Matt's eyes shone. "You're the best."

Aidan's heart was so close to bursting, he wasn't even sure he could speak. As he opened his mouth, he felt a hand on his shoulder.

It was Holly, dressed in a flowy light-green flowered sundress and smiling like she'd just won the lottery. The sight of her sent a rush of heat through him.

Her violet eyes glowed with excitement. "Look at you two. You're giving Bing and Frank a run for their money." She brushed one hand over Aidan's lapel and straightened Matt's pocket square. "Curtain in thirty seconds." She kissed both their cheeks and then swiftly exited stage left, tossing a whispered, "Break a leg," over her shoulder.

Set up below the stage, the small orchestra from the college played the first notes of the Cole Porter classic as the house curtain separated. The spots kept Aidan from seeing much except a sea of faces, and he shot an arrow prayer to Da that Matty wouldn't suddenly lose his nerve. Completely unnecessary as a startlingly suave and debonair Mateo Santos came in right on cue and belted out the first lines of "Did You Ever," exactly as they'd rehearsed it.

"OUR KID KNOCKED their socks off, didn't he?" Aidan stood behind the bar on the *River Queen* twisting a corkscrew into the last bottle of sparkling traminette to be had on the boat. He claimed the only reason he produced this one was because he'd tucked it into the kitchen fridge behind the tanks of diet soda. Holly didn't care how he'd managed it, she was just grateful it was there. She hadn't had anything at all to eat or drink since the show started. She'd been too busy helping her mom, meeting and greeting, and singing with Aidan in the second act.

She slipped off her sandals and settled onto a barstool. "Ah, so now that he's showing real promise as an entertainer, he's *our* kid? Is that how we're playing this?" She gave him a teasing wink.

Aidan raised his gaze from the cork to her, his expression unreadable, although he looked sexy as anything with his tie hanging loose and his shirt unbuttoned to reveal his tanned neck. "I'm pretty sure I've spent the last six months trying to convince you that he should be *our* kid." He poured two glasses of the shimmering wine, came out from the behind the bar, and tilted his head toward the theater. "Come with me."

"Why?"

He gave her a mysterious smile. "I want to show you something."

Curiosity aroused, she followed him as he wove his way around the many tables and chairs in the house and up the steps on the right side of the stage. A few lights were still on, including a gel-filtered spot that cast an opalescent circle center stage. As he walked into the beam, his whole body took on an ethereal quality that only emphasized his physical attractiveness. When he turned and crooked a finger at her in a come-hither motion, he took her breath away and desire pooled in her belly. Everything inside her quivered. No man should have this kind of effect on her. *But, oh, thank heaven and all the stars above, this one did.*

He held out one of the glasses. "C'mere, little one." His voice was rich and smooth and irresistible.

Slowly, she approached him, intrigued and frankly, turned on by the aura the light was creating around him. She accepted the wine, but didn't sip yet because she knew Aidan well enough to know that a toast was coming. She actually was hoping they'd have some time alone after the show to celebrate his success because, by God, he'd pulled this off with the kind of panache only Aidan Flaherty could achieve. A toast was definitely in order.

The evening had been a huge success. Every seat in the house was sold and the audience applauded until Holly was sure their palms had to be sore. Aidan and Matty's number opened the show fabulously, and the people shouted with laughter when Matty gave the house a wink and ad-libbed behind his hand, "Don't worry, folks, it's only ginger ale." The finale, all the summer students onstage with Aidan for a rousing rendition of "Anything Goes," brought the last of multiple standing ovations with the crowd reluctant to disperse after the final curtain.

Aidan had kept her and Matty close as he accepted congratulatory hugs and pats on the back from family, friends, and strangers alike. He was so happy to see some of his LA friends in the audience, and Holly had enjoyed meeting Phil, his former personal assistant, and her partner Chloe. His agent and publicist had made the trip in as well, which surprised and pleased Aidan.

He was most excited to introduce her to Harry and Sandy Watts, the couple who had jetted him back to River's Edge when she'd had her breast cancer surgery. Their bond was immediately obvious as Sandy kissed his cheek and Harry swept him into a fierce hug. When Holly expressed her gratitude for bringing him back to her, they waved it away as if it were nothing at all and hugged both Holly and

Mateo, extracting a promise from her to come out to their cottage in Old Saybrook soon.

Aidan even had Matty and her standing near when Marie Mills interviewed him for *Entertainment This Week*. He pulled Matty into the camera's view so he could tell Marie to keep an eye on *his boy* because he was headed to Broadway one day. Matty, of course, was thrilled to be on TV and played to the camera with charm and poise.

The moment had made her recall Clive and all the shows he'd produced on the *River Queen* when she was a child and all the kudos he'd received. Somehow, though, the memories no longer stung. Her dad would be so very proud. Aidan had brought fun and joy back to the *Queen* and back to her life and Matty's and Melinda's. How would she ever thank him for that gift?

Aidan raised his glass. "To us, little one. To you and me and Matty finally becoming a family. And hopefully to growing our family... soon." He touched the edge of his glass to hers and sipped before sliding his hand into the pocket of his tux. Carefully, he set his glass down on the wood floor, took a knee before her, and held up a light blue box. "I picked here and now to ask you to marry me—officially—because this stage, this showboat is so much a part of both our histories. I want it to be a part of our future... together." He opened the box to reveal a stunning square-cut sapphire solitaire with triangle-cut aquamarines on either side, all in a filigree-carved platinum setting. "I know we've got stuff to work out and maybe life won't always be easy because, love, I *am* an actor and that's not going to change. But I promise I will be right by your side any time you need me and I will love you to the last breath I take. Holly… little one… will you do me the honor and the great joy of becoming my wife?"

Holly gasped, not because he asked her to marry him; he'd been doing that regularly since January. No, it was the unexpected romanticism of *this* time. He'd planned it, and for a night that was supposed to belong to him alone, which was so perfect and so very much her Aidan that her legs went weak. She set her glass down and slipped to her knees so she could be eye-level with him. His amazing blue eyes, almost navy with emotion as he awaited her answer.

This marriage wouldn't be a walk in the park. They both had strong personalities and Holly was all too aware that she would struggle with his acting career and the work of the *River Queen*. There would be hard discussions about long weeks apart while he was on location and probably talks about Matty and exactly where he was headed because clearly, he would be following in Aidan's footsteps. There was her health, which at the moment was strong after radiation and a new clean mammogram, but that specter would always haunt them. When more children came along, and they would, because she couldn't imagine marriage to a Flaherty that didn't include a houseful of kids, more negotiations would ensue.

But the rest of her life without Aidan Flaherty in it—without him by her side, in her arms, in her bed—was unthinkable.

She threw her arms around his neck. "Yes, I will marry you," she whispered breathlessly after a long intoxicating kiss.

He touched his forehead to hers, his smile a sweet caress. "So, you're okay with taking a chance on another actor?" He slipped the ring onto her left hand, where it glimmered in the opal light.

She laughed with pure bliss as she covered his face with kisses. "I'm feeling lucky, rock star. Besides, how am I taking a chance when we're a sure thing?"

The End

If you enjoyed this book, please leave a review at your favorite online retailer! Even if it's just a sentence or two it makes all the difference.

Thanks for reading *Christmas with You* by Nan Reinhardt!

Discover your next romance at TulePublishing.com.

TULE
PUBLISHING

If you enjoyed *Christmas with You*,
you'll love the next book in....

The Four Irish Brothers Winery series

Book 1: *A Small Town Christmas*

Book 2: *Meant to Be*

Book 3: *Christmas with You*

Book 4: *Coming July 2020!*

If you enjoyed *Christmas with You*,
you'll love these other Tule Christmas books!

Christmas at Sleigh Bell Farm
by Kaylie Newell

A Texas Christmas Wish
by Alissa Callen

Long Lost Christmas
by Joan Kilby

About the Author

Nan Reinhardt has been a copy editor and proofreader for over twenty-five years, and currently works mainly on fiction titles for a variety of clients, including Avon Books, St. Martin's Press, Kensington Books, Tule Publishing, and Entangled Publishing, as well as for many indie authors.

Author Nan writes romantic fiction for women in their prime. Yeah, women still fall in love and have sex, even after they turn forty-five! Imagine! She is also a wife, a mom, a mother-in-law, and a grandmother. She's been an antiques dealer, a bank teller, a stay-at-home mom, and a secretary.

She loves her career as a freelance editor, but writing is Nan's first and most enduring passion. She can't remember a time in her life when she wasn't writing—she wrote her first romance novel at the age of ten, a love story between the most sophisticated person she knew at the time, her older sister (who was in high school and had a driver's license!), and a member of Herman's Hermits. If you remember who they are, you are Nan's audience! She's still writing romance, but now from the viewpoint of a wiser, slightly rumpled, post-menopausal woman who believes that love never ages, women only grow more interesting, and everybody needs a little sexy romance.

Thank you for reading

Christmas with You

If you enjoyed this book, you can find more from all our great authors at TulePublishing.com, or from your favorite online retailer.

TULE
PUBLISHING

CPSIA information can be obtained
at www.ICGtesting.com
Printed in the USA
LVHW091401141219
640498LV00002BA/611/P